the recipe box

SANDRA LEE

the recipe box

HYPERION

NEW YORK

Library of Congress Cataloging-in-Publication Data

Lee, Sandra.
The Recipe Box/Sandra Lee.—First Edition.
pages cm
ISBN 978-1-4013-1083-7
1. Self-realization in women—Fiction.   2. Cooking—Fiction.
3. Mothers and daughters—Fiction.   4. Family secrets—Fiction.
5. Life change events—Fiction.   I. Title.
PS3612.E34853R43   2013
813'.6—dc23
2012043233

FIRST EDITION

10 9 8 7 6 5 4 3 2 1

SUSTAINABLE FORESTRY INITIATIVE   Certified Sourcing
www.sfiprogram.org
SFI-00993

THIS LABEL APPLIES TO TEXT STOCK

We try to produce the most beautiful books possible, and we are
also extremely concerned about the impact of our manufacturing
process on the forests of the world and the environment as a whole.
Accordingly, we've made sure that all of the paper we use has been
certified as coming from forests that are managed, to ensure the
protection of the people and wildlife dependent upon them.

To my nieces and nephews—
Scott, Danielle, Brandon, Austen,
Stephanie, Taner, Blake, Bryce, and Katie—
May your lives be full of love, light, and
laughter, and may you grow strong and
happy wherever God plants you.

All my love always,
Moon and stars,
Aunt Sandy

the recipe box

chapter 1

As soon as she heard the ring, Grace knew there would be no answer. Every mother recognized that ring—the one where you could just sense your child wasn't going to pick up.

"Hi, it's Em, leave a message . . ."

Grace had hoped to reach Emma. She was hours late, but she still smiled at the sound of her daughter's voice as she raced through LAX, cell in one hand, wheelie handle in the other, veering past a food stand, around a woman pushing a stroller, and almost sideswiping a man in a motorized wheelchair. "Oh my God, I am so sorry . . ." Good grief, she was running down babies and seniors. *Grace, get a grip!*

"BEEP!"

"Honey, it's mom. I'm really sorry, Em. The plane was late, there was weather out of Green Bay, I missed my connection in Chicago and . . ." What was the difference? Grace thought. Emma would only care that her mother wasn't there again when she got home. "I'm going straight to the set, so don't worry if you don't see my suitcase when you get home. Just start your homework. I'll bring sushi for dinner, OK? I love you." Grace picked up her bag and raced down the escalator steps, breaking into a run as she dragged it to the parking lot. It was a perfect spring day in Los Angeles. Sunshine and bright blue sky a world apart from the foggy dawn darkness of New London, Wisconsin, where she'd started her day ten hours ago.

Grace's phone rang. Great, Emma was calling back. "Sweetie?"

"Don't sweetie me! We still have six scenes to cover today. Where is my trusty assistant? Are you back in LA?"

With the time difference it was only lunchtime in LA, so Grace still had a half day of work ahead of her. "Ken, I feel terrible, you were wonderful to have Emma stay with you, but the flight was late. I left you a message about the connection . . ."

"Yeah, I got it. Just glad you're back, and heads up—we're gonna run late. Artie's out of control again."

Grace sighed. Artie was the director of the show she and Ken were working on, *The Lost Ones*. He was a creative genius, but his management style was terrible. Ken was an amazing godfather, letting Emma stay with him while Grace was in Wisconsin. Ken adored Emma, and his domestic skills were, Grace had to admit, a thousand times better than her own, but Emma was only fourteen and the reality was that Ken had a very high pressure job as a head stylist for a hit TV show. "I tried calling Emma. She's probably at lunch. Leeza asked me to stay a bit longer, the flights were delayed, but I'm here now."

His voice softened. "It's OK, Grace. Just get here when you can, honey. How's our fighter doing?"

"Not great." Grace had managed to miss her connection, but she'd spent an extra day with Leeza, and right now that was what mattered. Ken understood. Grace and Ken were taking turns helping Leeza and her family. Back in high school in New London where they'd all grown up, Grace, Leeza, and Ken had joked they were closer than the Three Musketeers.

"I'll fill you in later." Grace sighed, thinking of that morning. "Be there shortly."

———

Pulling onto the 405 headed north, Grace groaned. The freeway was a parking lot. She'd have to get off at the first exit and take Sepulveda, or if that was blocked another surface street all the way to Century. This was going to be a long, painful exercise in stop-and-go. She looked at her reflection in the rearview mirror. Good lord, Grace thought. There were circles under her blue eyes. Her skin was paper white. She looked like she hadn't slept in three days.

This crazy schedule that left Grace exhausted and racing from LA to Wisconsin and back had started last fall during the annual Fall Family Fun Fest. The leaves were in full fall color. Music and the smell of sausages, cheese, and beer filled the air all week. Grace, Ken, and Leeza had been going to the festival together since they were kids, and even though Grace and Ken had moved away, they wouldn't have missed it for the world. Like New London's huge St. Patrick's Day Parade, the Fall Family Fun Fest was a town tradition. On the last day of the festival this year, Grace and Leeza stole a quiet moment to talk while they watched Grace's daughter Emma and Leeza's little Sara dance around the town square.

"I can't believe I actually live in LA," Grace had mused.

"Me, a die-hard Midwesterner. Now, Ken, that I can believe. He's taken to it like a duck to water. In fact, he *is* a duck on the water. You should see his houseboat." Grace had chattered on in the way lifelong girlfriends do, filling Leeza in on the latest annoyance with Brian, her ex-husband.

"I guess he's moving into a huge loft in Chicago," Grace had sighed. "Reclaiming his lost bachelorhood or something. LA is so far away, I worry about sending Emma to Chicago and Emma said he had a date over Labor Day."

"Who says you couldn't have a date, too?" Leeza said as she put a straw in a juice box for Sara.

Looking back, Grace realized she'd yammered on about her ideal man, Brian's issues, and other insignificant blather until Leeza had abruptly interrupted her.

That's when Leeza had told Grace about her recent doctor's appointment and the lump he'd found in her left breast. "It's probably nothing," Leeza had assured her. "I'm sure it's just a cyst. Lots of women get them." Then she added, "The doctor is just being careful because Jonathan and I want to try for a little brother or sister for Sara." Leeza flashed her famous grin at this confession, the look that said, Watch out world!

"I'm sure you're right," Grace agreed and added, "Still, I'm glad you are going in for the follow-up."

Before Grace could ask Leeza any more questions, Ken appeared with beer for everyone, and they'd toasted the happy news. "A new baby! How great!" Ken said. "Dibs on godfather. Emma got Sara. The next munchkin is mine!" They toasted, and the conversation turned to possible baby names, all thought of Leeza's follow-up appointment forgotten.

Grace had been absolutely certain nothing would be wrong, nothing *could* be wrong. It had been a perfect trip. She'd hugged Leeza good-bye at the airport, and she, Emma, and Ken flew back to LA.

A week later, Leeza called and said she had breast cancer, but it had been caught early and there was nothing to worry about. Just something to take care of before she resumed with the Baby Plan.

But it turned out it *was* something to worry about. Leeza actually had aggressive, stage three breast cancer.

Suddenly the friends were cast into an ocean of tests, radiation, surgery, chemo—and after all that, the cancer had still spread. Then more surgery, more treatments, and finally weeks of isolation during Leeza's grueling bone marrow transplant over the winter. It was finally spring, and after months of hospital rooms, Leeza was at last home with her husband and little girl, where she could recover and spend time in her beautiful garden.

Whether it was people or plants, Leeza was a caretaker. She had a gift for making things bloom. Just the day before, Grace and Leeza had sat outside admiring the forsythia banking the side of Leeza's house, a faint dusting of pale butter yellow starting to peek through.

Grace had tried to keep their conversation light to give Leeza a break. "Your garden is going to be stunning this year, Leeza. I still can't believe Claire designed it. Claire Howard, the meanest girl in school. Who would guess? Oh my God, do you remember the time Ken put a laxative in Claire's milkshake?"

Leeza laughed. Ken had been a devil in high school. "God, she deserved it, though." She rolled her eyes and added, "She was the absolute worst!"

"The number-one popular girl," said Grace. "I still think she's the one who stole my sweater and put it on that scarecrow at the festival senior year."

"How about the time she accidentally 'lost' your tennis racquet when she was in charge of the equipment at the regional championships?" Leeza added.

Grace and Leeza laughed, recalling what had seemed like the worst things in the world back in high school. "We were so clueless. It's hard to believe she's my sister-in-law!" said Leeza. "Will miracles never cease?"

They'd been quiet for a minute, and Grace had said a little silent prayer: *I hope not. Please let the miracles continue and let Leeza get well.* But she didn't want to scare Leeza, so instead she just said, "Maybe it was Ken's milkshake."

"Yeah, Ken gets total credit for the turnaround," giggled Leeza.

They talked for another hour about their girls, Grace's work, and about Leeza's husband, Jonathan. They were still talking when it was time for Sara to wake up from her nap. As she got up, Leeza turned to Grace. "How's your mother? Will you see her this trip?"

Grace said nothing. Leeza knew Grace didn't want to see her mother.

"She comes by the hospital, you know," Leeza added. "All the time. Whenever I'm there."

"You don't have to see her, Leez."

"I know. But she's just trying to help."

"That's Lorraine—soup kitchens and hospitals are her specialty." Unspoken were the words *Daughters are not*. Especially her own daughter. Grace hadn't really had a relationship with her mother for sixteen years. She hadn't stood between her mother and Emma, but her own estrangement put a distance there as well. When she went back to New London, Grace stayed with Leeza and Jonathan. They were her family now.

"Maybe it's time, Gracie," said Leeza, squeezing her hand. "Sometimes there's less time than we know."

"There'll never be enough time," said Grace firmly, hating that they were discussing Lorraine. "Now, about Sara's birthday—" She tried to change the subject.

But Leeza cut her off. "Gracie." Grace could hear their whole history together, the secret only they shared, the reason they were closer than any sisters, in the way Leeza said her name. "There is never going to be a right time, but it's up to you now. You're going to have to be the strong one."

"I don't see why . . ."

Leeza shook her head. "It's not about you and me anymore, Gracie, it's about Emma and Sara. As mothers we both have to do things that aren't easy, but we owe it to our daughters." She looked at Grace pointedly. "I can't help but wonder if maybe Lorraine thinks the same thing."

Leeza was right, but Grace could only shrug. Her relationship with Lorraine was complicated. Grace and Leeza had hugged, linked arms, and walked back to the house, each carrying her favorite mug.

At dinner that night, they had made plans for Grace to come back for the Fourth of July. "I'll be well then, you'll see," Leeza said as she picked at her food.

"You need to come visit us and get some California sunshine," said Grace. "We'll stay on Ken's boat and be California girls together." She sang the line from the Beach Boys' song: *I wish they all could be California* . . . Jonathan had joined in and they'd gotten Leeza to laugh.

"I'll get a tattoo like Emma's," Leeza had teased, and Grace had winced. "Oh, no, don't encourage her." Jonathan winked, took Leeza's hand with seriousness, then joked, "I don't know, I think a Snoopy tattoo would be fun," and they'd all laughed because Snoopy was the nickname Leeza had given Jonathan back in high school for following her around like a puppy.

Leeza was tired after dinner, so while Jonathan had finished the dishes Grace had helped her up to bed.

"Thank you for coming to visit and for staying this extra day, Grace," Leeza said. "I know it's hard for you to be away from Emma, but this time with you means the world to me. I wish you didn't have to leave in the morning."

"I'll be back soon. Fourth of July, and I'll bring Emma. It'll be here before you know it!" She'd settled the quilt around Leeza, and as she was dropping off to sleep Leeza squeezed Grace's hand and whispered, "Be strong, Grace."

It was Leeza who needed strength, Grace thought, but that was so Leeza, always thinking of others.

That morning Grace woke up grateful she'd spent the extra night, but dreading the drive to Green Bay, returning the rental car, then the commuter flight to Chicago's O'Hare Airport, where she'd connect with the flight to LA. Jonathan had gotten out of bed in the predawn darkness to turn on some lights and walk Grace to her car. He looked like a man who had been to hell and back.

"It's going to be fine now," Grace had assured Jonathan as she hugged him good-bye. "She's home with you and Sara. That's going to help her get better fast. Being home is the best medicine. You'll see."

———

Suddenly a space opened up in front of Grace, and a car veered into her lane, cutting her off. She slammed on the brakes and leaned on the horn.

Leeza and her family were not the only victims of Leeza's illness. Ken had made several trips out to see Leeza too, and Emma had bounced back and forth between Grace, Ken, and, on holidays, her father, Brian, in Chicago.

Grace reached for her cell phone to try Emma again. No answer. She checked her messages. Nothing.

At last, Grace saw the sign for the Culver cutoff and started inching the car over to the right lane. Driving in LA was a far cry from the streets of New London, Wisconsin. She still wasn't used to it. Truth be told, Grace still felt like a visitor. She had one foot in LA, trying to make a new life, and the other back in her hometown, New London, for Leeza. She didn't know if she was coming or going, and most days she didn't think she was doing anything very well. If she was with Emma, she felt she should be with Leeza. If she was with Leeza, she felt she should be with Emma. If she was with either of them, she felt she was leaving Ken in the lurch at work. Her whole life looked like a bad patch of traffic. It will get better soon, Grace thought. She gritted her teeth, zigzagged across three lanes, and merged onto the exit ramp.

chapter 2

An hour later, Grace was at work on the set of *The Lost Ones*, surrounded by a family of vampires.

"Grace, put these in the refrigerator and line them up for the next shot," said Ken, pushing a metal cart full of glass bottles of fake blood toward her. "The natives are hungry."

"Got it." *The Lost Ones* was the story of a vampire family that moved into a normal suburban neighborhood. The vampire kitchen looked like something out of *Leave It to Beaver*, but *The Lost Ones'* family was a far cry from Ward, June, Wally, and the Beav. Ken's eye for detail, his perfectionism and creativity, had made him a go-to name in Hollywood for set design, and Grace had him to thank for transforming her from a starving artist to a professional stylist with a union card who could now afford to rent a precious apartment overlooking a canal in Venice.

Grace stocked the refrigerator with decanters filled with cranberry juice, red food coloring, and a cornstarch thickening agent. The refrigerator looked normal enough, except it had no back, so the camera could shoot from the inside out.

"Grace!" Ken was calling her through her headset. "Where are the sparklers?"

"In the tackle box. I'll get them." Grace hurried to the team van. The tackle box held the answer to every problem from a loose screw to a special prop spray that killed the shine on surfaces to, Ken liked to say, the solution to total consciousness. It was indispensable and should have been on the set, but it wasn't there because she had been late. She raced back, hoping this wouldn't hold things up.

"Here are the sparklers," she said, snapping the box open. "We have three boxes."

"I only need one sparkler," Ken said as he opened a large rectangular cardboard box. Inside was a sheet cake.

"That is gorgeous," said Grace as she helped Ken transfer the cake to a large tray. "What is it? Red velvet?"

"Please! Nothing so common for the undead! It's a blood orange cake for our vampires. We're number one in our time slot! Isn't that great news? This means the show will get picked up again for sure. We're celebrating job security! I have some champagne to go with it. If this doesn't put old farty Artie into a good mood for a change, nothing will, baby cakes." He raised one eyebrow. "It's a good thing somebody around here bakes." He leaned in closer and lowered his voice. "The secret is never use anything but blood orange juice. Plain old O.J. is so last century."

"Even if I did bake, which you know is not my thing, it's a little hard to do at thirty thousand feet in the air."

"Excuses, excuses. I baked this on a boat. Anyhow, Emma

BLOOD ORANGE SHEET CAKE

Serves 24

FOR THE CAKE:

1 cup butter, softened

2¼ cups sugar

5 eggs

4½ cups cake flour

4 teaspoons baking powder

½ teaspoon salt

Finely grated blood orange (or regular orange) rind

¾ cup blood orange juice

1 tablespoon lemon juice

3 tablespoons red food coloring

¾ cup buttermilk

FOR THE FROSTING:

3 (8-ounce) packages cream cheese, room temperature

2 sticks butter, room temperature

4 cups powdered sugar

2 tablespoons blood orange juice

Finely grated zest of 1 blood orange or regular orange

Preheat oven to 350°F. Butter and line two 9-×13-inch cake pans.

MAKE THE CAKE: Cream butter and sugar. Add eggs one at a time and beat until well incorporated. In a separate bowl whisk together flour, baking powder, salt, and blood orange zest. In another separate bowl combine blood orange juice, lemon juice, food coloring, and buttermilk. Add dry mix to wet mix in three parts, alternating between the two, ending with the wet. Scrape down the bowl and mix on medium speed 30 seconds. Divide the batter between the prepared pans, spread evenly, and smooth the tops. Bake 30 to 35 minutes, rotating pans halfway through. Cake is done when toothpick inserted in the center comes out mostly clean with moist crumbs sticking to it. Let cool.

MAKE THE FROSTING: Whisk together the cream cheese and butter. Add the sugar. Add the juice and zest. Add more sugar or juice, depending on the consistency.

TO ASSEMBLE: Remove the cakes from the pans and cut them each into two layers. Frost the layers and sides.

helped me. She poured the blood orange juice and then iced the cake."

"Well, that in itself is incredible. She never sets foot in our kitchen."

"Like mother, like daughter." He winked. Everybody, especially Ken, knew Grace didn't cook, much less bake.

"Don't rub it in. I'm a busy single mom," Grace joked a bit uncomfortably as she positioned an honorary sparkler in the center of the cake. She wished she could love cooking, she really did. Something told her that if she cooked for Emma, she'd be a better mom. The sad thing was, Grace had actually been a great cook once, but she hadn't cooked or baked anything since high school. The kitchen was not a place of warmth and good memories for her.

Somehow Ken never bought her arguments. "And I'm a busy single godfather of two," he said. "Counting one cockatoo."

"I hope she didn't give you any trouble." Grace took the opening to steer the conversation away from cooking. She was dying to check her cell phone to see if Emma had called back. Something wasn't sitting right with her ever since she'd left a message on Emma's phone.

"We're talking completely spoiled, with a total potty mouth."

"Oh, God . . ."

Ken laughed hysterically. "Oh, don't worry, honey, I'm talking about Mr. Halo. Emma is giving naughty vocabulary lessons to that cockatoo of hers. Now Emma, she was fine. Perfect. No problems."

Grace's shoulders relaxed. Thank God; she'd been worried.

It wasn't funny about Halo's new vocabulary. Emma had been acting up so much lately, Halo had picked up her wisecracks. "*Seriously!*", "*God bless America!*", "*Really?*", "*I am begging you!*", and the one Grace hated the most, "*Your point?*" It was like living with two teens. "It was wonderful of you to take her again." Grace put the box from the cake on a shelf, in case there were leftovers.

"Not at all. Emma and I have an understanding."

"Maybe you should give me some pointers."

"Sweetie, it's a phase. Don't take it personally. She's a good kid. How could my goddaughter be anything else? Now, let's get this cake moving." With great fanfare, Ken lit the single sparkler and motioned for Roberto to open the champagne. "We'll have to use plastic glasses," Ken said sorrowfully. "Artie co-opted the real ones for the next shot. Anyway! Everyone! Everyone! Congratulations to all! No Krispy Kremes for us today! In honor of the momentous occasion that we have reached number one in our time slot, I have created a blood orange cake named '*The Lost Ones* Is Number One' cake." He waved his arms like Vanna White and pushed the cart containing the large sheet cake into the room while the crew and all the vampires applauded. Roberto and Grace handed out plastic cups and poured the champagne.

Ken's confections always made people happy. The *Lost Ones* cake was no exception. Even Carrie Flannery, the lead, a frosty star rarely seen between takes, seemed to have ESP whenever one of Ken's creations appeared. The tanginess of the blood orange cake combined with the sweetness of the frosting. "This is heavenly," Grace complimented Ken as she scraped the last crumbs off her paper plate.

"Or as close to heaven as these vampires are gonna get," Ken quipped, heading off with a plastic trash bag to pick up the paper plates and plastic forks. Ken was at the top of his field, but no job was too small or trivial. He was such a genuine person with a big heart. It was a wonder Ken hadn't found a good guy to settle down with, Grace thought. She grabbed a second plastic bag and circled the other side of the room. Artie had enjoyed his two slices of cake, but snapped that break time was over.

"Ken?" The assistant director, a young woman in skinny jeans and spike heels so high Grace wondered how she could walk in them, much less stand all day on a set, clicked briskly by, clipboard in hand. "Artie needs you. Can you do something about the glass decanters in the refrigerator? They were reflecting too much light during the close-up."

Ken nodded briskly. "On my way." Ken cocked his head in an aside to Grace. "I'm not changing the decanters. They're perfect. The backups look like beakers from Frankenstein's lab. Bring the tackle box."

Grace had just picked up the box when she felt her phone vibrate. She always set it on silent when she was working. She'd learned the hard way that hundreds of thousands of dollars and dozens of people's time and effort were on the line. She'd never make that mistake again. She checked her messages.

"Hello, Ms. Holm-D'Angelo? This is Pat Seiden at Santa Monica Middle School. We've been trying to reach you. Could you please call me as soon as you get this message?"

The phone buzzed again. This time, Grace got it on the first buzz. "Hello?"

"Hello. Is this Ms. Holm-D'Angelo?" asked a voice that, unfortunately, Grace recognized as Pat Seiden.

"Yes. This is Grace."

"Ms. Holm-D'Angelo, this is Pat Seiden, from the Santa Monica Middle School."

"Yes. Hello. Is Emma all right?"

"I was going to ask you the same question, Ms. Holm-D'Angelo. Does Emma have a written excuse for missing classes today?"

"Uh . . . Isn't she in class?"

"No. Is she at a doctor's appointment, perhaps?"

"No. Ms. Seiden, isn't Emma there, in school?" Grace closed her eyes and tried not to panic.

"No, Emma didn't come in today, and I'm afraid with her record recently, well, we have a three strikes policy, as Emma is fully aware. She is now on mandatory suspension. When are you and Emma available for an appointment? . . ."

"Thank you, Ms. Seiden. You see, I've been out of town for a family emergency and I'm sure this is just a misunderstanding. Let me check a few things and I'll get right back to you." Grace clicked the phone off. She had a knot in her stomach. Not in school! Where was Emma if she was not in school? Suspension from school wasn't going to be any kind of meaningful punishment. Emma would consider it a treat.

Grace knew she couldn't ignore it any longer. The warning signs were all pointing in the same direction: being perpetually late for school; cutting class; terrible test scores; hours online; missed curfews; older friends who hung out at the beach until all hours; Emma's beautiful blonde hair dyed black; the halo tattoo that appeared on the back of her neck. She knew, of course, that teenaged girls could be rebellious. Maybe all this was normal, but if it was a phase Grace didn't see an end in sight.

She had to talk to Ken, but he was deep in conversation with Artie. She couldn't interrupt, and she still had to deal with those decanters. She rushed across the room and reached into the vampire refrigerator to grab one of the glass decanters. Suddenly it tipped over and crashed into the rest of the decanters, causing glass and fake blood to explode in every direction.

Grace couldn't imagine a longer day than this, but she knew she had to get on with it. "There's an old saying," said Ken. "No use crying over spilled blood."

During the cleanup—or, as Ken dubbed it, "sanity break"—Ken insisted that Grace sit down and drink a bottle of water. "Hydration is key," he explained. "You're back in a desert climate. Don't be afraid, take it, the bottle's plastic."

"Very funny. I have a right to be upset. Our best friend may not make it—I think she will, but what if she doesn't?—and I just found out from the assistant principal that Emma cut school again. She's not there. I have no idea where she is."

"Viper Lady, you mean?"

"No joke, Ken. They're suspending her. This is the third time she's cut."

Ken's shoulders sagged. "This is all my fault."

"No it isn't. She's cut before, you know that."

"She promised me. We had a deal. No misbehaving—either of us!"

"A one-way deal, obviously. Well, don't feel singled out. She's lying to me these days too."

"She broke her word," said Ken. "I never thought Emma would do that."

"I don't know what to do."

Ken straightened up. "Well, I know what we're going to do."

"What?"

He pulled Grace out of her chair. "What are you sitting there for? We've got to find our girl."

Grace looked nervously over at Artie. He was busy chewing out the cue card girl.

"Ah," said Ken, nodding in their direction. "Another stop on Artie's endless quest for perfection. Well, let's go."

"What do you mean? We have at least three hours left on set. We'll probably go into overtime, thanks to me."

"MY GOD, GIRL," Ken said loudly. "Look at your arm! It's covered with blood! That's a nasty cut!" He put his hand in the middle of Grace's back and pushed her toward the exit sign, calling over his shoulder. "People! We're going to the emergency room! Roberto! Take over."

Grace frowned and whispered to Ken, "It's FAKE blood. They all know that."

Ken shrugged as he steered her toward the parking lot. "How can they tell? Workplace injuries need to step out of the shadows and be taken seriously. For all they know, I'm calling OSHA. We'll leave the van for Roberto, and we'll take yours.

Now, we're off to find that little juvenile delinquent. This time, she's going to answer to Uncle Ken, and I can promise you, it won't be pretty. Now, if you were Emma, where would you be?"

The Santa Monica Promenade and Mall weren't far from the studio, and Grace knew Emma often met up with her new crowd there—or at least she said she did. Grace didn't know what to believe anymore where Emma was concerned. What had happened to her sweet, innocent little girl? When had she morphed into this black-haired, sullen creature who could give the vampire kids on *The Lost Ones* a run for their money? Grace blamed herself for Emma's transformation. Before the divorce, Emma had been a typical, happy child. Sure, with Brian trying to launch his business in a recession, their family didn't have a lot of money, but their apartment in Wrigleyville was sweet. Emma had loved her school and her friends, and she was doing really well. Getting Emma to California had involved dragging, bribes, and threats.

Emma blamed Grace for her parents' divorce and for the fact that she had to leave her school, her friends, and the father she idolized. Her sobs seemed to echo nonstop in Grace's ears. Grace had often been tempted to tell Emma the facts, but she felt—with about 80 percent certainty—that would not be the right path to take. As disillusioned as she was with Brian, she did not want her daughter to feel the same way she did about him. Making this decision was one of the toughest things Grace had ever had to do. Grace knew firsthand what it meant to have a good relationship with your father.

"Why can't I stay with Daddy?" Emma wailed. "Daddy

didn't do anything wrong! He's only trying to make money for us. He's working so hard, and all you ever want to do is act mean to him! I hate you!"

It was gut-wrenching. Brian had broken her trust and destroyed their family, but there was no way a thirteen-year-old could or even should come to grips with the fact that her father had lost all the family's money gambling, and slept with another woman. Grace just told Emma that there were very good reasons for this move, that she didn't know everything, and that California had much better weather than Chicago. She'd even promised she could learn to surf—a suggestion for which Grace now berated herself. She should have talked up yoga, organic gardening, or maybe even watercolors.

She and Ken parked in a lot near the Promenade and spent the next hour peering into every store, Starbucks, and Coffee Bean and Tea Leaf. The outdoor Promenade, lined with shops and restaurants, was bustling with its usual mix of locals, California hipsters, and street performers. Grace dialed and texted Emma endlessly while Ken got them each a double iced latte to keep their energy up. There was no sign of Emma, so they headed for the next likely destination, the Santa Monica Pier. Emma wasn't at the pier either. Grace and Ken wound their way through the meandering couples, skateboarders, and a few stroller brigades, but there was no sign of Grace's daughter. They collapsed onto a bench. The sun was going down. "We're running out of options, at least the ones I know about," she said. "What's next? Do we call the police?"

"Don't overthink," Ken said. "She's just testing her wings

SANDRA LEE

like we did when we were kids. Or did you forget? We weren't
exactly angels one hundred percent of the time either."

"Oh, God, just what I needed to hear. What if she's with
some boy?"

"All kids do these things at Emma's age. Or did you forget
that too? I certainly haven't. I think I lived every fight you ever
had with Brian right along with you all through high school,
right down to the night you married him, and then fast-forward
to the night you left him."

Grace shook her head. "I was tragic. I can't believe you put
up with me."

"Neither can I. At least you didn't marry that Von guy. Such
a cliché, Grace. The hot foreign exchange student who sweeps
the innocent Midwestern girl off her feet. Then again, maybe
you should have, in hindsight."

"Von was just a fling, as you well know. I loved Brian. He
loved me. And besides, Von went back home to Switzerland and
is now engaged." Grace's cheeks burned whenever she thought
of Von, even all these years later. Talking about him made her
nervous. Good lord, if Emma had inherited anything of her
own reckless streak, they were all done for. "What if Emma
was in an accident or something while I was in the air?"

"There wasn't an accident, Drama Queen."

"What if she tried to reach me and I was in the air with no
signal? Emma's right I'm a terrible mother. I'm never there
when she needs me."

"Don't be so dramatic. That's my role! Let's walk up the

boardwalk. I bet we'll spot Emma and her crew before too long. Tell me about Leeza. How's Snoopy doing?"

Grace smiled. "She's still weak, but I think she's finally turned the corner. Poor Jonathan's still a wreck. Though he's holding it together for Sara. Did I tell you when the doctors give her the all-clear they're going to keep trying?"

"Well, at least somebody has some good news."

"Don't you ever wish we were back in high school, when life was so simple?" Grace asked.

Ken looked at her sideways. "Did we go to the same high school? Life was anything but simple, as I recall. Especially for you! Things were worse then. Way worse! Now that I think of it, Emma should be up for sainthood compared to us. Well, except for Leeza."

Grace agreed, "Leeza was something else."

"Still is. Oh my God, my phone!" Ken jammed the earpiece into his ear. "Hello?" Then he mouthed, *It's Emma!*

Grace grabbed his wrist and leaned over to whisper, "Tell her to call me this minute!" Why wasn't Emma calling her mother back, Grace wondered. It wasn't as if she hadn't gotten her calls and texts. She reached for Ken's phone.

He held up his hand and gave her a look. She knew that look. It was the look that said, *Brace yourself, girl.*

So Grace braced.

"Uh-huh, uh-huh, and where are you?" Ken didn't sound angry with Emma or even worried. His voice was soothing and calm. Too soothing and calm, Grace thought. He was using his it's-a-disaster-but-I'm-in-control voice. That alone was cause for panic. This tone meant something really bad was being said on the other end. "OK, sweetie. You stay right there." He paused. "No, I won't tell her." He looked at Grace apologetically and hung up.

"Tell 'her' what? Why didn't you just give me the phone?" Grace demanded.

Ken turned to her and took her hand. "Grace, there's been an accident."

————

How they got to the police station, Grace never knew. Later she'd only remember that for once Ken didn't try to make a joke out of the situation.

"Emma is OK, but someone has a broken clavicle, and I don't want to scare you, Grace, but the kid who was driving, Suki somebody, had been smoking pot."

Grace felt sick. Emma had always hated drugs, sworn she'd never be around kids who used them. Grace knew who Suki was—a boy from the surfer crowd who was at least three years older than Emma. A lot of Emma's new friends were older, but Grace had assumed the surfers were like athletes. Clearly, she'd been deluding herself. They were obviously more like a bunch of young hoodlums. Now she'd have to tell her ex, Brian. When he learned what Emma was up to he'd snap back into their lives. He might even demand custody. Right now, Brian had Emma on alternate holidays and part of the summer, but he'd been asking to change the arrangements. This was all the ammunition he'd need. Grace felt like crying just thinking about all the things that were falling apart around her, and how off-track her daughter had gotten.

"She didn't want me to tell you, Grace."

That, especially, stung.

"She wanted me to come get her by myself. I said I would."

"You lied to her?"

"Sweetie, when you're dealing with the police, all bets are off. Besides, who lied to whom, here? I feel terrible. This is all my fault. I was responsible for her." It was getting dark. Ken switched on the headlights as they turned off on the 101.

"Where did it happen?"

"Malibu. This Suki kid picked Emma up at school after lunch and they went off to Zuma Beach to surf. Apparently they were going to pick up stuff for a bonfire, but they hit someone going out of the parking lot near the Sunset Restaurant. The guy they hit called the police to file a report. The police got one whiff, and *bam*! Suki went to the hospital, apparently he didn't have on his seat belt and he got banged up pretty good. His next stop may be rehab."

"Oh, God," moaned Grace. If only she'd come home yesterday like she'd originally planned.

"Emma says she had her seat belt on. She didn't smoke pot. She wasn't drinking and she passed a Breathalyzer."

Grace had to stop herself from shaking. "I don't know what we can believe anymore. She was there, not in school. Well, at least she wasn't hurt. We think."

They drove in silence another half hour or so. Grace thought she'd go crazy sitting in traffic until it finally thinned out and they reached the Agoura cutoff. Ken pulled off the freeway.

"I thought the accident was in Malibu?"

"This is where the Malibu police station is—in Agoura. It's called the Malibu/Lost Hills Sheriff's Department." Ken had a house in the Malibu area hills just above Zuma Beach and knew the area. "This is a celebrity police station. You know—the facility for movie stars who drink too much and forget where they are? It's where they locked up that pop star when she had the nervous breakdown during a pedicure."

"Great, I feel much better knowing that."

They pulled into the parking lot, and Grace leaped out of the car.

A female officer brought Emma out from the back of the station. Emma's eye makeup was streaking down her cheeks. Her eyes and her nose were red from crying. She was wearing a vintage Sex Pistols T-shirt and a micromini over purposefully torn black tights and knee-high, lace-up platform boots. Her left ear sported four piercings. She stopped in her tracks when she saw Grace, then ran straight to Ken.

"I thought you weren't going to tell her," she cried.

"This is not about your mother, Emma," Ken said. "This is about you. You told me you were going to be in school. Instead, you were in a car with marijuana, and then there was an accident. Someone was hurt. Thank God you're OK." He kissed her. "You know I love you and so does your mom, obviously, but this has to stop, Em."

"It's not my fault," whispered Emma as Grace hugged her.

She could see the halo tattoo on the back of her daughter's neck. How had they become so distant? When Emma was born, Grace vowed she'd have a different relationship with her daughter than the one she had had with her own mother. She would be open. There would be no secrets between herself and her daughter.

"It's not my fault," Emma said again, pulling away.

"I know whose fault it is," thought Grace as she watched her daughter climb into the backseat. There was something other than the truth about her divorce that Grace was holding back from Emma, and this secret was causing them to pull apart.

chapter 3

Grace was so exhausted she fell asleep for most of the ride home, but she didn't miss anything. Neither Ken nor Emma felt like talking, so the ride home was quiet.

Grace's apartment in Venice Beach was one of Ken's finds. Four years ago, when her marriage had blown up, Ken realized how shattered Grace was and began pushing the idea that this was the perfect opportunity for Grace and Emma to move to LA. One of the crew members from a comedy he was working on happened to be moving to New York, and Ken overheard him saying the landlord, a producer who lived in France, was looking for a new tenant. Ken had been at parties in the apartment, so he was sure it would be perfect. The apartment was on the first two floors of a charming three-story building that backed right onto the canal. Like most of the houses in the area, it was small, but it was ornately trimmed, with pastel-painted wood, and sandwiched between a mix of other cottages and the occasional modern overbuilt designer show house. And the area, dotted with sun umbrellas and walking bridges, was enchanting. The apartment even had a small yard framed with multicolored flowers that looked like confetti from afar, but the water view was what made it really special.

"This place is a jewel," Ken insisted. "We can do so much with it, even on a budget. The Shabby Chic look—we can make slipcovers, and a few cracks and chips will only make it better. Emma's going to love living on the canal. And you'd only be a fifteen-minute bike ride from my boat in Marina del Rey. We can ride our bikes up and down the beach and borrow cups of sugar. You've got to take it!"

So Grace had, and with Ken's help they'd made it homey and even stylish. The first floor had an open kitchen with white scalloped cupboards and trim. The living area hosted a big overstuffed couch and chairs and white painted rustic tables, and ornately framed mirrors that Ken had scored as castoffs from the set of a cancelled sitcom. They'd made slipcovers with plain white sailcloth he'd gotten cheap in the boatyard and painted the drab wood floors white with waterproof high-gloss boat paint. On the second floor were two small bedrooms and a shared bath. When Grace first moved in, Ken donated a small collection of antique milk glass vases that he then placed throughout the living room to hold the roses they'd pick up on outings to the Santa Monica floral market. "Roses, roses, everywhere!" Ken exclaimed, and the effect was indeed lovely— when it happened. Recently, though, the vases stood empty; maybe this week she'd find time to get to the market. The third floor was Grace's studio—a work in progress. So far there was just a sheet of glass propped on sawhorses, and rolling racks for clothes that didn't fit in the tiny closets downstairs, but there was potential.

"I'm calling for sushi," Ken announced. "Roberto can bring it when he picks up my car from the studio lot."

"*I am begging you!*" Halo squawked. Emma's cockatoo always had an opinion, and tonight was no exception. Sitting in his cage on his perch, Halo was part lord of the manor and part resident court jester. His head tilted sideways as he gnawed on a miniature rawhide dog bone.

Emma went straight to Halo's cage and the large, snow-white bird stretched and dipped when he saw her. "Come here, Halo baby," Emma murmured, opening the cage door and scooping him out. She clutched the bird to her chest, and he clung there like an infant. Together they dropped into one of the big, overstuffed couches. Emma sat silently stroking Halo for a minute, but soon she started to cry. "I'm so sorry, Mom, Uncle Kenny. I'm so sorry." Halo hopped up onto the back of the couch, tilting his head, observing with his black button eyes. The cockatoo could articulate a dozen phrases, but even he was at a loss for words.

Grace rushed over and held Emma, soothing her as she had when Emma was little. "It's OK," she whispered, smoothing her daughter's faux-black hair. "We're a family. We're here for you."

Ken, who could never handle tears, sat at their feet, silently stroking Emma's hand. "We're here, baby," he said.

"I didn't mean it. I thought it would be fun." Emma choked out the words between sobs. "Now Suki is in the hospital. Oh, God."

"Suki is going to be OK, but a broken clavicle is no joke. Em, you have to see this is not good. These kids are dangerous," said Grace, trying to keep her voice soothing and supportive.

Emma sat up as if jolted by an electrical current. "They're my friends! Suki is my friend!" She pulled away. "You just don't get it! You never get it!" She scooped up Halo and ran up the short flight of stairs to her bedroom.

"Well," said Ken. "I guess we just don't get it."

"That's an understatement," sighed Grace.

Roberto arrived with the sushi and Ken's car. Emma refused to come down and have any food. How was Grace going to connect with her when Emma ran out on all of their conversations?

After Ken had left, Grace lay in bed staring out at the canal and the reflections on the water. She'd been almost the same age as Emma was now when she'd lost her way. It had been the end of a very hot summer, one of the hottest on record in Wisconsin. Like Leeza, Ken, and all their friends, Grace had been counting the days to her senior year. Grace's father, Derek, had died three years previously, and since then it seemed to Grace that their tiny house felt even smaller. Her mother still seemed lost without him. Grace had turned to Leeza, Ken, her boyfriend, Brian, and baking. She started by baking the family recipes from her childhood. Cinnamon buns, gingersnaps, saffron bread, and lingonberry pancakes. Grace knew she didn't have her mother's talent, but she tried her best and hoped it might also bring her mother back to earth. Maybe even bring the two of them closer.

One afternoon, Grace made a German chocolate cake. She decided to try something different, and added fresh local Door County sour cherries to the batter. When Ken tasted it, he'd fallen on the floor, exclaiming, "I'm dead, but at least I went to heaven: Death by chocolate!"

"Watch out Wisconsin State Fair cake competition," Grace had laughed, wiping the counter and taking aim with the sponge.

"What!" Leeza said, grabbing her. "Of course! You're entering. She's entering, isn't she, Ken?"

"Absolutely. That's an automatic blue ribbon."

"I was joking," said Grace. She had no intention of entering the Wisconsin State Fair. The people who entered were practically professionals. But once Leeza had an idea in her head she made sure it happened.

Ten practice cakes later, two weeks before school started, Grace Holm found herself at the Wisconsin State Fair, standing in front of her Door County German Chocolate Cherry Cake, holding a blue ribbon. Her mother had said how proud she was, and Brian took pictures from every angle. A reporter from the Green Bay paper even interviewed Grace and published the recipe.

For the first time since her father had died, Grace started to feel better about things. She had actually won something! Carefully, she hung the blue ribbon in her room, in a place of honor. Everyone heard about Grace's big win and stopped her in the street to ask her for the recipe, even Claire Howard's mother.

DOOR COUNTY CHERRY GERMAN CHOCOLATE CAKE

FOR THE CAKE:

1 pound Door County
   sweet cherries, stemmed
   and pitted

4 ounces German chocolate

1 cup butter

1 cup sugar

1 cup light brown sugar

4 eggs

1 teaspoon vanilla

2 cups plus 1 tablespoon
   cake flour

1 teaspoon baking soda

¼ teaspoon salt

1¼ cups buttermilk

FOR THE FROSTING:

1 12-ounce can evaporated milk

3 egg yolks

1 teaspoon vanilla

1½ cups brown sugar

1 cup butter

2 cups flaked coconut

2 cups toasted pecans,
   roughly chopped

1 ounce German chocolate,
   grated

Preheat oven to 350°F. Butter and line 3 9-inch cake pans.

MAKE THE CAKE: Pit and stem the cherries. Put them into a strainer to drain. Reserve 8 beautiful cherries for top of cake. Toss the remaining cherries with 1 tablespoon flour.

Melt the chocolate and let cool a bit.

Cream the butter and sugars. Add eggs, vanilla, and chocolate. Whisk together 2 cups flour, baking soda, and salt. Add the flour mixture alternately with the buttermilk. Fold in the cherries. Pour batter into prepared cake pans. Cook 20 to 25 minutes and cool.

MAKE THE FROSTING: Whisk together milk, egg yolks, and vanilla in a large saucepan. Turn heat to medium high and add sugar and butter. Cook, stirring constantly, until the mixture is golden brown and has thickened. Remove from heat and stir in the coconut and nuts. Let cool.

Frost the tops of the cakes and stack them up. Grate chocolate over the top. Decorate with reserved cherries.

Grace imagined she was poised to enter her senior year as a celebrity of sorts. She was truly in a mood to celebrate.

That Saturday, Lorraine had been at the local food pantry, where she often volunteered on her days off, and Grace was alone, bored in the empty house. Later that night, Leeza's family was having a welcome party for her cousin Von, who was coming from Switzerland to live with Leeza's family for his and Leeza's senior year. This was the perfect time, Grace had decided, to stretch her wings and make something really special for the party. After thumbing through cookbooks and magazines without success Grace decided she'd like to make one of their special Swedish family recipes, but not something she'd already made. She wanted to find something new to try. Her mother had the recipes memorized, but on the rare occasion she turned to a very special family heirloom. The plain, weathered, reclaimed-wood recipe box had been given to Lorraine by her grandmother in Sweden and was one of the very few things Lorraine had brought to America when she'd come over as a young woman. When she was younger, Grace had liked to read the family record of all the places the recipe box had been, only to end up in their kitchen in New London. The recipe box was of little value in itself, but, to Lorraine, it was precious—too precious to even keep in the kitchen, so she stored it on a shelf in her closet. Grace wasn't supposed to go in there, but tonight was an occasion, and her mother wasn't around to ask. It wasn't as if Grace were a little kid who might wreck the box or spill something all over the cards.

Growing up, Grace had always loved the kitchen, with its

speckled linoleum floor and buffed wood table. Paintings and cards she'd made as a child were framed and hung on the walls. Although unused now, her dad's collection of beer mugs still sat on a shelf. Grace poured herself a glass of lemonade and sat at the table. She opened the recipe box. It was crammed with bits and pieces of paper, scribbled notes, and the occasional birthday card. She pulled out a receipt for her mother's wedding ring and smiled. She loved that her mother had saved the receipt. Her mother and father had adored one another. They both really missed her father.

The recipe cards were faded, their edges fraying. Most showed grease-spattered evidence of loving use over decades, but they were like a family album. She pulled out a card, turned it over, and read "Astrid's Herring." Astrid was Grace's aunt back in Sweden, whom she'd never met, and never would, because her mother hadn't spoken to her sister in over fifteen years. Grace didn't know why, but Astrid was a closed subject in the Holm household. This card was as close as Grace was going to get to her aunt. Sometimes sisters just didn't get along, she supposed. Anyhow, herring was not what she had in mind. Grace recognized Grammy Marie's handwriting right away on the meatball recipe card. This had to be the recipe for her mother's legendary Swedish meatballs. Of course, Lorraine didn't have to look at that recipe. Grace had only met her mother's mother once, as a baby, and couldn't remember her at all. She scrutinized the pale, faded ink and faint but still elegant handwriting.

She continued rifling through the box, through the recipes and papers, and then she'd found it. How stupid she had been, Grace thought later. She'd just always assumed that her mother kept the recipe box on the back of the top shelf of her bedroom closet because it was a treasured and irreplaceable family heirloom. Now she knew better. And after what she'd found in the recipe box that afternoon, things were never the same, and were still not the same after all these years.

In shock, Grace had stuffed the cards back inside, slammed the wooden lid shut, and returned the box to the top shelf of Lorraine's closet. She'd never made the Swedish specialty and she never again made anything else much beyond a toaster waffle. When people asked about her sudden aversion to cooking, Grace would make a joke of it. "I retired at the top," she'd say. The truth was, whenever she set foot in any kitchen that wasn't a stage set, Grace came down with an instant migraine. The only reason she could tolerate the kitchen in the Venice apartment was that it was open to the living room.

Grace looked at the clock: 2:00 a.m. She wanted to be on that vice principal's doorstep when the school opened, so they could throw themselves on the school's mercy. After all, she was a single working mother raising a daughter. The school should be able to offer some solutions. They'd turn things around. She'd have to miss another day of work, but Ken said she could work on some proposals to make up for it. As these thoughts raced through her head, Grace thought about taking a sleeping pill, desperate to stop tossing and turning and get some much-needed rest. She'd need to be up in four hours.

A phone that rings in the middle of the night is always frighten-ing. Even half asleep, Grace got a pit in her stomach as she reached for the bedside phone. Outside, the sky was turning pink, and the bedside clock said 5:00 a.m. Her first thought was, "Oh my God, Emma has snuck out of the house and gotten her-self into trouble!"

"Hello!" she said hesitantly.

"Grace, it's—it's Jonathan." She could barely understand him. He was crying and nearly incoherent.

Grace was instantly wide awake and overcome with a sense of dread. *Leeza*. She'd meant to call when she'd landed, but with all that was going on it just slipped through the cracks. "Is every-thing OK?" Grace was already ticking things off the packing list in her mind.

"No," Jonathan's voice cracked. "She—she fought so hard, Gracie, but—she didn't make it."

Didn't make what? "What are you saying Jonathan?" she asked. Her hand was shaking.

"Gracie, Leeza died a half hour ago," he whispered, choking out the words.

Grace dropped to the floor and curled her knees to her chest as if to protect her heart. This had to be a terrible nightmare.

"She had a heart attack. The treatments—they took so much out of her." He paused, trying to catch his breath. "She was so strong, strong for all of us. But there was so much stress on her body. Grace? Can you come? Sara will need you. She doesn't know yet, but . . ."

Grace was too stunned to cry, but she let out a low moan. "Oh, Jonathan." All her questions were in those two words.

How could this happen?

How could we let this happen?

Was Leeza in pain?

Were you with her, who was with her?

Where was the doctor?

Why didn't you call me sooner?

What can I do?

Jonathan heard them all. "She was doing great when you were here, Gracie. I think she pulled it together for your visit, but this morning she was so tired, she couldn't even get out of bed."

"That wasn't so abnormal," thought Grace; Leeza had understandably been very tired these past few months. She was only just back from the hospital.

"I called Dr. Palmerston," Jonathan continued. "He came right over. We talked about taking her to the hospital. He did some tests and said her liver was shutting down. You know, she signed those papers, not to do anything, if it was the end. And Dr. Palmerston said . . ." Jonathan started to sob again. "I'm sorry, I'm sorry . . ." He took a breath so he could continue. "Dr. Palmerston said it wouldn't matter. She hadn't wanted me—us— to know. Her organs had been failing for the past few weeks."

"But I thought she was getting better."

"That's what she told you, and me. And that's what she wanted all of us to believe. But she wasn't getting better. She was dying, and she wanted to do it her own way, here at home, with Sara and her garden. She didn't want Sara to remember her with a bunch of tubes and needles. She knew it was only a matter of weeks, or even days. She'd come home to die, Grace."

"Oh, Leeza," Grace whispered.

"You know how she was, Grace, always thinking about others, and when she got something in her head . . ."

"And I didn't see that," Grace thought. She'd missed the cue from Leeza.

"She went to bed early. Sara and I sat on the bed with her. She seemed to be having trouble breathing, so we had the oxygen tank, just in case, but she just had no strength left."

Just hearing this was more than Grace could bear. Tears started to run down her cheeks, but she needed to let Jonathan continue.

"Before I put Sara to bed, Leeza kissed her good night. Then, a little while later, Leeza slid into a coma, and Dr. Palmerston said it was just a matter of hours. And, so . . ."

If Jonathan could pull it together to make this call, Grace decided, she could handle it the way Leeza would have wanted. She could hear Leeza saying, "Grace, Snoopy can't handle it. You've got to step up!" So she tried.

"Jonathan, I am so sorry. This is the worst thing in the world. I will be there as soon as Emma and I can get on a plane." Grace was already moving toward the bathroom. She felt like throwing up. She hadn't even unpacked her suitcase. She'd just throw in a black dress and book a flight. One thing Leeza would have laughed about—one thing they knew for sure was that Emma had a black dress. It was the only color she would wear anymore.

"And Ken? Do you think he'll be able to come?"

"Of course." In the next few minutes, Grace learned the funeral would be at the New London cemetery where Leeza's parents were buried. Jonathan wasn't ready to think further, but he didn't really have to. Leeza had left all her wishes in a letter, he told Grace.

"She spent the last three weeks sitting in the garden, writing letters," Jonathan said. That was just like Leeza. She had never been much of an e-mailer. Leeza wrote letters for birthdays, anniversaries, and any occasion that mattered, like spotting a cardinal in a fruit tree in her garden. She'd even written a letter to the cardinal about the beauty of "his" garden, and had sent it to Claire, since she'd designed the garden. And this, after all the mean-girl things that Claire had done to Leeza and Grace back in high school. Leeza didn't hold grudges, but you had to earn her love. And when you did, it was beyond boundaries. Grace wished now that she had kept every single letter.

"I have to go," said Jonathan. "The people from the funeral home just arrived. I have to talk to them so we can take care of Leeza before Sara wakes up."

"Go, of course, we love you and Sara, and we love Leeza so much." Grace's voice caught sharply as she tried not to sob into the phone. She couldn't bring herself to speak of Leeza in the past tense. "We'll be there as soon as we can."

How do you tell a child that someone they love has died? Grace forced herself to put one foot in front of the other as she walked barefoot across the wood floor to Emma's bedroom, knowing that this would be the end of innocence for her daughter. She gently shook Emma awake and told her the terrible news, and for a few minutes, mother and daughter clung to each other, Emma's head on her mother's shoulder, their tears mingling on each other's cheeks.

You have to be strong, she could hear Leeza saying, and so she tried.

"We're leaving for the airport as soon as we're packed," Grace said, patting Emma's back.

For the rest of the morning, Emma was silent. Only Halo chattered up a storm.

"Seriously!!! God Bless America!!" the bird squawked as Emma scrambled eggs to share with him.

Thank God for Ken, Grace thought, as she made the requisite call to the school. He was as shattered as Grace, but, being Ken, had responded by springing into action. Of course he was going to New London. He'd pick them up and they'd all go together to the airport. He'd arrange for Roberto to take Halo. Grace was relieved to have someone else make the decisions.

———

"I don't think I can take it," Grace said to Ken when he called on his way over. She folded her one good black dress, traded out her dirty laundry for a few clean things, and stuffed it all into her bag. She would buy a toy for Sara at the airport. Not that a toy was any consolation to a child who had just lost her mother. "But what are our options? None." Grace just wished she had time and space to mourn, but they needed to get to Wisconsin.

"I'm not sure what I can say to Sara." Ken's voice sounded

hoarse. Grace could tell he'd been crying. Ken always put his emotions right out there. He might be dramatic and sometimes totally over the top, but he was the most real person on the planet.

Ken and Emma sat together on the flight to Chicago. Emma slapped on her earphones and buried herself in Ken's playlist until she fell asleep on his shoulder. Grace had made this trip so often in the past few months that the flight attendant recognized her. Thank God Ken and Emma were with her this time.

To save time, Ken had splurged and chartered a small private jet out of O'Hare that cost a fortune but shaved precious hours off the trip. "This is not the time for a road trip," he had announced. "Anyhow, I'm sure I have business to conduct in New London. It's a write-off."

Emma remained silent. Grace tried to hold Emma's hand to comfort her, but after just a second, Emma let go and went back to her headphones. It was nearly sunset when they arrived in New London, and the small airplane taxied to a stop. Normally Grace would call Leeza to let her know she'd landed, but Leeza wasn't there to call this time. A deep sadness filled Grace, and she decided to call Leeza anyhow, so after Ken and Emma left the plane Grace took out her phone. "I'm insane," she thought as she dialed the familiar number just to hear Leeza's voice. *"Hi, this is Leeza. Leave a message."* She knew her call was pointless and sad, but she'd leave a message. Why the hell not? "Hi, Leez. It's me. I miss you. We all miss you. But Ken and Emma and I are all here, we'll be here for Snoopy and Sara. You know that. We love you." Grace knew she would never hear anything back from her dear friend again. Tears burned her eyes.

"Miss?" The pilot had come into the cabin.

There was no further avoiding getting off the plane.

Their few small bags had been unloaded right onto the tarmac, and as she walked down the stairs from the jet, Grace could see Ken and Emma picking them up a few yards ahead. They were talking to a man. As she got closer, Ken waved. "Look who came to pick you up—after sixteen years!"

The man turned around. It was Von Vasser.

chapter 4

The yellow-blond corn silk hair that in high school had fallen to his shoulders was now cut short, but otherwise he was still the six-foot-three, fit, well-dressed guy from high school who'd made Grace's heart beat a little faster. Von and Ken shared a quick hug, then he turned to Grace, his blue eyes filled with warmth.

"Grace. I am so sorry. I came as soon as Jonathan e-mailed that Leeza asked for me. I had no idea . . . We were making an acquisition in Germany and . . ." Von embraced Grace. She closed her eyes and put her head on his broad shoulders. For an instant she felt seventeen again, and in his arms under the fairy lights at their high school prom. Grace could feel his warm chest and his breath in her hair, and it seemed like all would be OK. She was surprised that after all these years, there was still such an attraction. An airport vehicle honked, and Grace came to her senses. They weren't alone or in high school anymore. She took a step back and pulled Emma forward. "Where are my manners? Von, this is my Emma."

Emma shot her a look that said she was nobody's anything, but she politely shook Von's hand. "H'llo. Nice to meet you."

Von also took a step back, shaking his head slowly. "Such a gorgeous girl," he said, looking past her gel-spiked hair and smeared black eyeliner. "Like her mother. Your mother is very beautiful, you know, Emma."

Grace could almost hear her daughter's unspoken comment to that: *Eeeeeww.*

"Please come with me," Von said. "I have a car to drop us off." He pointed to a sleek, black Escalade, and a uniformed driver leaped out to open the doors.

Ken leaned over and whispered, "Nice touch." Grace wondered when the last time was that New London had seen a chauffeur. Von must have booked the service through Green Bay. He always did know how to make the grand gesture. Like when he'd brought her three dozen pink roses to match her rose-colored chiffon prom dress. And then there was the crowning touch, a small box of fresh strawberries dipped in his family's legendary Vasser chocolate. She could still practically taste the berries, ripe and sweet, with the contrast of the bitter-sweet dark chocolate.

"Chocolate was originally a treat for kings and queens," Von had told her just before he gave her a kiss.

"I have a rental car to pick up, but I could use a ride over to Enterprise, if that's OK?" Ken asked, then added, "How is your mother? Is she here?"

Vanessa Vasser, Von's headstrong American mother, was Leeza's aunt, her late mother's sister who had met Von's father, from a wealthy Swiss chocolate-industry family, on a post-graduate vacation in Zurich. Vanessa was never far from her son's side. She even managed to make the huge trip from Switzerland to New London for almost every one of Von's choir performances. She came more often than many local parents, in fact, sometimes taking the entire choir out for pizza. Leeza had explained that her aunt Vanessa had lost her only daughter, Von's older sister, and so she had become ultraprotective of her son, as well as her niece, Leeza.

"Yes, a ride, of course, not a problem. And yes, my mother is here. She flew over with me," Von said. "She is devastated, of course. We all are." He picked up Grace's bag and placed his hand on the small of her back, gently leading her toward the car. He added, "I can imagine you are all devastated as well."

Von helped Grace and Emma into the car while the driver got the other side for Ken.

"How is Sara?" Emma asked.

"Of course, she's not really aware of what's happened." Von shook his head. "Only two! Imagine growing up without her mother. Poor angel."

"I have to be with her," Emma announced. "She's just a baby. She needs me." Grace noticed tears welling in Emma's ice-blue eyes, even though she tried to blink them back.

"Emma is Sara's godmother," Grace explained.

"She's truly beautiful," said Von, his blue eyes falling on Grace. "You and Brian must be very proud." Von touched Grace's shoulder. "It's sad I wasn't able to see you before now. Once I was back in Zurich, the business took over my life, and now so much time has passed."

DARK CHOCOLATE
DIPPED STRAWBERRIES

Makes 20 to 24

8 ounces semisweet
  chocolate

4 ounces milk chocolate

20 to 24 medium to large
  strawberries with stems

Pearlized sugar

Wash the strawberries and make sure they are very dry.

Add the chocolate to a glass bowl and melt it over a double boiler.
Let the chocolate cool a bit before dipping strawberries.

Dip the strawberries in the chocolate and place them onto a wax
paper-lined baking sheet. Immediately sprinkle with the pearlized
sugar before the chocolate starts to set. Refrigerate for 5 to 10 minutes for the chocolate to completely set. Store in the refrigerator and
use within 24 hours.

NOTE:

- Milk chocolate was added to the dark chocolate
  to sweeten it a bit.

- Any sanding sugar would work as well.

Grace had heard this from Leeza, but never from Von himself. She knew that Von's father had suffered a stroke right after
Von went back to Switzerland, and Von had been forced to take
over the family business.

"I had hoped to attend our graduation, then go to university,"

Von continued. "But life had other plans. Well, at any rate, now we've actually purchased two of our competitors and we're expanding. Things are going well. But still, things happen. I will never forgive myself that I wasn't able to come immediately when Leeza asked."

"When did she ask you to come?" Grace asked as the car pulled out of the parking lot.

"This week, but I had no idea it was so serious. Leeza never let on." Von wrung his hands and twisted at a gold ring that glinted even in the fading light. Grace recognized it right away—it was Von's family crest, the brand insignia that was on all the chocolate products Vasser Master Chocolatiers produced. Back in high school Von had let Grace try the ring on, and Grace had found it all very exciting—none of the Wisconsin boys she knew had a family crest.

On the short drive to Enterprise, Von explained that the funeral, followed by a reception at the home, had been arranged for the following day. Grace's mother, Lorraine, had volunteered to take care of the food. They dropped Ken at the rental car office and told him they would see him after he checked into his bed-and-breakfast. Then they made the short drive to Leeza's home.

Leeza's house sat on six acres across the beautiful Wolf River, which wound its way through all of New London. Grace sighed as they crossed over the Wolf. She never got tired of seeing the river that defined her childhood hometown, its peaceful blue water and tree-lined banks.

"The driver can take your bags to your mother's house now,

if you'd like, and then drive you there later," said Von. "I'm afraid my mother has taken over the guest room at Jonathan and Leeza's. Or, I'm sure you'd be welcome to the pull-out couch, of course. I know you often stay with Leeza when you visit."

Grace hadn't thought of that. Naturally, all of Leeza's relatives would be arriving, and Jonathan would want to put them up at their house. "The couch will be great for tonight. Emma and I can share."

"I'm sleeping with Sara," Emma announced, throwing open the car door and leaping out.

Grace followed her daughter up the drive to the house she'd left just two days before, which now seemed so long ago.

When did he arrive? Grace wondered. It had to be just the previous night. Von had said Leeza had asked him to come, but he'd been delayed. That meant Leeza had asked Von to come when Grace was still there visiting and she'd asked Grace to stay an extra day. Leeza's request of Von was not about Leeza, Grace suddenly realized. It was about Grace. As one of her last wishes, and without telling either of them, Leeza clearly wanted to bring Grace and Von together. As it turned out, she'd done it—just not the way she'd planned.

As she and Von stepped onto the porch, they greeted Jonathan's brother and law partner, David Ericksson, who was now mayor of New London and married to her high school nemesis, Claire. The house buzzed with activity. Everyone loved Leeza, and it seemed as though the whole town were scattered among the living, kitchen, and family rooms. People were even spilling out onto the wraparound porch, chatting in small clusters or sitting quietly with their plates of food. In the kitchen, the large, marble-topped island that had been Leeza's command center was piled high with food containers from concerned friends. Claire Ericksson moved through the crowd carrying a platter of sandwiches, taking her role as Leeza's sister-in-law very seriously. Grace spotted Von's mother, Vanessa Vasser, across the room, her unmistakable flaming red hair and dramatic hand movements accentuating whatever she was talking about. They could wait. She needed to find Jonathan first.

At last she found him, going through the motions of welcoming and comforting family and friends, but he was clearly struggling. Emma said hello and then ran off to help by putting Sara to bed. Grace gave Jonathan a hug and, although she tried her best, she could no longer hold back her tears. Jonathan and Sara were all she had left of Leeza, and she wept on his shoulder. Suddenly, Grace felt a hand touching her own shoulder, and her mother, Lorraine, was there. As always, her mother looked beautiful. She had the carriage of an aristocrat, the kind of looks that shone even in the simplest clothes, no makeup, and a low ponytail pulled back from her face with a scarf.

"Jonathan, Grace, dear, this is all so awful, I'm so sorry."

Jonathan added Lorraine to the hug, and they stood quietly for a minute. Then Lorraine spoke.

"Emma looks exhausted. I can take her home with me now."

Of course Emma was exhausted. They were all exhausted and heartbroken, but leave it to Lorraine, Grace thought, to find a way to pass judgment on her parenting skills at a time like this. "We are staying here, Mother," Grace answered, not noticing the flicker of disappointment that crossed Lorraine's face.

"Well, that's fine. I'm sure you'll be a help." She turned to Jonathan. "I left a platter of meatballs and a salad on the counter. I'll bring more tomorrow."

Jonathan simply nodded as he disappeared into the embrace of a large, white-haired woman, leaving Grace and Lorraine to continue the conversation on their own.

No matter how old she got, Grace felt like a girl around her mother. There were so many unspoken things between them. Where or how to start? Now certainly wasn't the time.

"Well, I guess I'll see you at the funeral, then," Lorraine said politely, breaking the silence and reaching into her purse for her car keys.

It was late when the last person left. Emma and Sara had gone to bed hours ago. Von had gone to his hotel, and his mother had gone up to the guest room. Claire and David left with the last friends, leaving Grace and Jonathan alone. It was strange being in Leeza's house late at night without her. Grace had always liked Jonathan, but she realized just then that she'd never actually spent time alone with him. Leeza had always been present. He was clearly exhausted, so Grace offered him a mug of warm milk and added, "I'll clean up. Why don't you get some rest."

"Thanks, Grace. I'm so grateful you, Emma, and Ken are here." And with that he shuffled off to bed.

After Jonathan went upstairs, Grace wiped down the kitchen,

SANDRA LEE

put the food containers away, then washed and dried the dishes. The final dishes to be put away were the two mugs Leeza and Grace thought of as their talking mugs. Grace's mug was red with pink dots and Leeza's was pink with red stripes. Grace held one in each hand and felt a deep sadness wash over her. Leeza and Grace had only just drunk from them a day ago, but that would be the last time. Grace sighed and placed their favorite mugs gently back into the cupboard. The house fell quiet.

The morning of the funeral started with a Midwestern downpour that would last the day. "What a cliché," Ken said under his breath as they joined the mourners at the graveside. The only nice thing about the rain was the bright bouquet of umbrellas hovering over the somber crowd. The cemetery had erected a large canopy, but it offered little protection against the blowing wind. It was Leeza's wish that the funeral be held as soon as possible so that, she had said to Jonathan, everyone, especially Sara, could get on with life. As if life would ever be the same. Leeza had been the glue in so many people's lives.

Leeza's funeral. The words just didn't make sense. Leeza, who had always been there, was just gone. How was it possible that Leeza, so full of life, of love, was in this white coffin? *She doesn't belong in there!* Grace wanted to scream. *There's been a terrible mistake!* Grace didn't know how she would make it through the day. She gripped her umbrella so tightly her hand fell asleep. She had to pull herself together. She remembered what Leeza had said during their last talk about doing difficult things for Emma and Sara, and this was a doozy, but she tried to find strength now for Emma. Thank God Ken was there, holding her other arm.

The group bowed their heads for the final prayers, and Grace, Emma, and Ken joined the others in placing a single pink rose on Leeza's casket. Jonathan held Sara in his arms, as she placed a tiny stuffed bear among the roses.

The burial site was beautiful, even in the rain, Grace thought. She would enjoy coming to visit here, to feel close to Leeza again. It made her wish that her father had a grave she could visit. Instead, she and Lorraine had stood, hand in hand, and scattered his ashes over his beloved Wolf River. She'd been thirteen when he died in a snowmobile accident. Grace wondered if Lorraine was remembering, too, as she looked at her across the circle of mourners and felt a pang of—what was it? Regret? Anger? Sadness? There were so many complicated feelings where her mother was concerned.

Directly next to Lorraine stood Von and his mother. David and Claire were nearby. And Brian, Grace's ex, stood next to Emma. Brian had driven up from Chicago for the day. Once Brian, Grace, Leeza, Jonathan, and Ken had been nearly inseparable. Now everything was different. Their friendship had splintered into a million pieces. Grace glanced down and smiled to see Brian's shoes. Even at the funeral he was sporting red laces. About ten years ago, he'd won a roulette jackpot while betting on red and wearing red shoelaces, and they'd been his lucky laces ever since. She looked at him. Brian's olive skin, dark curly hair, and dark eyes were a stark contrast to Von's

pale and tall, angular looks. They had always been polar oppo-
sites, and neither had ever had much use for the other. However, Grace couldn't help but thinking, they ironically had one
thing in common—both men had bitterly disappointed her. In
the end, she had ended up with Ken. Good old, trustworthy,
always-there-for-her Ken. He held the umbrella over both of
them steadily, as always. Funny how things had turned out.

Back at Leeza's house, Grace and Ken had barely taken off
their coats when Brian approached. "I have to get back to Chicago," he said. "But I think Emma should come with me."

"Well, that's not happening," Grace said, calmly hanging her
coat on the makeshift coatrack Jonathan had set up on the porch.
Inside, however, Grace was seething. She couldn't believe Brian
was bringing this up now, of all times. "Emma is going back to
LA with me, where she has school."

"I think she needs to be with her father for a while, and
Emma agrees."

Grace had no patience for this discussion right now. "Well,
you should have thought about that when we were a family. You
had plenty of chances to be with her then, but where were you?
Don't answer that, because we both know." She banged her
umbrella down. There was no point in recounting their years in
Chicago now, nor was this the place. It angered her that Brian
always did this—made her the bad one.

"You have so much on your plate right now," Brian said.
"And Emma wants to see her Chicago friends. Besides, it
sounds like she could use a change from the LA scene, what
with the accident and all."

"Today is about Leeza; we'll discuss this later." Grace's heart was pounding. But she wasn't feeling so secure, not at all. What if Brian decided to take legal action, sued for custody? Worse, what if he was right? What if Emma was better off with him?

"Let me send her a ticket," said Brian. "Once things are resolved with the school, it just makes sense for her to come to me for the summer."

"Well, we'll look into it," Grace said, trying, for Leeza's sake, to not escalate the situation.

Brian put his hand on her arm. "I don't want to argue, Grace. Emma needs both of her parents." He paused. "I've been thinking—why don't you both come stay for the summer?"

He had to be kidding. "Brian, we can't go backwards," Grace said. *And you blew it!* she wanted to add, but she knew he knew exactly what she was thinking. If nothing else, after four years of dating and twelve years of marriage, Brian D'Angelo knew Grace Holm.

When Brian finally left, she found Ken talking to a man she didn't recognize. Ken waved her over. "Grace, this is Tim Westerly from the bookstore in town."

"I'm sorry for your loss," Tim said, shaking her hand. "Leeza held her book club meetings at my shop, the Book Nook. We'll miss her terribly."

"Thank you," Grace said, but she wasn't paying attention. In a corner of the family room, Emma was in a large wing chair, with Sara asleep on her lap. Von was perched on the arm of the chair, leaning over and talking to Emma. She was showing him pictures, probably of Halo, on her phone. It was nice seeing

Emma getting along with another adult, but that it was Von made Grace uneasy. She excused herself from Ken and Tim and made her way over to Emma and Von. "Emma, would you like to put Sara down for her nap?"

Emma looked like she might argue, but for once she actually agreed with one of Grace's suggestions. She shut her phone and tenderly carried her goddaughter through the crowd and up the staircase. The sweet, loving Emma was indeed still inside the Goth Girl, and this gave Grace hope.

"Von, I've been wondering, did Leeza tell you to come when I was here?"

"Well, she mentioned it." Von looked at her.

"But not to me."

"I think she meant for us to see each other again. Just not the way it happened. She knew you would leave, I think, if you knew I was coming. But Grace, high school was a long time ago. I am not that boy."

"We're different people now, Von. I know I am." Von was gazing at her, and it was making her uneasy.

"I'd like to get to know this Grace," Von said, caressing her arm. "And her daughter, Emma. I must leave tomorrow to go back to the factory. But why don't you both come spend some time on my boat this summer? I am planning on a trip around the Greek Islands. I invited Leeza and Jonathan, but maybe now he will come with Sara."

What was going on? First Brian, now Von. This was crazy. Grace felt like she might be the butt of some great joke. She collected herself. "What an amazing invitation, Von, but Emma needs to be grounded this summer," she said. "And I have to work. Thank you, I'm sure it's lovely, and I'd love to meet your fiancée," she added pointedly.

"Of course you wouldn't have heard. I was going to tell Leeza. I've broken off my engagement."

Grace was so taken aback that she had not noticed Emma's return. "Mom! Mom!" Emma tugged at her arm. "Mr. Vasser invited us on his boat! Can you believe?"

"I can believe we're not going."

"What! We're not going? Well, I want to go. It sounds like fun." Emma crossed her arms in exasperation and turned to Von. "You see what this is? Total irrationality. Well, I'm beggin' you, don't take no for an answer."

Von laughed, and Grace felt flutters in her stomach as she looked at Von and her daughter standing together.

chapter 5

"I am not going back to that school. Ever. I hate it! I hate you!" Emma screamed, slamming the car door in Grace's face.

"Emma, come back here this minute!" Grace yelled before slumping in the front seat next to Ken. "I spent an hour on the phone to get the school to lift the suspension due to emotional hardship, and now she won't even go back. All she wants to do is go on Von's yacht."

"Let's see," said Ken. "Algebra class or a yacht in the Mediterranean, which would you choose? Duh! I seem to remember you skipping school to go bowling. At least Emma's got some taste. You know what? After the past month, a trip would do the two of you good. Maybe you should go."

"We're not going."

"Von's not so bad. You used to like him. And how many single guys with yachts are floating around out there anyhow? Why not have some fun? Leeza would have been the first to agree."

That much was true. Leeza had asked Von to come back when she'd thought Grace was going to be there. Leeza was the only person, aside from Grace, who knew she had unfinished business with Von. With Brian out of the picture, had Leeza thought Grace would fall for Von all over again and that Von, Grace, and Emma could become a happy family? Perhaps it was a good thing Von's trip to New London had been short and there wasn't time for anything other than family before he left again.

"Gracie," Ken interrupted her thoughts, "Earth to Gracie—I know you are in the thrall of higher education, but the fact is, we have to deal with some logistics. Jonathan has asked me if you and I could stay on for a few weeks to help sort out Leeza's things. And, of course, we must."

"But Emma has school," Grace said.

"Darling girl, we all know, nothing happens the last two weeks. Can't she do it from here?"

"From New London? How?"

"Well, people telecommute. Even to school. Say, she lived in Alaska, and a glacier kept her from attending class."

"Except she doesn't."

"Skype?"

"She's one cut class away from being expelled. They're not going to go for it."

"Let's think positive, Grace."

———

An hour later, Grace and Ken were huddled over mugs of hot tea at the Book Nook, a cozy shop in a gently used Dutch Colonial style house that faced the town square. At the turn of the last century, a prominent family had probably lived there; now the building had been converted to a commercial space, with a small studio upstairs. Behind cheery blue-and-yellow checkerboard cotton curtains, the ground floor was occupied by rows of books, some comfy couches and chairs where customers were encouraged to flop down for a good read, and small tables and chairs scattered about in the children's section. A wooden staircase, painted fire-engine red, led upstairs to the apartment of the proprietor, Tim Westerly. Ken and Tim had been seeing quite a bit of each other since meeting at the funeral. "You remember Tim from the wake. Leeza's book club met here," Ken said. "Trust me, Tim knows how to handle these academic issues—he has a PhD. He'll help us brainstorm."

Tim descended a ladder, balancing a box of books. A huge smile broke out across his face when he noticed that Ken was there. "I don't suppose either of you is into fishing?" he said. "This stock isn't moving. I might as well give it away."

Tim certainly didn't look like an academic, Grace thought, or like a typical resident of New London—at least not from her day. He looked more like an intellectual refugee from a punk rock band—skinny, pale, with spiky dark hair, skinny black jeans, horn-rimmed glasses, and tattoos of vines climbing down his arms from under the sleeves of his T-shirt to his wrists. "Ah, yes," Grace thought, "Ken is right. Emma would indeed listen to Tim."

"Well, it's a matter of marketing, clearly," said Ken, getting up to give Tim a kiss hello. "New London is one of the biggest fishing centers in the Midwest. Who's going to see those fishing books tucked away in the middle of the F's? Put them right in the window! Now, in exchange for that sage advice, let's talk school."

Two hours and one fisherman later, a plan was in place, and Ken was walking through the shop with Tim. They were talking and laughing as Ken made suggestions on how to spruce the place up. "Budget Bibliotheque," as Ken called it. They worked well together, and Tim was taking avid notes on his iPad. Grace was going to see if the New London Middle School would agree to supervise Emma's final exams. If only Emma could stay in New London, she would hopefully stay out of trouble, while Grace and Ken went back to LA and wrapped up the season on *The Lost Ones*. The school might refuse, Grace realized, but it was worth a try. A change might be good for Emma, Grace thought. And as many issues as she had with her mother, she knew from experience that Lorraine would keep an eagle eye on her granddaughter. Brian was begging for her to come to Chicago, but the social scene there, with all Emma's old friends, was bound to be so distracting she would probably never make up all the work she needed to pass into high school. And Brian had certainly not proved himself to be reliable, at least not in Grace's mind. His intentions were always good, but intentions weren't enough when it came to Emma. In New London, she'd be able to focus, and she'd have her grandmother to watch over her. No matter what Grace felt toward Lorraine, this option made sense for now.

"Is the end of this couch taken?" Grace looked up to see a muscular, thirty-something man with curly brown hair and deep gray eyes dropping into the couch beside her. He was smudged with red paint and had sawdust in his hair. A tool belt hung around his waist and he chugged from a bottle of water.

"Storage units," he said. "I've been installing storage units in the basement, in case you're wondering. We're moving the back stock down there."

"I wasn't, but thanks," Grace said.

"Ken, you remember Mike from the other day, and Grace, I see you've met our resident carpenter, plumber, painter, and jack-of-all-trades," said Tim. "Mike Lund, this is Grace Holm-D'Angelo."

"I've been meaning to tell you, the red stairs are a stroke of genius," said Ken.

Mike shrugged and wiped his hands on his shirt. "Thanks, leftover paint from the firehouse. The price was right. And, hey, Tim, when was the last time you checked the batteries on your smoke detectors? They were dead. I changed them, but you should get the hardwired kind."

"The wiring in this place is so old, it's from the Ice Age," Tim shrugged. "It's impossible to wire anything. Grace, can't you tell?—Mike's a volunteer fireman. Among other things. Lucky for me, he loves books. We made a deal."

"One paint job for twenty copies of *Last of the Mohicans*."

"What on earth would you do with twenty copies of *Last of the Mohicans*?" Grace asked.

"Give them to my class at the school."

"Mike's day job is teaching."

"English. Eighth grade."

"My daughter Emma is in eighth grade," said Grace. "En-

glish, well—I can't even go there. We've had some family issues, but if all goes well, she'll be finishing up the year here. I'm
hoping her school will send her final exams and let her take
them here. But she's cut classes and skipped school, and I'm not
doing a good job of handling it . . ."

"Emma is Leeza's goddaughter," said Tim.

"Really? I gave a talk to her book club once. Lovely lady, I'm
sorry. Is there anything I can do?"

"Maybe there was," thought Grace. She found herself asking
Mike Lund if he could possibly find time to meet Emma and just
talk to her.

"You know what?" Mike said. "I run a study group after
school. The eighth-grade curriculum is pretty standard. If you
meet with the head of the middle school and ask, maybe Emma
could join us. And we can set up a proctor situation if they'd let
her take her exams here. Sometimes, when there's a family
emergency, that's allowed."

Ken stood behind Mike, miming a big thumbs-up.

"Maybe we could discuss this over coffee sometime soon? If
you're free . . ."

"I have to go back to LA. Emma will be staying with her
grandmother." *Hopefully, that would work out.*

"Grace, can you help us over here for a minute?" Ken called
out, motioning her to the back. "The coffeemaker seems to
be—stuck." He pulled her into the kitchenette. "Missed opportunity, Grace." Ken wagged his finger at her scoldingly.

"Ken," she whispered. "I am not interested in dating. I can't
even think about it."

"Who said anything about dating? How about tutoring? You need this guy. Tim says he's great with kids. He's supposed to be an even better teacher than carpenter. Or fireman. And look at this guy. How hard would it be to look at him for an hour?"

"OK, OK, I'll meet with him." For some reason, Grace found herself smoothing her hair before she went back over to the couch. Not that this would be a date.

———

For the non-date the next day, Grace suggested the coffee shop a couple of blocks away, overlooking the river. She couldn't help but notice that even before they sat down, several kids came over and said hi to "Mr. Lund." They seemed to like him as well as respect him. That was a good sign.

"You didn't grow up here, did you?" Grace asked. "I'd remember you from high school."

"No, we're from Sister Bay; my family is all over Door County."

"It's beautiful there," Grace said. She soon learned that Mike had ended up in New London after the University of Illinois, where he played football. Now he coached the middle school team in addition to teaching English, and he was a volunteer fireman. He wasn't married, had had one broken long engagement with his college sweetheart. Grace didn't probe—after all, this was a non-date, and heaven knows she had enough issues of her own to deal with. Instead, they talked about Emma. Mike was easy to talk with, and she had to admit he had a great smile.

"Let's start with what she's interested in. What books did her class read this year?" Mike asked.

"Um . . . I'm not sure." Grace squirmed. This was pathetic. What kind of mother was she? She could not recall a single book that had been assigned reading for Emma's class. Between work and Leeza, she'd been too busy and preoccupied to be able to monitor Emma's homework that closely. "The thing is, I know it's important for her to finish the year, but I'm so worried about what will happen if she does go back." She found herself opening up about Emma's accident, and her bad-influence friends. And then, to her astonishment, Grace found herself crying, right in the middle of the café. She was crying for Emma, for Leeza, for herself—she'd had to hold it together for so long, and now the dam had a crack. A gap, actually.

Mike quickly gathered their jackets and walked her outside. "The psychologists say, don't make any major decisions when you're under stress," he said. "The death of a good friend is extremely stressful. Emma will be fine here, with your mother. You go back, do what you have to do, and then come back for her. I organized a high school tutoring squad. I've found kids respond better to other kids. She'll enjoy them; that makes a big difference. And she'll make new friends."

That all sounded promising to Grace. She'd certainly tried everything else. They were at the end of the plank in LA. This had to work. She nodded as she blew her nose. She didn't want to think about how she must look—no makeup, wild hair, red eyes, and now a nose to match. Thank God this was a non-date.

Talking to Lorraine, after Mike had dropped her off, was not so easy. Grace hadn't wanted to admit to her mother how badly things were going in LA. But now she had no choice. "She has some issues involving school," Grace began tentatively. She told her mother about the suspension, about the exams coming up, and, finally, about the older kids Emma was hanging around with. Telling her about the accident was especially hard. Every sentence made her feel like she'd failed as a mother. "So, can you take her? Just for two weeks?" They were sitting in the kitchen, at the same table that always brought back memories Grace would rather forget.

Lorraine sighed. "Of course I will. She's my granddaughter."

Grace expected her mother to be judgmental, but instead, Lorraine smiled. "Do you know who she reminds me of?"

"Who?"

"Me. She reminds me of me. And of you. We're alike, whether we like it or not, Grace, and whether or not you want to admit it to yourself. We're mother, daughter, and granddaughter. We're strong women, all of us. Sometimes that gets us into trouble. But that's also why we straighten ourselves out in the end. Why we can handle so much." She offered Grace a piece of pie and, in a natural reflex, Grace took it and began taking bites. Her mother's strawberry pie, once a rite of spring in their house. These were the same dishes she'd eaten off of while she was growing up, the turquoise Fiestaware that was Lorraine's pride, displayed on a wooden rack flanking the door. Grace recognized this very plate, an old friend with a chip on the underside of the rim. She even remembered when she had caused the chip, accidentally banging the plate on the rim of the sink, and the chagrin she'd felt, because she knew her mother was so proud of this set, a rare garage sale find. She could remember how the chip had felt, and how she'd tried but failed to glue the piece back on again. Now the chip was smooth, like those rocks on the shore of Lake Michigan, once sharp, but softened over time. She could practically see the card for strawberry pie in her mind's eye. She couldn't help wondering, where was the recipe box now?

"It will be good for us to spend some time together," Lorraine said.

Grace wished she could believe what her mother was saying, but she wasn't so sure, so instead she focused on the practicalities. "I've arranged for a tutor." Grace told Lorraine about Mike. Amazingly, Lorraine already knew him.

"Mike's a teacher? He fixed the porch steps last summer. And he put in a birdhouse. Let me show you." She walked Grace outside. The birdhouse was adorable, a little turquoise and yellow construction perched on the outside of one of the porch columns. "There are finches nesting in it already," Lorraine said. "Emma will like that."

"Stay here? You've got to be kidding. I'm going back to LA with you," Emma stated, her hands planted firmly on her hips.

"Emma, please," said Grace. "I'll be back in two weeks."

"I am not staying in this place."

"It's all arranged. You can take your exams here."

"I'll flunk."

STRAWBERRY PIE

FOR THE CRUST:

2½ cups flour

2 tablespoons sugar

¼ teaspoon salt

1 cup cold butter

6 to 8 tablespoons
ice water

FOR THE FILLING:

3 tablespoons flour

3 teaspoons cornstarch

½ cup sugar

4 egg yolks

1½ cups milk

2 teaspoons vanilla

2 quarts small strawberries

Sugar, optional

1 pint strawberry jam, optional

Powdered sugar, optional

FOR THE CRUST: Whisk together the flour, sugar, and salt. Cut in the butter with a pastry cutter or two knives until it is the size of small peas in the flour. Add the ice water a tablespoon at a time until the dough just holds together. Turn it out onto a board and separate it into 2 pieces. Form each piece into a disk and cover with plastic wrap. Put one in the refrigerator for a half hour; put the other into the freezer for another use.

When ready to bake, preheat the oven to 450°F. Remove the crust from the refrigerator and put it onto a well-floured board. Roll it out about 2 inches larger than a 9-inch pie pan. Put the crust into the pan, fold over the excess, and crimp the edge. Prick some holes with a fork in the bottom of the crust. Line the crust with foil and fill with beans. Bake in the oven for 15 minutes. Remove the beans and bake for another 5 minutes or until the crust is golden brown. Cool.

FOR THE FILLING: Whisk together flour and cornstarch. In a medium bowl, whisk together sugar and egg yolks until the mixture has lightened. Whisk in the flour mixture, working out any lumps. In a medium pan, heat the milk until hot but not boiling. Slowly whisk the milk into the egg mixture. Pour the egg mixture into the pan and return to the heat. Bring to a simmer, stirring constantly. Let it simmer for at least one minute or until thickened. Turn off heat and stir in the vanilla. Pour through a sieve into a clean bowl. Put plastic wrap or wax paper directly on the surface, let cool a bit, and refrigerate.

TO MAKE THE PIE: Spread the filling evenly into the pie shell. Taste your strawberries and gently stir in a little sugar if they are not sweet enough. Mound the berries on top of the filling. You can serve this immediately as is.

You can make a glaze by warming the strawberry jam and straining it through a sieve. Gently brush over the strawberries. Or you can just sprinkle with a little powdered sugar.

NOTE: This pie could also be made with raspberries, blueberries, or blackberries. Or any mix of the berries.

"No you won't. There's a great tutor here. You'll have a lot of help."

"What about Halo? Halo needs me!"

"Halo is fine, he's home with Roberto, you know he loves going on vacation."

"Dad says I should stay with him," Emma countered defiantly. "He'd let me bring Halo."

Brian had visitation rights, but Grace did not want to give him any more leeway with Emma. She knew that he was already unhappy about the situation in LA, and she did not want to add any more fuel to the fire. The last thing Grace needed right now was for Brian to think she didn't have things with Emma under control. She had to stand firm. "Emma, do you understand that this is your last chance? If you don't pass those exams, you're repeating the year. You won't graduate middle school with the rest of your class."

Emma looked around the kitchen in a panic, then stomped over to the counter, grabbed a bag of chips, and started stuffing them into her mouth.

"And you know what? There's a paid summer internship available at the Book Nook. Tim says he needs help with all the kids who come in over the summer. "

Did Grace detect a flicker of interest at the word "paid"?

Lorraine walked over and put her arm around Emma. "Once you're settled in, we can bring Halo. It will be wonderful to have you," she said. "I've been lonely, you know. I don't get much chance to be with my granddaughter."

Emma said nothing.

"I know you love birds . . . there are so many beautiful wild birds here in New London, and . . ."

"They're not Halo." Emma stomped back to the table, snatched up her iPad, and stormed out. "I've got to Skype my friends and tell them I'm being held prisoner."

Lorraine and Grace sighed.

Maybe Halo would help. Ken was commuting back and forth, finding an increasing number of "important" design decisions for the Book Nook that translated to an increasing number of reasons to be with Tim. He could bring Halo on his next trip. But that was just a temporary Band-Aid. Grace could not imagine how she was going to keep things together. Once again, she was leaving her daughter, just when she needed her, but she had to get back to LA and straighten out her own life, her job. Grace was a single mother now, so she couldn't afford to lose her job. If she didn't work for Ken, she'd probably have been fired by now. Grace knew that her job skills were tenuous. Being a stay-at-home mom was the toughest job in the world, but all those years devoted to raising Emma did not translate in a tough job market. Working with Ken had given her a foundation, and he'd trained her well, but Grace knew this was a transition period. She had to think about the future. She needed to protect her current job and also think about her next steps. Ken could only cover for her for so long, and she would never want to let him down.

Then there was the school issue. Grace had to meet with Emma's school and tell them her daughter was at risk if she came back. She had to convince them to let Emma take her exams in New London, and she had to make sure Emma passed.

chapter 6

"**M**alibu is the cure-all for everything," Ken announced as he waved a bunch of fresh mint at Grace. "And what Malibu can't cure, my Mojito will. The secret is to bruise the mint leaves."

Grace was enjoying the sunset. After the tough talk with the vice principal, who finally agreed to let Emma take her exams in Wisconsin "in exchange for my left arm," as Grace told Ken, plus a full schedule of work during the top-rated Werewolf Week, Grace was exhausted. Ken hadn't had to argue to get her to agree to stay at his house above Zuma Beach for the weekend. He drove them up the beautiful Pacific Coast Highway overlooking the surf, in his 1970 280 Mercedes SL convertible with Halo perched in the back in his "Wingabago" acrylic car cage. As he drove, Ken chewed her ear off about Tim and the Book Nook. She couldn't remember Ken ever being so excited about someone. It sounded like Ken wasn't just helping Tim with a few display tips; they were really starting to become close. From the moment she spotted Ken's house, an ultra-white, modernist wood structure jutting out from the top of a moss-covered cliff above the beach like the prow of a ship,

Grace felt the tension start to drain away. Spring in LA could be foggy along the coast, but this evening was beautiful.

The velvety ocean air settled over Grace and Ken as they hauled the grocery bags through the front door and walked straight toward an unbelievable view of the Pacific. Deep blue-gray water and sky as far as the eye could see. The view was nothing less than breathtaking.

The house itself had every modern convenience, but Ken preferred overhead fans to air-conditioning. "The ocean is na-ture's AC, baby," he liked to say. The décor was all Ken. It looked simple, but there was a backstory to every piece. No treasure escaped him. There was a wall of framed, autographed black-and-white movie star photos from the fifties and sixties that Ken had unearthed in an album he got for a song. Ken liked to say that Clark Gable, Marilyn Monroe, and Elizabeth Taylor were his "house guests in residence." And he had scored big-time with the twig table in the living room. It looked like some-thing that might have been thrown out in a yard sale, but Ken had immediately recognized it for what it was: a masterpiece of Adirondack crafts, which had once graced Topridge, one of the legendary camps in upstate New York in the early 1900s.

They unpacked the fresh vegetables that they'd picked up at Gelson's and fell into their well-practiced teamwork, slicing the vegetables and throwing them onto the patio grill. Grace manned the tongs, but she could barely focus on the food, the sunset tonight was so spectacular. Within minutes, Ken arranged the vegetables over a bed of greens on a board, and, with a drizzle of dressing, a sprinkling of crumbled organic goat cheese, and a handful of pine nuts, dinner was ready. Ken could always make the simplest setting look photo shoot–ready. "This salad is guaranteed to pull you out of that pity party. It's so fresh and good for you, you can eat it without any guilt whatsoever."

"Good thing," Grace thought—she had enough guilt already.

"So—what do you hear from that hunk, Mike the tutor?"

"So far, so good. Emma seems to like him. She did the study group three times this week. That's a record." Grace sipped her Mojito as the sun dipped below the surface of the ocean, just as a large school of dolphins emerged on their travels to Santa Catalina, an island off the Southern California coast.

"That's it?"

"What did you expect? He's the tutor."

"Well, he could be more. Tim says he's a really nice guy."

"Just what I need. A virtual romance, to go with my virtual daughter and, unfortunately, nonvirtual ex-husband."

"And let's not forget the virtual ex-boyfriend with the very real yacht. Just keeping score! Besides, I'm getting reports from Tim that Mike seems to enjoy your talks."

Ken was bringing up Tim quite a lot in conversation, "Ah, Tim. Things seem to be heating up between you two."

"As much as things can heat up across half of the continent." Ken made a face. "Leave it to me to move across the country and find love on my childhood doorstep. Go figure."

"Not that I'm one to give relationship advice," Grace said, "but Tim seems like a keeper."

Ken nodded and his usual curtain of sarcasm dropped. "You know, this is the first time I've felt this way about anybody,

MALIBU MOJITO

Makes one drink

4 mint leaves, plus one for garnish

2 chunks fresh pineapple, plus a spear for garnish

2 lime wedges, plus more for garnish

1 teaspoon sugar, or more to taste

2 ounces white rum, such as Captain Morgan Silver

Club soda

Put the 4 mint leaves, pineapple chunks, 2 lime wedges, and sugar into the bottom of a bar glass. Muddle everything using a muddler or a wooden spoon. Add rum and fill with ice. Cover and shake 10 to 12 times. Pour into a clean tall glass. Top with a splash of club soda and garnish with a lime wedge, pineapple spear, and mint leaf.

NOTE:

- For a darker flavor, substitute the Captain Morgan Silver with Captain Morgan Original Spice Rum.

- Add a splash of Ciroc Coconut Vodka along with the club soda to give the mojito a little something-something.

Grace. At first I was just helping him out a little with the store, but the more we've talked, I've really fallen for him. We each fill in what the other doesn't have. He's about words, I'm about visuals; he's academic, I'm artistic. With Tim, I don't have to be somebody I'm not. So I'm learning how to have a relationship. I don't want to screw that up with a bunch of Hollywood crap. I want to keep it real. So, actually, I was thinking of going back for a few days next weekend myself. I'm thinking of becoming Tim's business partner; he needs some help."

It didn't surprise Grace at all that Ken would offer to help Tim, as he'd done for her, but she was delighted to hear there might be more. Ken deserved a nice guy in his life.

"I want to help Tim figure out a way to keep the shop solvent, and of course I'll check on Emma when I drop off Halo. Not that I've performed my surrogate parent duties so flawlessly in the past." He grimaced.

"You've done everything you could. What would I have done without you? Sometimes I think that Emma wouldn't have the problems she's had if she'd found even one friend like you and Leeza."

"I lucked out when I found you and Leeza," Ken agreed. "You can't imagine what it was like back then, growing up gay. Even my parents thought I was a freak show." He poked at the mint in his drink. "Now that they're retired in Florida, they're a little more—'accepting'—but in those days . . . I remember, when I came out to them, Dad wouldn't even talk to me."

"Then there was me: my mother and I weren't talking, either. With Dad gone, I was so lonely."

"Well, my sweet girl, we made our own little family, didn't we? But now maybe we need to open it up a bit, you think?"

Yes, now we're like a table missing a leg, Grace wanted to say. Carrying her secrets around for so many years had been nothing but a burden. And what did it matter now, really? Times had indeed changed, but with Leeza's death, she realized she hadn't changed along with them. Ken had moved on from New London and built his life, and now he'd found someone special, but she hadn't. Ken, of all people, would understand, would have understood all along. Like dipping into a pool, you have to start at the shallow end, Grace thought.

"Ken, I have to tell you something," she said. She closed her eyes and took a deep breath. *It's only Ken*, she told herself. *It's OK.* And as she began to remember, Grace was seventeen years old again and back in her mother's kitchen.

Grace was looking for something different in the recipe box; she wanted to bake something that would impress Von. And it had to be better than good, because his family was, after all, in the chocolate business!

Wait! Here it was, at the very back. A card for Swedish chocolate coconut balls. A classic! Grace had been making these since she was a child.

Then it happened. Directly behind the card for Swedish chocolate coconut balls, Grace found a folded paper. Most of the recipes were on cards, but maybe, she thought, this one was too long to fit on a card, so it piqued her curiosity.

It wasn't, as it turned out, a recipe at all. It was a birth certificate—her birth certificate. Grace had never seen it before. What a strange place to keep a birth certificate, she thought. Then she noticed something odd. The name in the space for "Father" wasn't her dad's name, "Derek." It was her uncle Carl. Maybe she was reading this wrong, Grace thought—hoped—maybe there was a mistake. But no, there it was.

FATHER: CARL ALMQUIST. Carl Almquist was the husband of her aunt Astrid, the older sister her mother never talked or wrote to. All she knew about her Uncle Carl, aside from his name, was that he had died two years ago, and she only knew that because she'd overheard her mother talking about it on the phone with her grandmother. Since Astrid and her mother never talked, Grace had never met either Aunt Astrid or Uncle Carl.

How could this be? It was impossible, it had to be some kind of mistake. A stranger—an *uncle*—couldn't be her father! But what if he was? Grace didn't know what to do. She felt sick. She sat in a daze until the kitchen had gotten dark and, finally, her mother came home from work.

The confrontation was brief. Lorraine was tight-lipped, Grace accusatory. But there was no denying the truth. The story her mother told her only made her feel worse. Lorraine had been very young, living with her sister and her brother-in-law while she finished college at Stockholm University. It was a college town, and Carl ran a bakery, where Lorraine worked after school. She was young and Carl had seduced her. He convinced Lorraine that he wanted to leave Astrid for her, have a life together. It had been a horrible scandal, Lorraine said, emotionless, when she realized she was pregnant and that Carl had misled her. To save the family's reputation, she'd been sent to America, where she'd met the man Grace thought of as "Dad" at work in Milwaukee. By this point, Lorraine's pregnancy was showing, so he had always known the truth and welcomed Grace as his own. He was a kind man, Lorraine said, and she

SWEDISH CHOCOLATE BALLS

Makes about 30 pieces

½ cup heavy cream

3 tablespoons dark spiced rum, such as Captain Morgan's Black

12 ounces semi-sweet or bittersweet chocolate

1 tablespoon butter

Cocoa powder, to coat

Put the cream and rum into a pan over medium heat. Do not let it boil.

Chop the chocolate into small pieces and put it into a shallow bowl with the butter. Pour the hot cream over the chocolate and let it sit for a minute or two. Then stir the chocolate until it is all melted and smooth. Let cool and refrigerate for 1 to 2 hours to harden.

Using a small scoop or teaspoon, scoop out some of the chocolate and quickly roll into a small ball. Put onto a wax paper–lined cookie sheet. When all the chocolate pieces are rolled, roll them into the cocoa powder or leave them plain. Store in the refrigerator but bring them out about a half hour before serving.

NOTE:

- Other items that can be used for coating chocolates: finely chopped nuts, such as almonds, walnuts, or pistachios; coconut, regular or toasted; sanding sugar; cookie or cake crumbs, finely chopped; a few grains of flaky sea salt.

- Use a combination of semi-sweet and bittersweet chocolates or milk and bittersweet chocolates for the ganache.

- Flavor the chocolate with other flavors: whiskey, brandy, or aquavit.

knew he would be a good husband and father. But Lorraine's family was not so forgiving. Her sister had never spoken to her again, and Lorraine didn't blame her. She'd never seen, or spoken to, Astrid or Carl again.

From the minute she realized that it was true, that her real father was her uncle, that the man she thought was her father wasn't even related to her, she had felt like some kind of alien, dropped into a false family. She didn't know who she was, who to trust, what to believe. Her life had been a lie. She'd never even had a chance to know her real father, and now he was dead. He may have been a jerk to his family, but he was still her father. It was like she'd lost her father twice. And now, Grace felt like she'd also lost her mother. *Who was this woman who could not tell her own daughter the truth?* She felt abandoned on all sides. The rest of senior year, she'd felt disconnected from everyone. Her grades dropped. She'd wanted to quit show choir, but Leeza had talked her out of it. Hating the bad memories of the kitchen, she'd stopped cooking. She'd retracted into a shell. It had been Leeza who had rescued her. Leeza with whom she shared this secret. When Leeza was alive, at least there was someone else who knew, whom Grace knew she could turn to, and that was something of a comfort. Now, she realized, she felt so alone. But Ken would understand. *Of course he would.*

Ken's reaction was not what Grace expected. Not at all.

"Well, that was a nice ancient history lesson, Gracie," he said.

"Meaning what?"

"Meaning, that is a lot of heavy stuff for a teenager, no question about it. But you're still you. That's never gonna change. And that's a good thing. What's not so good is that you're still raking yourself over the coals about this. Here's the headline: This issue has passed its sell-by date. It is what it is. Now it's up to you. "

"But you don't understand, I never knew my father."

Ken picked up her hand and held it, giving her his most level gaze. "Yes, you did. And he loved you. He chose you. He could have walked away, but he didn't. My dad didn't have a choice, he got me, he was stuck with me, and he was never so disappointed in anything in his life. *Now that's sad*. What happened to Leeza and Sara is a *tragedy*. What happened to you . . . that's ancient history. So suck it up, beautiful girl. Suck it up and get over yourself. You have my goddaughter to think about. And give that poor woman who raised you a break. If I had a mother who was there for me, no matter what, I wouldn't be sitting here now, I'd be walking over hot coals to get to her. The thing you can't stand, and I love you so I can tell you this, is that you are more like your mother than you'll ever admit."

"I'm not like her."

"You're not?" Ken arched an eyebrow.

Suddenly Grace wondered—*maybe I'm like my father*. Her real father. Carl Almquist. The man she had never known. What she did know was that he was a cheat and a liar. *Good lord, what if she took after him?*

The cell phone rang in Grace's purse across the room. The perfect excuse to end an uncomfortable conversation. Grace ran to it.

"Grace! Grace!" Lorraine was breathless. Grace felt a prickly feeling on the back of her neck. Something was seriously wrong. "Emma's missing. She's gone."

"What? How did you let her leave?"

Ken sat bolt upright.

"I didn't 'let' her leave, Grace. She left on her own. I think she may be trying to get back to LA. She misses Halo."

"She can't afford a plane ticket."

"She's been saving her money from the Book Nook and working overtime. She probably has enough."

Grace tried frantically to calculate. This pit in her stomach was becoming way too familiar.

"Maybe that boyfriend in LA dropped her."

"What boyfriend in LA?" Grace widened her eyes in Ken's direction. "She didn't have a boyfriend."

Lorraine sighed. "That you knew of."

"Do you know his name?"

"No, no I don't."

Grace signaled Ken to get up. "We're leaving. We'll find her." Driving back down the PCH to Venice, with Halo hastily stuffed in the backseat, Ken said, "I don't know about you, but I could swear I just did this. Maybe because I did."

Grace spent the hour it took them to get back to Venice calling and texting Emma's friends, or at least those she knew. Nobody had heard from Emma. She got a name and number for the so-called-boyfriend and called it. A girl answered the phone, and Grace hung up. "There was the reason," Grace thought. Maybe the same thing had happened to Emma.

Ken called Tim to see if he had seen her or knew anything. "How was she after school? Did she seem especially unhappy?" He listened for a minute. "I'm driving, I'm putting you on speaker. Grace is with me."

"Hi, Grace," said Tim. "Mike is here. He says Emma made it to study group tonight. Then she left. She had a large backpack. I'm calling the police."

"Wait . . . I'm sure she's headed to LA. My call-waiting is buzzing." She peered at the phone number. "It's Brian!"

"Grace? Emma's with me."

"How . . . ?"

"She took a bus."

Grace gasped. "Oh my God!"

"I know, I know . . . she just showed up at my door. She just misses Chicago so much, Grace. And it's Kimmy's birthday."

Kimmy was Emma's best friend from Chicago. Thinking of Leeza, and how much she missed her, Grace knew how Emma must feel lonely. "She never mentioned it."

"She said she figured you'd refuse to let her come. She's in a negative frame of mind, but she's OK. Our daughter can live by her wits, I'll tell you that much."

"She doesn't need to live by her wits. She's a minor with a family. Put her on. This minute." Grace thought she'd explode with fury. *Live by her wits!* Brian had to have lost his mind. Or maybe he was just being Brian. Where was Emma's grandmother? How had Lorraine let this happen?

There was a pause. Then Brian got back on the line. "She's fine here. She's being taken care of."

"By who?"

"By me and my mother."

His mother. Or, as Ken always called her, the Great Enabler. Grace loved Brian's mother, but it was true she always had a ready excuse for everything her son ever did, whether it was never being home ("investing in the future") or gambling ("letting off steam"). Even his affair ("It takes two to tango"). "I'm coming to Chicago," Grace said. "If you let Emma out of your sight, I'll never forgive you."

Grace clicked back to Tim. "Thanks, Tim, but we found her. She's with Brian in Chicago." Grace hung up, and Ken wrapped an arm around her. "I'm going with you."

Grace tightened her lips. What she wouldn't give to have Ken there with her, but she knew she had to handle this one by herself.

chapter 7

Grace trudged up the third flight of stairs to Brian's loft in Chicago's Little Italy, dragging her trusty wheelie. A framed canvas backpack with a mesh front was strapped to her back. "Halo," she muttered, "next time we're trading places." As she reached the top step, Grace could smell the rich, garlicky aroma of Sunday gravy—Brian's mother's specialty. Even after all these years, the smell of Marie's meatballs and gravy reminded Grace of Sunday dinners with Brian's family. These were good memories. For a young girl who felt adrift from her own family, it was not just the food that was so intoxicating. Marie D'Angelo had been a second mother to Grace. She never judged her, never criticized, and had always been there as a sounding board.

After their divorce, Brian moved out of their apartment in Wrigleyville into his office, a loft on Taylor Street. Chicago's once-thriving Little Italy section had morphed into more of a memory, but in the past few years, the area had sprouted new condominiums and town houses. Brian's loft was two floors above a pasta café named Michaelangelo's. She missed Marie and those family dinners. Whatever was on the menu at Michaelangelo's,

MARIE'S MEMORY-MAKER MEATBALLS AND SUNDAY GRAVY

Serves 8 to 10

FOR THE MEMORY-MAKER MEATBALLS:

½ cup milk

6 slices Italian bread

½ pound ground beef

½ pound ground pork

½ pound ground veal

1 medium onion, finely chopped

4 cloves garlic, finely chopped

½ cup chopped parsley

½ cup grated parmesan cheese

2 large eggs

Salt and pepper

Olive oil for frying

FOR THE SUNDAY GRAVY:

10 pounds Roma tomatoes

Olive oil for frying

1 large onion, chopped

6 garlic cloves, chopped

1 6-ounce can tomato paste

Salt and pepper

16 fresh basil leaves, chopped

4 sprigs fresh oregano, chopped

START THE GRAVY: Quarter the tomatoes. Put some olive oil into a large pot over medium-high heat. Add the tomatoes and cook until they collapse. Process them through a food mill to remove the skin and seeds. Set aside.

In the same pot, add some more olive oil and cook the onion until soft. Add the garlic and cook for a minute. Add the tomato paste and cook for another minute. Add the reserved tomato puree to the pot. Season with salt and pepper and add half the oregano and basil. Cook on low until it thickens up, at least 1 hour.

MAKE THE MEATBALLS: Pour the milk over the bread and let it sit until all the milk is absorbed. Combine the beef, pork, veal, onion, garlic, parsley, cheese, and eggs and season with salt and pepper. Add the soaked bread, squeezing out any excess milk. Mix together lightly but thoroughly. Form into 2-inch balls. Heat some more olive oil in the skillet and brown the meatballs on all sides. They will not be cooked through.

Finish cooking the meatballs in the hot gravy for 20 to 30 minutes. Just before serving, stir in the remaining basil and oregano.

Serve the gravy and meatballs over your favorite pasta shape.

NOTE:
- Spice it up: Add ½ pound hot Italian sausage meat in place of the pork for the meatballs.
- Use 2 28-ounce cans whole tomatoes in juice in place of fresh tomatoes.

Grace bet that Marie D'Angelo's meatballs and Sunday gravy would be better. In New London, Marie was legendary for her twenty-bushel summer canning marathons, and every bite of Marie's "gravy" had the taste of summer. Nobody did it better.

Sure enough, when Grace got to the third-floor landing, the door swung open and there stood Marie in her apron, her hair a bit more gray, her face a bit more lined, but the same Marie. Years—and a divorce—evaporated as she held out her arms to her former daughter-in-law. "Hello, my Gracie," she said. "Brian! Take this suitcase from the landing." She pulled Grace into the loft, which, Grace noticed with a start, seemed to have actually been decorated. Bleached wood floors, sleek black and beige furniture contrasted with rough wood shelves framing the largest flat-screen TV she had ever seen. Black-and-white blowups of Emma hung on the walls. A large tree, leafless but sculptural, stood near the front windows. Brian appeared to have, at long last, organized his life, or at least his apartment. Her own memories of life with him were not quite so orderly.

At the back of the loft, a glass brick wall sectioned off a small open kitchen. Emma and Brian stood side by side, he tossing a salad, and Emma stirring the tomato gravy in a large stainless-steel pot. Marie's sausages were famous, but there was of course no meat in this meal; ever since she'd gotten Halo, Emma had refused to eat meat. Brian wiped his hands and strode over to Grace's side, where they exchanged a polite kiss.

Grace unstrapped the travel cage, set it on the floor, and unzipped the mesh. Two black button eyes peered out. *"Seriously?!?"* Halo squawked as he tilted his head, checking out his new surroundings.

Emma dropped her spoon into the gravy and whirled around, all pretense of being cool vanished. "Halo!" she shrieked, racing over and scooping him up to her chest, where he snuggled like a newborn. Halo looked so sweet, but Grace was well aware, from experience, that if anybody else tried to cuddle him like this, they could lose a finger. "Did you keep the mesh covered on the plane?" Emma demanded. "Birds are very susceptible to drafts."

"Emma, Halo is OK. Let's talk about you. You can't keep taking off like this. I had no idea where you were. I've been worried out of my mind. Imagine if Halo simply disappeared? How would you feel?"

Emma looked down, but said, "I want to stay here, with Dad. My friends are all here."

"Your dad isn't set up for you to be here, Emma."

Emma tucked Halo under her sweater. "You're just saying that. You just want to dump me somewhere so you can take off. You wouldn't even go on that cruise together."

Grace sighed. "Oh, Emma, I wish we could just take off like that, but you have schoolwork to finish and I have work. Neither of us can just take off for the Mediterranean right now."

"They could have gotten a tutor on the boat."

"Emma, be realistic."

"You got a tutor in New London, why couldn't they get one on the boat? I know they could have. Von would have done it. "

Von? "What Von would or wouldn't have done is not the point, Emma. You are on very thin ice with your school, and I don't think they would have understood your phoning it in from the Mediterranean."

Emma set her chin defiantly. Those blue eyes, that gaze, made Grace squirm. A shiver of recognition ran down her spine. *Don't even go there, Grace.*

Marie appeared carrying a tray brimming with gigantic bread-crumb-topped, baked mushroom caps, dotted with flecks of fresh basil—another of her specialties. "Stuffed mushroom, anybody?"

Dinner was dominated by Marie's chatter of the latest New London gossip, updates from the nursing home where Brian's dad was living now, and inappropriate asides from Halo.

Marie chattered on. "I tell you, Melissa swears she can talk to plants. Who says such a thing? But there's no arguing with her results. She brought me three huge azalea plants to bring down to the nursing home. I have never seen such blossoms. I asked her what her secret was, and you know what it is? A penny! She buries a penny in the soil next to the plant." She spooned more pasta onto Emma's plate as Emma tried to stop her. "Emma, you are wasting away."

"Grandma M!" Emma moaned in protest.

Brian ate silently, glancing occasionally at Grace over the top of his glasses. While Marie and Emma cleared the plates, he walked her to the front of the apartment. Grace could hear faint music coming up from the café below.

"Has she been calling her Chicago friends?" Grace asked. "Is that what's behind this?"

"She talked to Kimmy about the party," said Brian. "But she's spending a lot of time online—Skyping, Twittering. Let's call a spade a spade, Grace."

"Apt metaphor," Grace said to herself, but as snide references to Brian's gambling—now a former habit—were off-limits, she resisted the impulse to make that particular comment. "I'm listening, Dr. Phil."

Brian set his jaw, in the determined way Grace knew so well. "You know, Grace, there comes a point that, no matter what we've had—and there's no question it was great and we got a super kid—we've got to move forward. We have to put our lives back together now, but the trouble with you is you can't be happy because you're still distracted by problems from the past. I know it's important for you to work things through, and for

GRANDMA M'S MUSHROOMS

Serves 8 to 10

Italian bread for crumbs
 and croutons

Extra virgin olive oil

½ pound sweet or hot Italian
 sausage

1 pound medium
 mushrooms

1 cup grated parmesan

12 basil leaves, chopped

Salt and pepper

Preheat the oven to 350°F.

Slice the bread and cut out circles a little smaller than the mush-rooms. You will need as many circles as you have mushrooms. Brush them lightly with olive oil and place them in one layer on a baking sheet. Put them in the oven until golden brown, turning them once. Remove and set aside. Finely chop up remaining bread for crumbs and set aside.

Add the sausage to a skillet and cook, breaking up any clumps, until no longer pink. Remove the sausage and take out all but one tablespoon fat from the pan. Remove stems from mushrooms and chop them finely. Cook them until they are nice and brown, about 8 minutes. Add ½ cup bread crumbs and cook for a minute. Return the sausage to the pan and cook for a minute or two. Remove from heat and stir in ½ cup parmesan and basil. Taste and season with salt and pepper.

Fill the mushrooms with the sausage mixture and sprinkle over ¼ cup of the parmesan. Bake until they are almost cooked through, about 15 to 20 minutes. Top each with a crouton and sprinkle over remaining parmesan. Bake until cheese is lightly browned and mush-room caps are cooked through, about another 5 to 10 minutes.

some people that can take a lifetime. God knows, I've got my own issues, but the point is, I've faced them and I'm on to the next part of my life. We both have to think about what's best for Emma. She needs stability. You can't drag her along while you work things out. She can't go back to LA, with all those kids that are taking her down the wrong path, and you know it. She's just too vulnerable. Don't you see that?"

Grace started to open her mouth, then shut it. Brian was right, and in a way it was a huge relief to have him share in the realization that their daughter needed help. That she, Grace, needed help. But in another way, it also felt like a crushing defeat.

Brian knew her well. He stepped forward and put his arm around her. "My business has really taken off. The crunch is over. I have people working for me now. That means I can spend time with Emma. There's no reason why she shouldn't come here and be with her father, and back with her old school friends. What do you think? I'm prepared to change my life, Grace. In fact, I'm planning on it. Are you?"

Now Grace could not remain silent. Who was he to challenge her ability as a mother? His track record as a father hardly gave him the right to judge her. She stiffened and shrugged off his arm. "Being a mother is not a state of mind, or a mood, Brian. It's what I am. Emma is a young girl and she needs her mother. You like the idea of being Father of the Year now. Today. I'm not saying you don't love Emma, I know you do. We both do. But what's she going to do here? Sit in this loft and watch you program computers? She needs a healthy, active life, school, friends, activities."

"Like surfing?"

That did it. Some gate in Grace's feelings became unhinged, as if a latch blew open. She found herself snapping, "And then, Brian, how can I be sure . . ." She caught herself, but the words left unsaid, hanging in the air, were as clear as if she'd shouted them across the room: *How can I be sure you won't stay out late gambling and leave Emma unsupervised, or be off with some woman, or* . . . When she looked at Brian, Grace saw many Brians, in the way that long-term relationships between two people always involve not two people, but the many things they were, are, and have been to each other. There was the shy Brian whom she and Leeza had met in eighth grade, when his family had moved to the ranch house on the outskirts of town, the little boy on the first day of school who didn't know anybody, and they had taken him under their wing. There was the Brian who had been a math whiz in the days before geeks were cool, the kid who could solve any equation in his head, who helped Grace with her homework and was solely responsible for the fact that she even got a passing grade in algebra. Another Brian held her hand under a tree in a spring rain, pulling his jacket around her before their first, tentative kiss. The Brian who broke her heart when he ended their relationship on the eve of senior prom and the boy who she found love again with after they both realized how much they meant to each other. The Brian who was her first love, who was also the first to draw blood in the relationship, the first to hurt the other, the stranger who'd pushed her away when they'd been so close for so long.

Fifteen years ago, only days after Brian had crushed her heart by breaking up with her, Grace had swanned down the steps to her house in her strapless prom dress, engulfed in a cloud of Calvin Klein Eternity perfume. Her long hair had been blown dry and pinned up in an elaborate twist at the beauty shop, and she and Leeza had given each other manicures and pedicures. She was still tender from her first heartbreak, but Grace felt beautiful, or at least Von said she was. Von looked like he'd been ripped from a fashion magazine, decked out in a tuxedo that he actually owned, daring pink socks, and shoes that were polished until they shone. Pinned to his lapel was the boutonniere that Grace had given him.

"You look like a fashion model," Von had said, and Grace had melted right then and there. Nobody ever complimented her on her looks, which, to her, were entirely unremarkable. She swished her skirt, gave an exaggerated take on a catwalk walk, and felt pretty. She felt a pang to have her arm looped through someone's other than Brian, but she was determined to show everyone she was OK, and that Brian had not broken her, so she slid a steel door across her heart and blocked the thought. It was prom. She was with Von. She looked like a model. He looked great and everyone would see Brian was not the only boy who thought Grace was special. They were graduating. Next fall, she knew, she'd be at junior college in Madison, and he'd be at Oxford. But for the moment—or the night—nothing else mattered. She didn't even know if Brian was going to the prom. Anyhow, what business was it of hers? He hadn't asked her. She hadn't asked him. They were broken up. *Moving on.*

The giant mirror ball twirled over the gym floor, right under the banner that said CONGRATULATIONS GRADUATES! LOOKING FORWARD TO LOOKING BACK! The official class photographer snapped their pictures in front of a flower-decked backdrop as they walked in. The band was already rocking. Leeza, in a short pink dress and teetery high-heeled sandals, boogied over with Ken in tow. "You guys look great!" the photographer shouted. Ken and Leeza were co-chairs of the dance committee.

"Isn't she incredible?" Von had squeezed her waist.

Suddenly Leeza had yanked Grace aside. "He's here!" she whispered urgently.

"Who?" Although Grace already knew.

"Brian."

"He didn't have a date." Grace tried to appear nonchalant.

"I know! Still, he came by himself. That's bold. Can you believe! And I think he smuggled in a flask." She gestured toward the refreshments table.

Sure enough, there was Brian—in a tux jacket over a pair of jeans and a T-shirt. Alone.

The dance floor had quickly filled up, but out of the corner of her eye, Grace could see Brian. He would periodically disappear, then return, and each time his expression was more of a glower, a poorly contained storm cloud at the edge of the room.

Von smiled and chatted on as they danced, oblivious. "Let me tell you about Monte Carlo," he was saying as he dipped Grace, and she laughed. "Did you ever see that movie with Cary Grant and Grace Kelly, who is named after you?" For a while, Grace forgot all about Brian. *Brian who?*

That lasted until Brian had danced by with Claire in his

arms. *Huh!?* Brian knew that Claire was the Enemy. What was he trying to prove, anyway? Obviously something, from the way he was holding Claire close in the slow dances. Grace tried to avoid looking at them, but somehow she couldn't stop.

Well, she'd show him! Grace turned on all her femme fatale wiles, flirting, laughing, tossing her hair, twirling sexily on the dance floor—like Madonna, she hoped—clinging to Von in the slow numbers, whispering in his ear. *Take that, Brian.*

But he hadn't noticed because he'd disappeared. With Claire.

When one of the kids who had smuggled in some vodka of-fered to spike their punch, Von had refused—he had a bottle of champagne tucked away in the car—but Grace went for it. It seemed like the cool thing to do. And do again. The rest of the evening would remain a blur. At least the prom part.

But Grace would never, ever forget the part after the prom, by the lake, lying on the damp early-summer grass, wrapped in a blanket with Von. He'd brought real crystal glasses for the champagne. Her head spun, and not just from the drinks.

"To my girl," he toasted.

His girl.

His kisses were like she imagined those of a man would be, not a boy, and Grace had lost herself in them as easily as she'd lost her dress, and then all common sense.

The next morning, when she'd crept into the house at dawn, shoes in her hand, she'd felt the best and the worst she'd ever felt. Her head was pounding, her mouth was dry, her dress was askew, but she'd convinced herself that she was in love with

Von, and he with her. A bouquet of flowers arrived that day, but she'd waited in vain for Von to appear.

Instead, Leeza told her he'd left the country. His dad had had a stroke. No one knew how bad it was, but Von had to get home immediately to help his mother. According to Leeza, who'd spoken to Vanessa, everything was up in the air, including Von's plans for Oxford. But surely, Von would be calling her any minute, from Switzerland.

Except the days, then the weeks went by, and there had been no communication from Von.

"Why don't you just pick up the phone and call him?" Leeza had asked. "This is dumb."

"I can't call him. He'll think I'm chasing him across the ocean! Don't you dare tell your mother that I even mentioned his name! And why isn't he calling me, is the question?"

Leeza grew quiet, and Grace knew something was up. "You're holding out on me. What is it? I know you're his cousin, but I'm your best friend."

Leeza sighed. "I think he has a girlfriend in Zurich. From school there."

Grace didn't want to show how upset she was. "Oh. Who cares?" But inside, Grace was screaming at herself: *I cannot believe I was so stupid! He didn't even care! Why did I let myself fall for a total jerk? How could I have slept with him? I wish I had never met him! So I'll never see Von again. That would be just fine. Ideal, in fact. Let him drop dead.*

When Brian showed up at her summer job at the pool, Grace

looked at him and forgot why they'd broken up. He'd brought her a tiny bouquet of daisies from his mother's garden. Those flowers meant so much more than the elaborate flower arrangement Von had sent, just before he'd vanished from her life.

"I think I love you," he said. "I'm sorry. I guess I had to find out the hard way. Seeing you with Von . . ."

"He's not in my life," she said quickly. "You are." And she meant it. She couldn't imagine life without him.

When she'd missed her period, Grace thought she'd just forgotten to keep track. When she'd missed it a second month, and began to feel sick at the sight of her favorite cheese, she had to admit to herself that something was off. Telling Lorraine was out of the question. Telling Leeza was an absolute necessity.

"What about Von?" she'd said.

"What about him? He's not in the picture, obviously."

"You don't want to tell him?"

"I don't even know if it's his. It probably isn't. It was only that one time."

"I think it only takes once."

"Do not tell Ken. Do not tell anybody! Ever!"

"I swear it, I won't."

And Leeza had kept her word, to the grave, so now Grace was alone with her secret. Even Brian didn't know. The minute Grace told him she was pregnant, he'd proposed. They'd gotten married in Madison, just the two of them. Brian had deferred college, and his scholarship, to start his business to support them, and Grace had waitressed, with Emma in day care. The move to

Chicago had been on a wing and a prayer, a plan to get Brian's software business to catch on.

Grace had tired of her mother's constant "suggestions" and cut off communication with Lorraine until months after the baby was born. Grace and Brian had fallen madly in love with their perfect baby girl.

The idyllic scenario Grace had conjured up did not quite materialize though. As a young father trying to get a business off the ground, Brian was swamped with responsibilities. This Brian was scrambling to survive, desperate to pull a trick out of a hat, sure he could outsmart the market. When that didn't pan out, he resorted to gambling. He became someone Grace didn't know, yet she didn't know what to do to make things better.

Very occasionally, late at night, when she was awake after Brian had not come home, her little girl sleeping in the next room, Grace had let her guard down and allowed her mind to wander. Without being able to help herself, she would think of Von, of how they had laughed, sung, and danced together. How they'd made love. She'd think of Von's ice-blue eyes—and Emma's—and she'd wonder.

Now Grace had to admit to herself that in spite of the separation, the angry words, the divorce—she still cared. About Emma, of course, but she still cared about Brian, cared enough for it to still matter—still hurt. Cared enough to not be with him or let Emma be with him because she couldn't trust what would or wouldn't happen. There was something about your first love, Grace thought, that a woman never forgets or loses. But because she had resolved that it had to be over with Brian, over forever, she had closed that small crack in the door to her heart—firmly shut, with a reverberating click.

Grace said nothing of her feelings to Brian. Dredging up the past would be pointless. "The best thing for Emma is having her stay with my mother," were the words she'd said instead. Her hands were suddenly shaking, so she clasped them in front of her. They were the hands of a woman who worked with them—no manicure, short, practical nails. No jewelry—it had been two years since she'd taken off her wedding band and, one day soon after her move to LA, in a fit of resolution, Grace had thrown it over the side of Ken's boat, into the Pacific Ocean. "You can visit her whenever you want."

Actually, Grace couldn't bring Emma back to a summer of hanging out aimlessly in LA; Brian was right. This was the best option. She'd take Emma back to New London tomorrow, drop her off, and then she'd join Ken back in LA and work there until the show wrapped in June.

Brian sighed. He knew when he'd lost. He'd lost years ago, and never regained his footing with Grace. "Fine. I intend to visit her as often as I can. But you tell her—I can't disappoint her."

With impeccable timing, Marie appeared. "Surprise! We have cannelloni!"

There was nothing more to say, so Grace and Brian dutifully followed her back to the table, as if they were sixteen again and having Sunday dinner at his parents' house under the D'Angelos' watchful supervision, before they started their homework. Except now their daughter sat waiting for them, a bird on her shoulder, and two families were splintered, for different reasons.

Later that night, as Grace lay beside Emma on the futon in the loft's balcony bedroom, she stared at her daughter's back, bundled beneath the covers. Telling Emma she was going straight back to New London had not gone well at all, and Emma had stormed up the stairs, texted madly for about a half hour, and cried herself to sleep. Brian had left to take Marie home. The dishwasher hummed and sloshed softly below the open loft space. A phone rang below and Grace realized it was her cell. She pulled back the covers, and clambered down the balcony ladder.

"Grace?"

"Hi, Ken," she said softly.

"I am so sorry to bother you, but I stopped by your place to pick up the mail for you. You have a letter."

Probably from the school; they'd said they would send a confirmation of their conversation. "Ken, it's been such a long day."

"Grace. It's a letter from Leeza."

"What? How can that be?"

"I called Snoopy. Apparently she left a series of letters with instructions for them to be mailed at certain times. Should I open it, or do you want me to hold on to it?"

A letter from Leeza! "Open it, read it, oh my God, this is unbelievable."

"It's dated two months ago," Ken said. As he read the letter over the phone, Grace heard Leeza's words as clearly if she were speaking them herself.

"Dear, darling Gracie. You have just left to go back to our wonderful Emma. I am so sorry to see you go but also glad you will be with Emma. I know how precious it is for me to be with my Sara. I have so valued and treasured the time we spend together now that I know time is short."

"She knew it," Grace said. "Leeza knew it all along." How could she not have realized that all the optimistic talk was not for Leeza's benefit, but for hers? Tears rolled down Grace's cheeks.

Ken continued: *"I need to write this down and put it in a safe place to tell you when the time comes that I am not here to say it for myself. Grace, we made a promise, and only death would force these words from me, but here they are: You must stop running. Not from me or Emma or Brian or your mother, but from yourself. It is time to find forgiveness and peace within yourself. Time to go home. Life is not a rehearsal for show choir, my dearest friend. It's opening night every day. Always remember, I'm here and I'm in the audience applauding you. Bravo, Grace."*

"She signed it xxxT3M—our secret signature, the one we always used in high school—love, The 3 Musketeers." Ken's voice broke. "She left this letter . . ." His voice trailed off. "I'll save this for you."

Grace stood rooted to the spot. Leeza had reached out and been there for her, as always. The Three Musketeers were still an unbroken force, a friendship even beyond death. After a while, Grace was able to speak. "Ken? Would you mind sending Leeza's letter to my mother's house? I think I need to ask for a brief leave of absence."

After she hung up, Grace sat perfectly still on the stairs to the loft. She blotted her face with her T-shirt. Leeza was right—there were no more rehearsals. The curtain was up and it was about Emma now. Grace would do whatever was best for her daughter.

chapter 8

Emma sat on the bed in Grace's childhood room, Skyping with a friend. Grace could picture herself in the exact same spot years ago, on the phone with Leeza. Nothing had changed. Even her childhood room was like a time capsule. Her treasured tape collection sat in a box in the corner. Heavy Wisconsin winter clothes —a never-again size 6—still hung in the closet. The rainbow she'd stenciled on the wall behind her bed was faded, but still there, and the once-coveted state fair blue ribbon still hung on the shade of her bedside lamp. She'd been out of the house for sixteen years, but her room still stood ready for her to return. In a way, she was glad that nothing had changed, but this weekend, even this room was going to get a new life. Lorraine had asked Emma to help her redecorate it. Emma was allowed to choose any color to repaint the walls, and they'd pick out a coordinating bedspread and curtains. Grace smiled to herself, knowing that Lorraine had imagined they'd pick out a fluffy pink-and-white gingham or a radically stylish violet together, but Emma planned to paint the room red with a red shag throw rug. The bedspread, headboard, and curtains were going to be black—even Grace's old bookshelves would be painted black.

Welcome to my world, Lorraine. Still, Grace had to admit, her mother had gained a certain level of street cred with Emma by being cool with her plan.

Emma looked up and noticed her mother standing in the doorway. "Gotta go," she said hurriedly, snapping off-line.

"Who were you talking to?"

"Nobody."

"What were you talking about?"

"Nothing."

Grace sighed. Ensconced in New London between her daughter and her mother, Grace thought it was entirely possible she would lose her mind. Thank God, once the show wrapped in mid-June, Ken had decided to come back to New London for his summer hiatus—although Grace knew that wasn't entirely due to her and Emma. Ken and Tim were spending a lot of time together working on a plan for the Book Nook.

Emma, on the other hand, had still not forgiven Grace for forcing her to stay in Wisconsin.

Grace had tried to explain that this was the best option for all of them, that she was taking time off so they could bond. That conversation had completely backfired. No sooner had she dropped her backpack on the floor of Grace's old room than Emma had grabbed the now somewhat-faded state fair blue ribbon off the lampshade and waved it in her mother's face. "Well, this proves it," she says. "I have actual, physical proof that you lie!" she exclaimed.

"What are you talking about, Emma?"

She shook the ribbon, then tossed it on the bed. "This, you

won this when you were my age. A state fair blue ribbon for a cake YOU baked, but my whole life you've made it über-clear that you do not cook. You won this, but you never even cared enough to bake me a birthday cake. It's always store-bought!" She hissed the last words at Grace.

The next day, Grace had come across Emma and Lorraine talking in the kitchen. She paused outside the door, where she heard her daughter downloading a litany of complaints about her. Her mother didn't say a single thing in Grace's defense.

"Why can't we go back to Chicago?" Emma sulked. "She doesn't like my LA friends anyhow. And she complains about what I eat, but she's never home to make dinner and all she ever buys is junk food. Unless we're eating sushi, our house is a walking saturated fat."

"Well, look at it this way," Lorraine said. She was rolling out dough for *kanelbullar*, the Swedish cinnamon buns she brought every week to the food pantry. "Your mother is like these cinnamon buns. She's one thing on the outside, but there's something else going on in the inside. Watch how I do this, Emma." She rolled out the dough.

Kanelbullar. Just the thought of the traditional Swedish buns made Grace's mouth water. She still remembered making them with her mother when she was a little girl. Grace could see the recipe card on the table and, of course, there it was on the counter beside the card: the recipe box. Grace went cold. Good lord, what if her birth certificate was still in there and Emma found it! A surge of fury washed over her. She marched into the kitchen and slapped the top of the recipe box shut.

"Thank you for the culinary analysis, Dr. Freud." Grace looked at her mother.

Emma tossed her wooden spoon in the sink and stomped out of the kitchen. "I have to go." She spat the words at Grace, and a moment later her bedroom door slammed.

Lorraine shot Grace a look. Grace knew her mother would never have allowed a slammed door in her house when Grace was a girl, but she was giving Grace room to lay down the law with Emma.

"Please don't discuss me with my daughter," Grace snapped. "I don't think it's necessary for you to dissect my motives with her. I'm her mother, not a character in a book you're reviewing with your book club."

Lorraine kept rolling out the dough. "Grace, do you intend to punish me forever for the fact that you were born? Because if that's the case, don't you realize you are also punishing yourself—and Emma? You don't even recognize that you've been pushing her away. She's rebelling to get your attention." She wiped her hands on her apron and fixed her gaze on Grace. "I'm not saying I did things perfectly, God knows. And I know you've never forgiven me for my mistakes. Well, here's the newsflash, my dear daughter—people make mistakes. Life isn't the same as baking a perfect cake or getting an A on a test. All of which came easy for you, but life is about what happens after the mistakes we make. If I hadn't made my mistakes, you wouldn't be here. Sometimes, mistakes work out. What matters is the rest of the story."

Grace picked up the recipe box. "Where is it?"

She didn't need to explain. "All the important papers are at the bank now. Where they should have always been."

Grace ran her hand over the smooth wooden lid, gaining courage. "I never knew my father," Grace said softly. *There. She'd said it.*

Lorraine stepped over and placed her hand on Grace's arm. "Yes, you did. And he loved you. The man whose name is on your birth certificate did not. He didn't love me and he didn't even care to know you. I was very unhappy about that once, and instead of dealing with my feelings, I pretended like the whole thing hadn't happened. Your dad made it easy for me. He took care of us all."

"Well, things didn't work out that way for me. My husband didn't make things easy. I'm on my own and I have to work."

Lorraine looked at Grace with understanding. "I know, but maybe Emma could help with your work. Did you ever consider including her, instead of working around her? I thought I was protecting you by keeping things to myself. Don't do what I did."

At this point, Grace's discussions with Lorraine usually fell apart, but this time she remembered her conversation with Ken, and Leeza's letter. Ken had brought the letter with him to New London, and she'd read it over and over. She'd promised herself: No more running. So, this time, Grace stayed in the kitchen. She picked up the bowl that Emma had put down, and, from memory, measured and mixed the correct amounts of cinnamon and sugar. *Cooking was like riding a bicycle,* Grace thought. *Once you learned, you really could get right back on the bike at any time. You might be a little wobbly at first, but off you went.*

"Maybe you're right," Grace said.

Lorraine brushed the flattened rectangles of dough with melted butter. Then, together, without saying a word, mother and daughter spooned the sweet cinnamon mixture over the dough, working from the opposite sides of the table. Next, they rolled each rectangle up into a cylinder. Grace separated the brown paper cupcake wrappers and set them in rows on the cookie sheets. Then she picked up a sharp, serrated knife and cut slices that Lorraine set into the individual cupcake wrappers. Grace took a stack of cloth tea towels from the drawer by the sink, wet them with warm water, wrung them out till they were just damp, and covered the pans of dough. They would sit like that until the dough rose and doubled in size. Only then would the buns be ready for the egg wash, the scrumptious crushed sugar-cube topping, and their trip to the oven.

"About forty-five minutes, right?"

Lorraine nodded, and a certain understanding passed between them.

Next, Grace decided to deal with the stomping and door-slamming. This couldn't go on. In fact, she was sure that Emma was really begging for boundaries. Well, she'd set them. Emma's door, the door to Grace's old bedroom, was still closed. Grace gave a perfunctory tap and walked in. Maybe if it hadn't been her old room, she would have knocked louder, or longer, but she walked right in. Emma was Skyping.

SWEDISH CINNAMON BUNS

Makes about 20

FOR THE DOUGH:

1 package dry yeast

1⅓ cups milk, room temperature

½ cup sugar

½ cup butter, melted and cooled

1 egg, beaten

2 teaspoons ground cinnamon

½ teaspoon salt

5 cups flour

FOR THE FILLING:

1 stick soft butter

2 tablespoons sugar

2 tablespoons cinnamon

FOR THE TOPPING:

1 egg, beaten

1 cup brown (demerara) sugar cubes, coarsely chopped

FOR EMMA'S ICING:

1 stick (½ cup) butter, softened

2 ounces cream cheese, softened

1 cup powdered sugar

½ teaspoon pumpkin pie spice

1 teaspoon vanilla extract

MAKE THE BUNS: Dissolve the yeast in 2 tablespoons of the milk. Whisk together the milk, sugar, butter, egg, cinnamon, and salt. Add in the dissolved yeast. Stir in 1 cup of flour at a time until you have a soft dough. Knead until the dough is smooth and elastic, adding more flour as needed, about 8 to 10 minutes. Put into a buttered bowl, cover, and let rise until doubled, about 1 hour.

Gently punch down the dough and turn it out onto a floured surface. Roll into a 12×19-inch rectangle. Spread the butter over the dough. Stir together the sugar and cinnamon and sprinkle evenly over the surface. Starting with the longest side, roll up into a log and pinch the seam together. Cut into 20 to 24 pieces, about 1-inch thick. Put them cut side down into a buttered 9-×13-inch cake pan or 2

9-inch cake pans. Cover and let rise until doubled in size, about 1 hour. Preheat the oven to 400°F.

When ready to bake, brush the tops of the buns with the egg and sprinkle over the chopped brown sugar cubes. Bake for 15 to 20 minutes, or until the tops are well browned.

MAKE THE FROSTING: While the buns are baking, beat together the icing ingredients until smooth. Remove the buns from the oven and let them sit for 5 minutes. Spread the icing over the warm buns. Serve warm.

At first, Grace couldn't believe her eyes. *How on earth did Von Vasser get onto Emma's computer screen?* Emma tried to slam the screen shut, but Grace leaned over her shoulder and grabbed it. Von waved. "Hi, Grace! We're having a lovely chat. Emma and I have become Skype buddies. She couldn't come to the Mediterranean, so I brought the Mediterranean to her!" The image on the screen whipped around to show a glorious, azure blue seascape, with islands in the distance. "We're heading into port at Crete. You should have come, maybe next trip?"

"Von, how long have you been Skyping with Emma?"

"Well, since Leeza's funeral. We are all so upset by her death. I told Emma she could reach out to me anytime. And you know, we are having a lot of fun, aren't we Emma? I'm showing her sites from the *Odyssey*, firsthand."

Emma nodded. "I saw the rock where the Sirens sang," she said. "And the Acropolis."

"If you can't come to the Mediterranean—it can come to you," Von explained, as if it were an everyday occurrence for Emma to be touring ancient Greece by Skype.

Grace was incredulous. Surfers were one thing, teenage friends from Chicago another—but Skyping with Von from the Mediterranean was definitely not on the agenda.

"Skyping from the Med!" Ken yelled when Grace recounted the Skype story later that day at the Book Nook. Pilot season had ended in LA, and he was spending a few days in New London with Tim. Grace had brought over some of the cinnamon buns while they were still warm, and now she and Ken sat on the porch talking while they waited for the buns to cool enough to eat. Grace would never get over Leeza's absence, but thank goodness Ken was here, and Tim was fast becoming a dear friend.

"That is amazing! I told you, you should have gone on that cruise with him."

"What? You know I needed to be back in LA helping you, and Emma had school. You'd think with a chocolate factory to run and a boat to cruise on, he'd have better things to do. Emma's probably figured out by now that I cancelled her Skype account. You don't think she'll try to run away to Europe? Her finals are next week."

"Well, she won't risk having to repeat the year," Tim said. "All the kids are so excited about high school."

"I wouldn't worry about it," Ken agreed. "Von's just showing off with Emma and trying to make a good impression to get to you."

"Well, it's working." Grace felt more uneasy than she let on. If this door opened, there was no telling where it could lead. But even Ken couldn't really understand that.

"Let's not waste any more time on that hunk of Swiss cheese," Ken proclaimed. "The Fourth of July is fast approaching, the town is planning a parade, a parachute fly-in onto the town square, and fireworks at dusk. In the immortal words of George Washington, I see this as a sales opportunity. A chance for the Book Nook to proclaim its independence from debt. Think of it—all the people who will be passing by—kids, tourists, patriots . . ."

Tim clicked to the town calendar on his laptop. "If the Book Nook can't pull in some numbers during a big holiday like this, we might as well close up shop."

"I will not permit negativity!" Ken scolded Tim playfully. "Now—logistics. The Book Nook is right across from the square. We have to have a strategic plan to pull people in."

"We could dress in costume, like the founding fathers," Tim suggested. He nodded toward Grace. "And mother."

Ken winced and closed his eyes. "I'll pretend I didn't hear that. What about running an ad?"

"Buy one, get one free?" suggested Grace.

Just then, a woman pushing a stroller came up to the porch. "Wow," she said, smiling. "I have to tell you how good this smells. What on earth are you cooking in there?"

"You must mean these cinnamon buns," Grace said. She

offered the plate heaped with the *kanebullar*. "Please take one."

After a single bite, the woman was motioning the other young mothers from the park to come over. Within minutes, several women were milling around on the front porch, cups of coffee in hand, eating cinnamon buns, and five children's books had been sold.

Grace was busy helping out at the cash register when she noticed a red fire department car pull up outside. Mike got a warm welcome from the ladies on the front porch.

"Hey, these are great," Mike said, demolishing a cinnamon bun. "Can I order some for the firehouse?"

"Sorry, we don't have a real bakery," Grace apologized. "These are just some treats my mom whipped up."

"Come back for our Fourth of July Parade Party," Ken said. "We're having red, white, and blue cupcakes, and bring some of those cute firemen with you."

"Ooh, we'll come back then for sure," said one of the young moms.

Mike blushed, but tried to hide it with a laugh.

"We're having a Fourth of July Parade Party?" Grace asked.

"We are," Ken announced, firmly. "A Parade Party," he announced, using his best Music Man voice. "Come one, come all!" He turned to Tim and stage-whispered, "I smell the sweet smell of revenue."

"Cupcakes, firemen, and a Parade Party—a way to have fun and hopefully bring in the customers."

"Well then, if it's for the bookstore, I'm sure I could get a few of the guys to come," Mike said and with that, the Book Nook Cupcake Brigade was born.

The two weeks running up to the Fourth were an avalanche of sugar, butter, flour, red and blue food coloring, and sign-making. Grace's hands and fingers were permanently stained purple. Lorraine commandeered every refrigerator, oven, and freezer in the neighborhood to store ingredients and ramp up "the production line," as she called it. Emma and Ken hit the computer and sourced tiny American flags on toothpick poles.

Grace was in the middle of frosting yet another batch of cup-cakes when Mike knocked. Lorraine and Emma were down the street in a neighbor's kitchen, so Grace quickly wiped her hands and opened the door. "Hi, Mike! What's up?" Mike was staring at her.

"Looks like you're blue today?" he said.

Grace didn't get the joke and shook her head. "What? No. I'm doing great."

Mike laughed. "You've got frosting just here," and he brushed a bit of blue frosting from her cheek and licked his fin-ger. The gesture was playful, yet so intimate that Grace blushed and stepped back. Mike was cute and awfully nice, but he was also Emma's tutor, so Grace didn't want to blur any lines. Grace touched her cheek where his finger had been and quickly wiped at the frosting. "Oh, I guess I'm a bit of a mess."

They were in the homestretch leading up to Emma's final exams, so Mike had been over more often, making sure every-thing was going smoothly with Emma's studies. "Emma's not here just now," Grace explained.

"Actually, I wanted to show you something, Grace." He gestured for her to come outside while he returned to his van. He unloaded some red-white-and-blue bunting onto the porch, then he went back and pulled a folder out of the glove compartment.

"Emma's English paper." He handed it to Grace with a very serious look on his face.

Oh, no. She steeled herself.

"It's amazing. She put an incredible amount of research into this. It's one of the best I've seen. It shows what she can do when she applies herself." The paper was marked A+.

That's my girl! "I knew it! I knew she could do it." Grace was so happy she hugged Mike. "What's the topic?"

"*The Odyssey.* She wrote a poem about the Sirens. It's very impressive. Almost like she was there."

"*The Odyssey.*"

"Yes, that's the book we were studying."

"She had a—friend of mine—Skyping her from Greece."

Mike nodded. "Bringing the story to life, that always makes a difference."

Grace decided not to elaborate further on her friend in the Med. Emma had done well, and that was what counted. Maybe sometimes the end justified the means.

chapter 9

The day they got the news Emma had passed her finals, Mike arrived with champagne and sparkling cider. They called Brian on speakerphone to share the good news, and he let out a big whoop. "Hey, Emma—congrats. You're a high-schooler now!"

"This is going to be the best time of your life." Grace smiled, and she meant it. High school had been, after all, the beginning of everything for her.

Emma was, for the first time in months, her old happy self. "I can't believe I got a B-plus in English! I thought I was going to flunk!"

Mike nodded. "It was the essay on *The Odyssey*. You're a very good writer when you put your mind to it, Emma."

Emma shot her mother a look. "Maybe I was inspired."

Well, maybe she wasn't *completely* back to her old self. Maybe she never would be. And maybe that was the point. A lot of things were different now. It was as if Leeza's death had triggered a chain reaction.

Tutoring was done for the summer, but Mike seemed to be around more often. He'd help with a carpentry job, sit on the porch and take a break, or go for a stroll through the park at the end of the day. Once after they were closing up the Book Nook, Mike took Grace for pizza. She started to look forward to his visits. *But I'm not interested in dating*, she told herself. Life was complicated enough.

It was ironic, Grace thought, that even Claire had heard what they were doing to save the Book Nook, and arrived one afternoon with a carful of window boxes containing red and white geraniums. "Adam is in Tim's reading group," Claire said as Grace helped her unload the car. Grace remembered Adam, Leeza's nephew. He was about Emma's age. "We love the Book Nook!" In high school Claire and her gang of popular girl-friends had never even talked to Grace. Well, being Leeza's sister-in-law must have rubbed off, Grace thought, because, she had to admit, Claire was almost a different person. Or maybe Grace herself was. So much had changed in such a short time. It was unrealistic, Grace knew all too well, to expect miracles, but small steps were a beginning. A special grocery store run was in order.

"I have a really good recipe for German chocolate cupcakes," she said, bursting in on a frosting assembly line in Lorraine's kitchen carrying an armful of grocery bags. "Do you think a state fair award-winning recipe might bring in a few extra cus-tomers?"

And just like that three generations of Holm women were baking together. But there was one small problem. It had been so long since Grace had worked with this recipe, she found it hard to get the measurements exactly right when baking in such quantity. She'd overestimated, and now there was enough frosting to feed a small army. What would they do with it all?

Whack! A glob of frosting splattered onto Grace's shoulder. Another flew across the table and landed in Emma's hair. Grace and Emma stared at each other in disbelief. Lorraine, stiff-upper-lip, straight-laced Lorraine was starting a frosting fight! Suddenly, in soft focus, like an old, faded family film, it all came back to Grace—the crazy food fights she, her mother, and her father had had when she was a little girl, right here in this kitchen. Her dad had always been the instigator, and it had become a bit of a tradition. But when he'd died, a light had gone out in the house, and that had ended, along with many other things. Until now. Grace scooped up a wad of frosting and lobbed it at Lorraine. Emma whipped a big spoonful that hit Grace smack in the face. They were laughing hysterically.

"*God Bless America!*" squawked Halo, not to be left out of the action.

"Did somebody call the fire department?" Mike walked into the kitchen, slipping on sugar and frosting. "Good grief, ladies!" He ducked as a barrage of frosting flew in his direction. "Truce! Truce!" He picked up a white dish towel and waved it. "I surrender!"

Grace cringed. She'd forgotten—Mike had asked her to dinner and a jazz concert at the high school tonight, and here she was, coated in icing. Well, there was no time for the Miss America routine. Five minutes later, she'd run herself through the shower as if it were a car wash, thrown on a pair of heels with black skinny jeans, and dashed back down the stairs, hair wet, but ready. She didn't mind not spending too much time on herself—after all, this wasn't exactly a date. It was just Mike.

"Your carriage awaits." He chivalrously opened the door—the door of the bright red, twenty-eight-foot-long fire engine. Grace looked back at the house. Both Emma and her mother were peering through the edge of the curtains.

"Um—where's the fire?"

Mike turned to her and fluttered his hand over his heart. "Heart's on fire."

Grace laughed and climbed up into the cab of the fire engine. There was no graceful way to do this, she realized, especially in heels. No wonder firemen wore those boots. She had just settled somewhat awkwardly into the seat when a ball of black-and-white fur leapt toward her from the floor—a Dalmatian puppy, complete with wet nose and wagging tail.

"Down, boy." Mike grabbed the puppy by its collar and settled it into his lap. "This is Spotty," he said, stroking him. "His mom had puppies at the firehouse. I sort of inherited him. I thought it was better to leave him in the truck, since we don't know if he's bird-proofed yet."

"Good call. Halo is a real prima donna." Spotty's pink tongue flicked in her direction. "This is the world's cutest puppy." She reached out and stroked his soft fur.

"He's a good guy. We can leave him at the firehouse after dinner while we go to the show. He can visit his mom tonight."

People on the block were staring as the huge fire truck lumbered away from the curb. They probably thought Lorraine's house had been on fire. "You know, I thought this was going to be kind of a low-key evening," said Grace.

"What do you mean? This is low-key. I'm not turning on the siren."

Sitting there with a squirming puppy on her lap, Grace couldn't help but smile. She could see why kids liked Mike. Being around him was easy and fun. It had been a long time, Grace thought, since things were easy and fun. Ever since her marriage had fallen apart, she'd taken everything so seriously. For the past two years, she'd felt like she had to prove herself worthy of raising Emma on her own every single day. Like every day was a test for the two of them, one that she rarely felt she passed. No wonder Emma longed to escape. Did it really take a big red fire engine driving into her life to see this?

Mike drove past the football field, and a bunch of kids waved and called out, "Hi, Coach!" "Hey, Coach!" "Where's the fire, Coach!"

He waved and rang the bell. "Why don't you ring it?" he asked Grace.

Grace hesitated. Was a civilian allowed to ring the bell?

"You know," Mike said, "there's a story to these fire truck bells. The purpose of the siren was to clear the way and let people know the truck was on its way to an emergency. The bell was rung on the way back, to let the men in the firehouse know the truck was on its way home." He looked at Grace with a grin. "I'd say that describes the situation, wouldn't you?"

Yes, that describes the situation pretty well. Maybe a fire truck was showing her the way home, too, Grace thought. She smiled back and rang the bell. And then they both started laughing, and laughed about anything and everything the entire way back to the station.

At the firehouse, Spotty was reunited with his mother, while Mike escorted Grace upstairs to the living area. "I was just filling in for Jake today," he said. "I told him I'd take care of dinner, then he could take over. We're having my special chili. The guys love it."

The firehouse resembled an overgrown fraternity house, Grace thought. There was a workout area with weights, a bench and a stair-climber, a bunk room, a locker room, a TV area, and a small, open kitchen. Two firemen sat in sweats and jeans, playing poker in the living area. The kitchen was empty.

"What can I do to help?" Grace asked.

"Nothing. Only trained firemen are allowed in this kitchen."

"Ooh," teased Grace. "The rest of us might burn something and start a fire. How would that look?"

"It would be a public relations disaster, no question about it," Mike said as he unloaded the groceries and started chopping onions. "We wouldn't want that, would we?" He tossed Grace a can of kidney beans. "Can opener's in the drawer by the sink."

As the chili simmered, Grace watched Mike as he popped a large sheet pan of corn bread into the oven with a flourish. "I had no idea we had a four-star chef in the firehouse," she said.

One of the guys on the couch swiveled his head from the game on TV. "Yeah, he's a regular Chef Boyardee."

"Thanks, Tommy." Mike flung a wet towel at his buddy's head.

FIREHOUSE CHILI

Serves a firehouse full!

3 pounds ground chuck

2 pounds sirloin, cut into small pieces

2 tablespoons olive oil

3 large onions, chopped

4 jalapeno peppers, seeded and chopped

12 garlic cloves, chopped

2 tablespoons chili powder, or more to taste

1 tablespoon dried oregano

Salt and pepper, to taste

Tabasco, to taste

2 (28-ounce) cans crushed tomatoes

2 (15-ounce) cans kidney beans, drained and rinsed

2 (15-ounce) cans black beans, drained and rinsed

5 cups water

In a large pot, cook the ground chuck until it is no longer pink and has browned a little. Remove from the pot and drain off all but 2 tablespoons of fat. Cook the sirloin until it is lightly browned. Remove from the pot and discard the fat.

Add the olive oil to the pot and cook the onions until they are soft and translucent, about 8 to 10 minutes. Add the jalapenos and cook for a minute. Add the garlic, chili powder, oregano, salt, pepper, and Tabasco and cook for another minute.

Pour in the tomatoes, beans, and water and return the meats to the pot. Bring to a boil then reduce the heat. Simmer for at least one hour or until the chili has thickened. (Add more water if it is too thick.) Taste and adjust the seasonings.

NOTE:
- Ground turkey or chicken can replace the beef.
- Serve over rice or tortilla chips.
- Topping suggestions: sour cream, grated cheddar cheese, chopped scallions, chopped jalapenos, chopped onion, chopped bell peppers, cilantro leaves.

As Grace rinsed lettuce and tomatoes for the salad, she couldn't believe how comfortable she felt in this kitchen, with Mike. Then again, maybe she was comfortable with Mike, and they just happened to be in the kitchen. There was no agenda, no pressure, no past. Without a backstory, they were free to start fresh. They ate their chili from firehouse mugs, standing up. It wasn't gourmet, but it was about as good as it got, Grace thought, as they loaded a gallon into the freezer and another into the refrigerator for the next shift.

I am on an actual date, Grace suddenly realized, as she climbed onto the back of Mike's motorcycle, the designated transportation to the concert. Somehow, this non-date had morphed into the actual thing. Or so it seemed. Because Grace's dates had been so few and far between, she wondered if she would actually recognize one if it hit her in the face. Suddenly, she panicked. She didn't want the fact that this was a "date" to get in the way of what looked like a promising new friendship. "Mike?" She squeezed his shoulder from behind.

"Just hold on tight."

"No, it's not that." She hesitated, hoping he wouldn't take it the wrong way. "It's—this isn't a date, is it? It's still a non-date?"

He laughed and gunned the engine. "Absolutely, this is not a date. This is a non-date if there ever was."

"Good," Grace said firmly. "I'm glad we cleared that up." Still, she had to admit, leaning into Mike, her arms around him, it didn't feel totally platonic.

After the concert, they went for ice cream.

"How's it feel to be back home?" Mike asked. The night was

warm and quiet. Crickets could be heard even there in the center of town.

Grace licked butter pecan off her hand and thought for a moment. "Coming back, it's sort of like stepping into a time capsule. Like the school—so much is still the same. It brings back a lot of memories."

"Isn't that a good thing?"

"It's mostly good, but everything sort of collapsed in on me when I was in high school. A lot of things didn't turn out to be what I thought they were, so I'm still trying to understand how I feel about them."

Mike stopped and looked closely at Grace. He reached out, touched her cheek, and quietly told her, "You are truly beautiful, Grace Holm-D'Angelo." Then he leaned in and kissed her.

It was a two-cone kiss. A kiss that lasted long enough for both of their ice cream cones to melt.

"Well, then," Mike said finally. "I'm sorry to tell you this, Grace. But I think our non-date just became an official date."

"Can't we just call that a non-kiss?"

"Let me think." He paused. "I think we have to count it. Maybe even enter it into the national register of great kisses."

Grace had to agree. The kiss had been amazing.

"Maybe we need to check that national register part out, though," Mike said, into her hair. "We should conduct a little more research, just to get the facts right."

"For verification purposes only," Grace agreed.

But before he could kiss her again, she kissed him.

chapter 10

F*lag, cherry, gumdrop.*
   Flag, cherry, gumdrop.
Flag, cherry, gumdrop.

Grace's hands flew as she frantically added decorations to the last trays of the Fourth of July cupcakes: mini American flags on toothpicks, red candied cherries, and blue gumdrops. She felt like she was guest-starring in the famous *I Love Lucy* candy assembly-line episode. Emma had found a recipe in the recipe box, and the Cupcake Brigade had adapted it, baking so many cupcakes that racks covered every surface in the house. Still, it was impossible to keep up with demand.

She was racing against the clock. The first round of cupcakes had disappeared even before the parade had begun. The second and third vanished when, following the patriotically decorated stroller, wagon, and tricycle section of the parade, the stroller moms stormed the porch and spread the word. Nobody spreads the buzz like moms, Grace knew. They were a social network unto themselves. Within minutes of their onslaught of the Book Nook, the shop was awash in crumbs and smears of red, white, and blue frosting. Then there were the tourists, following a mob

INDEPENDENCE CUPCAKES

Makes 36 cupcakes

FOR THE CAKE:

1 cup softened butter

1½ cups plus ½ cup sugar

3½ cups cake flour

1 tablespoon baking powder

½ teaspoon salt

1 cup milk

2 teaspoons vanilla

9 large egg whites

FOR THE FROSTING:

2 sticks softened butter

4 cups powdered sugar

1 teaspoon vanilla

Pinch salt

4 to 5 tablespoons
  half-and-half

TO DECORATE:

Red, white, and blue jimmies

Red, white, and blue jelly beans

Red, white, and blue sugars

Raspberries and blueberries

Preheat the oven to 350°F. Line cupcake pans with 36 paper liners.

MAKE THE CUPCAKES: Cream butter and 1½ cups sugar. In a separate bowl whisk together flour, baking powder, and salt. Mix milk and vanilla. Alternate adding flour mixture and milk to batter in 3 parts, ending with the milk. Scrape down sides of bowl and mix for 30 seconds or until well incorporated. In a separate bowl whip the egg whites until frothy, slowly stream in the remaining ½ cup sugar, and continue to whip until soft peaks form. Gently fold egg whites into batter in 3 parts. Fill cupcake liners ¾ of the way to the top. Bake for 20 minutes, rotating pans halfway through the baking time. Cupcakes will be lightly golden on top when done and a toothpick inserted will have moist crumbs. Let cool.

MAKE THE FROSTING: Whisk together the butter and sugar. Add the vanilla and salt and whisk again. Add the half-and-half, a tablespoon at a time, until you get the spreading consistency you like.

that must have looked, from the park across the street, like Brad Pitt had dropped into the bookstore. Emma sat on the floor with Sara on her lap and Halo on her shoulder, reading stories to a spellbound group of kids. Halo became an instant tourist attraction and minor celebrity. People were snapping his picture like paparazzi. Spotty was a big hit too, and clearly loved the attention. Ken was burning rubber at the cash register, Mike and a few other firemen were hauling in jugs of pink lemonade, and Tim was in heaven. Suddenly, the Book Nook was the place to be. The problem was, they were running out of cupcakes. Ken had called up the emergency reserve, and Grace had sped around the neighborhood collecting the final trays—only to discover that they had forgotten to decorate them. The flags and gumdrops were a little crooked, but the product would probably last about thirty seconds, so Grace figured perfection was not a priority.

By the time the precision parachute team had landed in the town square, the last cupcake had been eaten. But, as Tim declared triumphantly, they had set a sales record. "Probably for all time," Tim said. "This is going to be hard to top."

Following an epic cleanup, for which Grace seriously considered asking Mike to just aim the fire hose into the shop and be done with it, the Cupcake Brigade adjourned to the ice cream parlor, followed by the fireworks. Emma was parked on a blanket with her new friends, Grace noticed, and she'd been invited to a party. Grace crossed her fingers. *This just might work out.* With a unanimous vote, it was decided that this was the template for success for the Book Nook. "We need another pop-up café at the 3F," said Grace, using Ken's nickname for the Fall Family Fest. "That'll be even bigger crowds. Ken and I will come in for it, won't we?"

Ken agreed. "Yes. Start baking now, everybody." He winked at Tim and looked at his watch. "Let's synchronize. Go!"

As they closed up the shop, Mike insisted on asking Lorraine to join them for a few beers at O'Malley's Irish Pub. "Tell me all about the food pantry," he said, genuinely interested, as they settled into one of the big wooden booths at the back. He squeezed Grace's hand as she sat beside him in the booth across from Ken, Tim, and her mother. *Mike thinks we're this typical American family. Little does he know. Little does he know* me. *If he knew everything, would he still care?* Grace wondered.

The Fourth of July had broken the ice, and as of July fifth the Book Nook seemed to be the anointed "in" spot for the young moms of New London. While the moms had coffee, browsed books, and gossiped on the comfy couch, Emma and Halo led a story-reading circle for the little kids. Emma had found a purpose, something she loved, and, Grace noted, she stepped up to it. On Friday night, instead of going out with her friends, Emma had a couple of the girls over to help her bake cupcakes for the weekend crowd at the shop. On their way to a movie, Grace and Mike walked into the kitchen to find Emma demonstrating a basket-weave piping technique that Grace didn't even know Emma knew. Two teenaged girls leaned over the counter, watching closely.

"Wow! Where did you learn to do that, Emma?" Grace asked, amazed by her daughter's talent.

Emma expertly maneuvered a pastry bag full of icing into a crisscross pattern.

"I saw it online," Emma said without looking up, her spiky black hair bobbing along with the movements of the pastry bag. "There was a video. I figured, how hard can it be? And Grandma has the pastry tips and tubes for decorating with frosting."

"This is so cool," said Maura, one of Emma's friends.

Later, as they waited in line for their movie tickets, Grace asked Mike if he'd noticed the change in Emma. "I wish I could take credit for this. I'd be Mother of the Year. But she's doing it all herself."

"She's invested in something," said Mike as he swiped his charge card through the scanner. "So she cares."

"She's already a better baker than I ever was," said Grace. "She's got a feel for it."

After the movie, Grace sat on Emma's bed.

"You're doing a great job, Em. I am so proud of you."

For once, Emma didn't squirm away. Instead, she asked, "Do you think I could be a teacher one day?"

"That would be wonderful. You'd be very good at it."

"Maybe a nursery school teacher," Emma said. "Really little kids. Like Sara, or the kids at the Book Nook." She twirled a strand of dark hair thoughtfully. "Or, I've been thinking, kids like my stories so much—maybe I could write an online children's book. I have an idea about a hip-hop cockatoo who saves the rain forest. Named Halo, of course. I have some drawings for the pictures for the first book, it's called *Hello, Halo*. You have to keep the words simple, then they get it." She pulled up some drawings saved on her iPad.

Grace could barely believe what she was seeing. The drawings were adorable cartoons, and showed a lot of discipline. Emma, who never stuck to one thing for more than five minutes, must have been working on them for days. She had always doodled little figures on the edges of her notebooks, but this was something else, an idea with real potential. It almost looked professional. "What a great idea! The cockatoo in the sunglasses is crazy; kids will love him. You know, Mike thinks you're a really good writer, and so do I. And you can draw this well! Why don't you bounce the book idea off of him?"

Emma's phone buzzed and she jumped to grab it. The moment was over, but it was a start. *More than a start. It was a miracle*. Grace was thankful for this time in Wisconsin, and while it was still only July, *The Lost Ones* was set to go back into production August 8 and she and Ken were expected on set. Emma would be starting school two weeks later, after they returned. Yes, before they knew it it would be time for them all to return to LA.

chapter 11

"I swear to God I'm going to kill Artie right here and right now," Ken fumed. If he were a cartoon character, Grace thought, smoke would have been coming out of the top of Ken's head. "Our esteemed, Emmy-winning director can join the undead because I'm gonna put a stake through his nonexistent heart."

Grace was busy making notes in the production book, synchronizing it with the script changes. It was her job to make sure that the set notes were up to date and complete, including any last-minute changes. "What now?"

"I'll tell you what's now. Give me that script," Ken said. "You see these three pages? Scene six? The one we spent all morning setting up?"

Grace nodded.

Ken grabbed the pages and ripped them out of the script.

"Ken! My notes!"

He tossed the pages into a garbage can. "Won't matter. Artie just called for an on-set rewrite of the entire scene. He's changing everything. He's decided the season premiere of *The Lost Ones* has to have more edge for the ratings. The writers are going nuts. They're threatening to call the union. Well, we're going to have to redo everything. He has this idea that the door opens, and as the vamps walk in, a freeze suddenly coats everything with a layer of ice. So we have like an hour to turn this entire set into the North Pole. What I wouldn't give to be back in New London working on the Book Nook with Tim—something meaningful rather than this silly show."

Grace knew Ken missed Tim and for the first time hadn't looked forward to returning to LA. Artie's outbursts weren't helping Ken feel better about being home. Grace sighed. "And where do we find the prop ice?"

"That, Grace, is why I have an assistant—namely you. I'm going to deal with the A.D. You are going to create ice. Call Dairy Queen, for all I care. Just figure it out. Oh, and he wants a vulture. A white vulture, mind you, to sit on the Queen's shoulder. Call that bird wrangler; he's on my speed-dial. Do vultures even come in white? Oh my God, I'm going to kill him!" Ken continued to rant as he jumped into a golf cart and sped off across the set with Roberto at the wheel.

Instant ice. White vulture. Another day at the office. Grace located an acrylic ice source fairly quickly. The white vulture was another matter.

"You're talking the Egyptian vulture here," the bird wrangler said over the phone. "Check 'em out online. They're indigenous to Egypt and Sri Lanka. They're practically endangered. I have other vultures, but they're turkey vultures. Turkey vultures are gray."

"Can you spray paint them white?"

"You've got to be kidding. And by the way, they have a six-foot wingspan; they're not going to sit on somebody's shoulder."

"Just asking, thanks." Grace dreaded telling Artie she couldn't find what he wanted. He never took that sort of thing well. Then she had an idea. She grabbed her iPad and pulled up some pictures to show him.

"Artie, look at this. Your idea of the bird on Carrie's shoulder is brilliant. But vultures are so large, she's going to say the bird is stealing her scene. What about a white cockatoo? They have this gorgeous crest on their heads; it would show up in the shot."

Artie adjusted his glasses and scrutinized the screen. "Hmm. You may have something there, actually. The crest is sculptural. It's more—organic. Let's do it. People!" he commanded, although only Grace and the A.D. were standing there. "Go with the white cockatoo."

Grace ran to call Emma. "Get over here with Halo," she said. "You guys have a job!"

Yes, they were back in LA, a place where stars shone and pigs flew.

Grace thought Emma would be glad to get back to her life in Venice, but in fact, she was upset at leaving her new friends in Wisconsin. The Book Nook had become a refuge for Emma, Grace realized. Working with little kids, Emma had come into her own. It was the first time in years Emma seemed to really care about anything. Once more, Grace was responsible for Emma's latest round of discontent, but school was fast approaching. The reading list had been e-mailed and preseason sports tryouts were coming up. Emma would be in high school shortly. Grace could hardly believe it.

Telling Mike they were going back to LA had been the hardest part about leaving. Grace knew she'd miss him, but there was no point, really, in letting things get serious. His life was in Wisconsin and her life was in LA. She'd miss Mike, but she just didn't know saying good-bye to him would feel quite this painful.

"I've never been to California," Mike had said as they went for one last walk along the Wolf River Trail. He'd brought a picnic, tossing together his own recipe for BLT salad, packed in Mason jars, and a firehouse blanket. "Ant-proof, and everyone knows bacon is a food group."

It was a perfect July day, and the water shimmered as they wandered after their picnic along the myriad of beautiful, shaded paths that New London was famous for. The rainy spring had painted a lushness across the summer greenery, and butterflies danced above the flowers. There was a peacefulness that Grace had to admit she'd never experienced anywhere else.

"LA is a crazy place," she said. "The weather in winter is definitely an improvement to Wisconsin's, but you spend most of your time in the car."

"I could come and visit in a couple of weeks, as soon as you're settled again. Once school starts, it's a little harder, but there are vacations. Do you want to make a plan?"

"Let's see how things go." Grace was being vague.

Mike stopped and stared at her. "Whoa." He shook his head.

MIKE'S MASON JAR BLT SALAD

Makes 4 servings

FOR THE SALAD:

2 avocados, sliced

2 heads Bibb lettuce, coarsely chopped

1 pint cherry tomatoes, halved

8 slices cooked bacon, chopped

16 basil leaves, sliced

FOR THE PARMESAN TOASTS:

12 ¼-inch slices from a baguette

4 tablespoons butter, softened

4 tablespoons grated parmesan

Freshly ground black pepper

FOR THE VINAIGRETTE:

¾ cup champagne vinegar

1 teaspoon Dijon mustard

1 small shallot, finely chopped

Salt and pepper

Pinch sugar

¾ cup extra virgin olive oil

PARMESAN TOASTS: Preheat the oven to 350°F. Place the bread slices onto a cookie sheet and cook them until lightly browned, turning once. Turn on the broiler. Stir together the butter, parmesan, and black pepper. When the toasts are cool enough to handle, spread each with some of the butter mixture. Put under the broiler until melted and lightly browned. Set aside to cool.

VINAIGRETTE: In a pint mason jar, shake together the vinegar, mustard, shallot, salt, pepper, and sugar. Add the olive oil and shake again. Refrigerate until ready to use.

SALAD: Toss the avocados gently in a little vinaigrette to preserve the color. In 4 wide-mouth quart Mason jars, make a layer in the bottom of each with ¼ of the lettuce. Add a layer of tomatoes on top, then a layer of avocado, then a layer of bacon. Top with basil, cover, and refrigerate until ready to serve.

To serve, pour some dressing into each jar, put the top on, and give it a shake. Serve with long forks and the parmesan toasts.

"Grace, I really care about you and Emma. If you need to be in LA, that's fine, I understand. But what are you saying?"

"I'm not saying anything." *Why can't you just say it, Grace?*

"Well, then what are you not saying? I need to know—is there a way forward for us?"

Grace wasn't used to such a direct approach. "I don't know, Mike. It's too soon to be definite about anything."

"What's really going on, Grace? You're like these butterflies, landing here, flying there, taking a little bit from everywhere you set yourself down, but never settling for long. You're so beautiful, inside and out, and there's so much to you, but you won't let yourself make a life. I'm not criticizing you. I just want to understand where we are. I like you, and I don't want to be left on the outside, looking in. Can we talk about this?"

"You know the show is starting production—"

"Not the show. *You.*"

SANDRA LEE

Grace was used to her focus being everywhere but on herself. There was Emma, Brian, Leeza . . . Mike was putting her at the top of the list. And, if he knew the truth, she probably wouldn't even be *on* his list. She felt worse than ever. She'd twisted herself into some hideously complicated knot that there was no way to untangle. Grace knew, rationally, that wherever she was on the planet would not be far enough away to escape from her past. She needed space to think through what she was doing this time. She leaned into Mike and put her head on his shoulder.

"Mike, it's not that I don't want you to come."

"What then? Is it Emma?"

"No. She's doing great, thanks to you. It's me."

"There's no answer I can have for that, you know, Grace."

Mike exhaled a long, slow breath, like the wind being taken out of their relationship. " 'It's not you, it's me—' That sounds like a hack line from one of those dating reality shows. Can't you do better than that?"

"We'll just have to see how it goes . . . I wish—"

"Yeah. I get it." Mike cut her off. Then he sighed and kissed her forehead. "I'll drive you and Emma to the airport."

Something precious was at stake here, Grace knew. She struggled to open up to Mike. What did she have to lose?

Only Emma. Thinking back all those years ago to that day in her mother's kitchen, Grace knew she couldn't tell Mike her secret without first telling Emma, or Emma would never forgive her. That much she didn't need to wonder about; she knew it firsthand. Which would mean settling the question that had unsettled her life for fifteen years:

Who was Emma's father?

Which meant telling Brian. And Von. And risking losing Emma just when they were getting along again.

Other than checking to see if they'd gotten home safely, Mike hadn't called since they were back in LA. Grace was sure that she'd crushed him and she felt terrible.

———

"Coming through! Heads up!"

Two union guys wheeled a huge wind machine past Grace on a cart, snapping her attention back to the set.

"Emma's here," Ken announced.

"This is so great," Emma said. "Halo is going to be a star. First, the book, now the TV show." Passing her finals with good grades had given Emma a new confidence, and her children's book idea had given her her first real goal, something to work for and dream about.

"I wouldn't tell him to give up his day job yet, sweetie," said Ken, unzipping the carrier. "This is just a guest appearance. He's only in one scene. He could end up a beak on the cutting room floor."

"What does he have to do?"

Ken showed Emma and Grace the new script pages. "He's basically playing himself. He rides around on the Queen's shoulder. Here she comes now for the run-through."

Carrie Flannery glided across the room. In her black Prada pantsuit, with flared legs and nipped-in waist, she was a fashion icon's take on a vampire. Veteran of dozens of Shakespeare productions and star of movies and the fashion pages, she'd seen it all. She was one of those actresses who appeared larger than life on any screen, but was in person surprisingly small, with a tiny frame and delicate bone structure. Her mouth was meticulously painted a dark blue-red, her eyebrows bleached, and she was wearing a platinum-blonde wig with a wide black streak. You could tell this woman was a star, Grace thought, and had been a star for a long time.

"W. C. Fields said never work with children or animals, and here I am doing both," Carrie said with an acid twist. "Where is this winged creature?"

"We padded Carrie's shoulder in case it has sharp claws," informed the wardrobe assistant.

"This is Emma, my daughter," Grace said.

"How perfectly charming. How do you do?" Like many successful performers and politicians, Carrie had honed the skill of looking intently at whoever she was speaking to and making them feel like that person was the only person in the room worth talking to. She turned her laser focus on Emma, only for a minute, but that was enough.

"Hello," said Emma, thrilled. "The show is so great."

"My dear, you have gorgeous eyes. You should always play them up."

Grace could see that Carrie had gained a fan for life.

"Well, where is my godbird?" Ken asked impatiently. "A bit camera shy, it seems."

Emma reached into the carrier and carefully lifted Halo out, cupping him to her chest and stroking his white feather crest.

"OK, let's try it," Ken said.

Emma placed the bird gently on Carrie's shoulder, while Grace held her breath.

"*Gimme a break!*" the bird suddenly squawked.

Carrie gasped and winced away from Halo. "My eardrum! Did that bird just say, 'Give me a drink?'"

"Break. It's *break*. He needs elocution training. Now let's go see Arnie."

Emma took out her phone and videoed Halo as he took his place under the lights. "For his blog. I'm starting it tonight: *Halo in Hollywood*."

"Genius," Ken proclaimed.

Grace marveled as she watched Emma bustling around the edges of the set, taking pictures and making notes, yet under the radar. She was a natural. Lorraine had been right, it seemed. The answer had been under Grace's nose all along. When given something meaningful to do, Emma had risen to every occasion. Grace had gauged it completely wrong, she realized. Emma didn't need sunshine, the beach, and surfing to succeed. She needed structure. *Wait till Mike hears about this*, Grace thought, and then—*Wait, Mike's not here*. Bringing Emma back had been a team effort, but a key member of Team Emma was missing.

"Tim is going to hate this," Ken said from across the set into Grace's earpiece. "He thinks he discovered Halo."

Grace motioned Emma over to check the monitor with her. There on screen sat Halo, preening on Carrie's shoulder. Grace could see that Carrie wasn't entirely at ease, padded shoulder or not. She walked cautiously, her eyes darting nervously to the side, monitoring the bird as if she feared he might mistake her earring for a piece of fruit and grab for it at any minute. But the minute Artie said "Action!" her posture changed, her back arched, the distinctive gliding gait returned, and Carrie became the vampire Queen. It was magic. And Halo was her consort. He looked positively regal, with his snowy white feathers arching distinctively over his forehead.

Please God, don't let that bird swear on camera, Grace prayed.

But it was a perfect take, and a star was born. Emma was swept off the set by her new friends in a rush of giggles and congratulations.

They were wrapping for the day when Grace looked over and saw a young woman in a flowy chiffon dress, sandals, and sleeked-back hair opening Halo's cage. Her first thought was, "Oh no, now we'll need bodyguards for Halo!"

"Excuse me!" she called out. "Please don't touch—"

The young woman turned around. At first, what Grace saw just didn't compute. Who was this stranger in the pretty long skirt, chic wide belt, and tank top who seemed to be so interested in birds? Maybe one of the new summer interns whom she hadn't met? Wait . . .

Oh, my, God. It's Emma. Emma!!

Emma looked like a completely different person. She had always been beautiful, but now her spiky hair, still dyed black, had been tamed, flat-ironed to a satin gleam, her eyes flickering with new prominence under short bangs cut straight across her forehead. A faint flush crossed her cheeks on a face that needed no makeup whatsoever to be fresh-faced but distinctive, a girl entering young womanhood. Her Emma.

"Hey. They gave me a new look. What do you think?"

Ken emerged, followed by the show's stylist interns. "Sophie and Randy couldn't resist," Ken said. "Sophie's hair and makeup, Randy's wardrobe." He nodded to each of them in turn. "They work with our teens on the show. Will you look at our girl now?"

Emma lifted the back of her tank top to reveal a huge sunburst tattoo. Grace almost fainted. "No problem, Mom. It washes off. They have a whole library of temporaries here. They're like really nice decals. It's so cool." She, Sophie, and Randy all burst into laughter.

"Meet the NBFs," Ken said to Grace.

"What?"

"New Best Friends. Sophie is actually quite an artist. She's a sophomore studying fine art at Carnegie Mellon—and she loves animals. She and Emma hit it off right away. I think I see a collaborator in her future."

"You are incorrigible." Grace shook her head. She wrapped her arms around her daughter. "You are so gorgeous. You always were, but now you're a star."

"Halo's the star. I'm going to be his manager. I needed a new look for that."

"It was a 'must intervene' situation," laughed Sophie. "Sorry, Em. But if you're gonna manage Halo, you've gotta man up."

"Thanks, you guys." Emma smiled shyly. Grace saw now that her bravado and edge had been driven by a yearning to fit in, to be accepted. Being different meant, she knew from experience, that if they aren't going to accept you, you can always reject them first. Emma had found her groove; she was still different, but now she was doing it her way, not following a crowd. Going into high school, she had it all over what her mother had at the same age, Grace thought. Grace had had the Three Musketeers. But Emma had something much more important, something that would carry her for the rest of her life. She had herself. Not based on a boy, not based on a friend, or a group, but on her own talents, looks, and future. "This girl will own the future," thought Grace. This was just the very beginning, but with so much going for her, how could it be otherwise?

"You go, girl," said Ken, giving a fist-pump. It was amazing, Grace thought, how wonderful Ken was with young people. He always seemed to relate to them, at any age, and now that Emma was growing up, he was growing right along with her.

As if reading her mind, Ken looked at Grace. "If anybody knows that a kid needs confidence going into high school, it's me. And you were there." Grace knew that he'd wanted to give that gift to his goddaughter and he'd come through for her. Grace herself had been unable to even get Emma to run a comb through her hair, she thought wryly, so this was all the more amazing.

"Wait, there's more," Ken said excitedly. "You know Jaxon Kerrig, the kid who plays the vampire son? Idol of millions of teen girls? Emma introduced him to Halo, and now he thinks Emma is great, and as a little surprise, he is going to give her a ride to school the first day of high school."

"You have got to be kidding."

"*Shh*—it's a surprise."

Grace grabbed Ken's arm and squeezed it. "I can't believe all you've done for her. Thank you."

"Look at this gorgeous little thing. You did it, Grace. She's your daughter. The potential was always inside her; we just helped let it out. Anyhow, it's the least I could do after letting my goddaughter slip out of my clutches and skip school. I seriously thought I would have a stroke that day."

"*Seriously!*" squawked Halo.

"Speak when you're spoken to, bird. You're talent now. Actually, it was this, or hardwire a GPS system to her. The makeover was actually easier." He sighed and looked across the set to where Artie was waving his arms and chewing out the location scout. "Here we go again. Life as a punching bag. God, don't you just miss New London?"

"No, not really."

Ken leveled a look at her. "Maybe not *everyone* in New London. How about certain people in New London?"

Mike. She was still trying to convince herself that she didn't miss him. Grace knew that she wasn't the only person who had left a bit of their heart in New London. Ken was thinking about Tim. She couldn't remember another time in their lives that Ken had let his guard down and really thrown himself into a relationship. When he was around Tim, Ken was almost as different a person as Emma had become. It was as if the Book Nook was some magical gateway that had opened things up for all of them to take that next step in their lives, the one they'd been waiting for, but hadn't known it. The question was— would any of it last, for any of them?

Of course, Leeza had been right, as usual. It was more than a little aggravating that she could be right even when she was dead. *But that was the thing about Leez.* While everyone else on the planet always seemed to be endlessly competing for something, jostling for space and attention, she'd never been in that game. Grace had always wished she could be more like that, and maybe, if things had been different, she might have absorbed more of her best friend's selflessness. But when a woman hit her thirties, Grace thought, she'd better have a pretty good idea of what she wanted to be when she grew up. A mother, that much had been clear from the beginning. A wife? She'd thought so, but marriage had been more Atlantic City than honeymoon city. A stylist? More like a survivalist. Now, looking at her beautiful Emma, just coming into her own and, after some typical teen missteps, suddenly gaining ground on a firm idea of who she wanted to be in life, Grace had to admit that she was defining herself more by what she wasn't than what she was—or could be. She needed to focus on the positive. One day, before she knew it, she was going to wake up, and Emma would be off on her own, out of high school, and Grace was going to be alone.

At least the job was going well, so, yes, Grace could say she had succeeded in her career. She'd been worried that her absence from Hollywood would kill her career; instead, she'd found a new way to work. After a few false starts, she'd designed a computer program that allowed all the production resources on a given job to document their workflow on one master file. It had been a system born of necessity, because she'd been managing her job remotely, from Wisconsin, but it significantly streamlined the process. Grace's system was working so well, the production company had asked if she could adapt it for other jobs, and she found herself in demand in cyberspace as well as on the set. She was earning a decent living. That was a huge step. Now that her living was sorted out, it was time to sort out her life.

That night, as she turned off her bedside light, Grace flopped onto her pillows and closed her eyes, and Leeza was there. They were sitting on Ken's thirty-foot vintage powerboat in Marina del Rey. It was sunset, and the Unbiased Panel of Judges had convened in special session.

In high school, the Three Musketeers had created the U.P.J. to deal with the many real and imagined injustices and decisions they encountered. The panel had consisted of Grace, Ken, and Leeza sitting in judgment on any person, place, or thing. Whatever was in question or open for discussion, the Unbiased Panel of Judges would be role-called to vote.

Should Leeza go out with the basketball team captain, even though he had the IQ of a gnat? The Unbiased Panel of Judges would vote. The answer to that was consistently no.

Should Grace get a perm? The Unbiased Panel of Judges voted NO.

Should Claire's sweater be made to "disappear"? YES!

Should Jonathan attend law school? This was mixed. The time and expense were discussed, but YES won out. No decision was too large or small for U.P.J. scrutiny.

In the dream, the three of them were drinking a bottle of wine and watching an orange ball of sun sink below the horizon.

Leeza looked perfectly healthy, with all of her beautiful dark hair. It was so real, Grace could hear the soft clinking of the boat fittings as it rocked gently in its slip.

"The U.P.J. is now convened," Ken intoned, raising a glass.

"*Here, here,*" squawked Halo, suddenly appearing. He didn't belong in the dream, but whatever. It was a dream.

"The issue before us," announced Ken, who was serving as arbiter, "is Emma. Should Grace tell Emma that Brian may not be her father?"

"Should she tell Brian?" Leeza asked. "Or Von?"

"I'll take the pros," Ken said, reaching into his pocket and unfurling a Post-it with some notes. "Pro: This uncertainty does indeed exist."

"Con," said Leeza. "Nothing is certain at this point. Why upset Emma without all the facts?"

"Pro," Ken retorted. "Keeping secrets like this has not had a good track record with Grace."

"Pro!" Leeza jumped up. "Emma deserves to know the truth."

"Ooh, let's rock the boat," Ken jibed.

"Con," interjected Grace. "She might hate her mother for-ever after."

"Hmm," muttered Ken. "Sounds familiar. Pro: It is better to be in control of the situation than to just let it happen."

"Pro," Grace interjected. "I always want to be honest with my daughter. Con: Brian would never get over it. Or forgive me."

"Yes, he would," said Leeza. "You can't vote both sides of the issue. But I will say that Brian is a very big Pro here. He knows what it's like to live with the consequences of a mistake, after all."

Grace started to cry. She told herself to stop it, it was only a dream, but it all seemed so real, especially Leeza. "All I wanted was to have a family and to do my best for my little girl. She's been so confused since we left Chicago, and now that she's started to come into her own, I'm going to pull the rug out from under her. She'll hate me. She'll think I lied to her, her whole life." Grace's eyes were streaming.

"Didn't you get my note?" Leeza asked. "Emma is not you, Gracie. Hasn't she been telling us that in every way possible? Think about it—she's showing us that she's her own person. And when we let that happen, wonderful things go along with it. Just because you feel one way doesn't mean Emma will feel the same way. Look what happened when you brought her into your life a little bit more, at work. She just wants to be included. Not telling her is excluding her from your life. Maybe she should be part of the decision of whether or not to tell Brian and Von. Maybe you can decide together."

Ken clapped his hands. "I call for a vote. All in favor of Grace telling Emma the truth?"

Leeza raised her hand. Ken raised his own hand, too.

"Well, that's a majority," he announced.

The sun was setting. "It's getting late. I think I have to go now," said Leeza.

"The Unbiased Panel has spoken," intoned Ken.

Grace started awake. It was pitch dark outside, and the bedside clock said 3:15 a.m. Her pillow was soggy with tears, so she tossed it over the side of the bed. The dream had felt so real. Yes, the Unbiased Panel had spoken, and, Grace realized, she had written the script herself. The dream was only an expression of something she herself already knew, how she really felt deep inside. She would tell Emma. She would take her to their favorite sushi place for dinner tonight, the one close to the beach, and afterward they would walk on the sand, and she would tell her. She would tell her about the love she'd felt for Brian, the passion she'd had for Von, and Emma would learn that her mother had been a teenager herself, with the same kinds of dreams and impulsiveness that Emma had herself. She would hold back nothing. She would give Emma the choice to be tested, or not. That had been Leeza's point, she now realized. That it was Emma's right, Emma's choice. She was crossing that blurry border, from little girl to the entrance of young womanhood, coming to a place where she was better able to handle what life would throw at her. *Yes, I'll tell her.* They would hold each other, and they would be closer than ever.

chapter 12

"Fire! There was a fire!" It was lunch break, and Ken ran up, breathless.

"What fire?" said Grace, her heart suddenly racing at the tone of Ken's voice. "On the set?"

"No . . ."

Was Emma all right? "My house? Emma's there, working on her book!"

"The Book Nook! A major fire! Tim called this morning. Oh my God! It's horrible, Grace. Some electrical thing shorted out in the middle of the night. You know how prehistoric the wiring was in that place. Anyhow, thank God nobody was there or hurt, and the smoke alarm kicked in, but it almost burned down."

"Oh my God!"

Ken flipped through pictures on his phone. "Look at these shots Tim took."

The pictures were heartbreaking. The place was a charred wreck. "Here you can see the entire front porch is toast. The windows are broken out. Tim said the fire department had to go in with hoses and foam. If it hadn't been for Mike changing those smoke alarm batteries, can you imagine? They used the hook and ladder, and Mike had to get Tim out through his second floor bedroom window. There was too much smoke on the stairwells." Ken looked like he might cry.

He clicked on a video taken from across the street, in the park. The building was partly obscured by the numerous fire and police trucks, but an orange-yellow blaze could clearly be seen licking skyward, ravenously devouring the building.

"The only thing that escaped fairly unscathed was the basement. It's like a bomb shelter down there. But still there was some water and smoke damage. Tim could have died! Mike is an absolute hero. Tim said Mike saved the back stock downstairs by telling them to foam the basement entrance, so the fire didn't get there. This is terrible. Poor Tim." Ken's voice trailed off and they stood silently looking at the picture. Grace hadn't seen Ken so sad since Leeza's funeral. Then he snapped to. "We're going back. Right away. We have to help Tim. We have to save the Book Nook. We'll file for insurance and we'll rebuild."

"Well, of course we have to help. This is a tragedy. But what do you mean—right away?"

"I mean, you see that man over there, that mean, nasty creature in disguise as a person who calls himself our director?"

"Yes. You're talking about Artie. Who *employs* us."

"Employed, past tense. We are quitting. Resigning. Now."

"W-wait, Ken, we can't just quit!"

"I'll tell Roberto. Roberto!" he called into his headset.

Grace put her arm around Ken. He was hysterical. She knew

he was more concerned about Tim than the Book Nook, but resigning . . .

"Emma is going to be so upset, I have to talk to her."

"She knows. Tim e-mailed us all. There's an e-mail waiting for you, too," Ken said grimly.

"Ken! You can't just quit!"

"Grace, I've been thinking about this since we got back. Think about what we left behind in New London."

Grace did: She'd left her mother, Mike, Jonathan, and Sara, and new friends. From New London, Brian was just a drive away. She had no job in New London, but without Ken, what would happen to their production design business? It was just the two of them, Roberto, and an assistant.

"Grace, sometimes it's just not worth it. The revenue is great, but being in New London, working on the Book Nook, meeting Tim—Leeza dying. Coming back here, I realize—it changed how I look at things. Who knows how long any of us has left? I don't want to spend the rest of my life with people who don't care about me, much less abusive drama queens. Look, you don't have to go with me, Gracie. But I have to go. Tim needs me. Do you know how good that feels?"

"I need you, too," Grace said softly.

Ken hugged her close. "No you don't. Not anymore. You created a money-making program. You know the business from all sides. I've trained you well. You're fully capable. The only one who doesn't know it is you. If you stay here, I'm absolutely certain you'll do me, and yourself, proud."

"Don't you want to make this temporary? See how it works out?"

"Grace." He flashed her the screen shot of the Book Nook. "We know how it's going to work out." He handed her his clipboard. "You have my passwords. I'll e-mail you the rest of my files. I'll call a Malibu Realtor from New London. Meanwhile, you can use the house and the boat; just don't take the boat out. I'll keep the boat for vacations. Tim will need a break."

Grace was incredulous. "The fire is terrible, but I can't believe you're just walking away like this and going back to Wisconsin."

"You know what they say—life is what happens when you're making other plans."

"Are you going back because of the fire, or is that just an excuse?"

"Neither. I'm going back to have a real life. I love Tim. I've been thinking about how to make it work, and the fire just solidified everything. You'd have to be selfish not to see I have to go back, and I don't like to think that about you, but . . ."

But you are. What was he saying? Ken had always supported her. "Selfish? I don't do much of anything for myself, you know that."

"I'd reconsider that statement, Miss Non-Transparency. I always feel like you have a hidden agenda. At least I tell it like it is. Maybe Emma senses the same things I do. Maybe that's been part of the problem with her. You have a hidden agenda, Grace, and it's your agenda and nobody else's. Which is fine, for you. But other people need things, too. Look at these pictures. Tim's life is in ashes. Ashes! If you'd be honest with yourself, you'd admit this is more important. This is where I should be, and it's where you should be too."

Grace felt as if Ken had slapped her in the face. The only thing missing was the handprint on her cheek. Of course, he was right. She had always had a hidden agenda. Yes, she'd been busy protecting her secrets. She was like the recipe box—a hard, weathered shell hiding a heart-shattering truth in plain sight.

"Tim and the Book Nook aren't Hollywood, but they're real life," Ken said. "You have Emma. I don't have anyone."

In that moment, Grace realized that Ken had a secret, too—at heart he was still the same insecure, lonely teenage boy she and Leeza had known. "You'd better go, then," she said softly. And she nodded. They each had something to protect.

Grace watched the resignation from across the room. It was anticlimactic. For once, Artie was calm and professional. He simply signaled the line producer, who stepped in immediately. "We hired your company," he said to Grace. "As long as the company delivers on the specifics, the contract is fulfilled. Your staffing at this point is not a material issue. Everyone has turn-over in this business. Now let's not lose time. We have a love scene to shoot."

Grace couldn't believe Ken had actually done it, but he had, and now she had to make an instant gear-shift to focus on the business at hand. For a minute, she was torn. She sent Mike a quick text: *OMG!* But she'd have to deal with the fire later. Mike was a wonderful man, but it was good that she didn't have a relationship to deal with right now. Ken had left the set, and now Roberto was waiting for direction. Right now, there was a job to do. She'd always thought of herself as more of a trainee, a wing-person, a professional and personal number two, following the lead of her mother, then Leeza, then Brian, and then Ken. Now there was nobody in front of her. The internship was over. In life and in work. Grace had just received a battlefield promotion.

Grace knew that some women would be exhilarated, empowered, by this kind of opportunity. She wished she could be a woman like that. But she realized she had never felt more alone. Ken, Leeza, Lorraine, Brian—none of them could prop her up now, in any way. There was nobody to turn to.

Breathe. Yes, that was the first step. That she could do. She took a deep breath. "Roberto!" she ordered into her headset. "Change of plans!"

chapter 13

The next weeks turned into a blur. After leaving the set, Ken tied up what he could in LA and flew back to New London. The talk Grace had promised herself she'd have with Emma didn't materialize, as she had more to do than ever at work and the time was never right. At night, Mike would call, and she barely had the energy to talk to him. In addition to *The Lost Ones*, the producers had been given the green light to develop a spin-off for the spring season. Grace couldn't afford to turn that down, so she was working overtime on the proposal. Ken was pretty wrapped up with the Book Nook, but thank God Grace had still managed to reach him for a pointer or two. Emma hung out on the edge of the preproduction activities, protectively managing Halo, who now had his own Facebook page and blog. She was working on her Halo story and tagging along with her new buddy, Sophie. Artie pretended not to notice Emma's presence on the set, but Grace knew he noticed everything.

Brian still wanted Emma to come to Chicago, but the first day of high school, with Emma's celebrity chauffeur, loomed large as she and Sophie went into overdrive figuring out the appropriate outfit. Sophie had come by the house and done a complete wardrobe makeover for Emma. A pile of black Goth clothing had been whisked off to the local Goodwill, and Sophie and Emma had spent a Saturday scouring the vintage shops for some blazers. They cut the sleeves off the blazers and belted them to create what Sophie called "blazer swagger." Grace snapped a photo for Ken so he could see his goddaughter in her new outfit, and sent it to him. He absolutely loved her new look.

There were school supplies and reading-list books to buy. It was just overwhelming. Whoever told women they could "have it all" was delusional, Grace decided. Her mother hadn't had it all, she didn't have it all, and if there was any shot for living a fairy tale, Emma would make it, but she was pretty sure Emma wasn't going to ever have it all, either.

———

Grace knew she couldn't put it off any longer. For once, Artie hadn't scheduled a postproduction crisis meeting, so she was able to leave the set on time. On the drive home, inching south on the 405 through the inevitable parking lot traffic, she rehearsed what she'd say, a rehearsal she'd been through dozens of times before. The script was never the same. She'd started writing it when Emma was born, holding the small, perfect rosebud-child in the pink blanket, whispering the words she knew she'd one day have to say. That first time had been the most complete, most honest explanation, from Grace's heart—and the one she wondered if she'd ever have the guts to say when her daughter was old enough to understand and, hopefully, forgive. There had been another script when Emma was seven, another when she was ten, and then the variation composed when Emma was thirteen, and finally the one she recited to herself and then stored in her mental filing cabinet when she decided to leave Brian. Now, so much had happened. She was different, Emma was different. Emma had met Von, was even friends with him. By the time Grace reached the cutoff for the 90 toward Marina del Rey, she had perfected her speech.

Grace parked under the little portico next to their house, slung her bag over her shoulder, and put her key in the front door lock. At that minute, she knew she was going to pull an Artie and tear up the script.

"Emma?" Halo was in his cage. A sure sign Emma was not home. This was not good. Emma was supposed to get permission, or at least inform Grace, whenever she went anywhere. She was supposed to be at home. "No reason to worry," thought Grace. A package with a FedEx label, addressed to her, sat inside the door. Emma must have accepted and signed for it. Under the plastic label protector, the return address was the New London house, in Lorraine's handwriting. "I must have left something at the house," Grace thought. Distracted as she scanned the room for clues to Emma's whereabouts, she pulled off the tape and opened the box. Inside were layers of newspaper, and inside that, wrapped in bubble pack, was something else. Digging under the packing, her fingers touched worn, weathered wood. Grace knew what it was immediately. She didn't even have to see it.

The recipe box.

Well, there it was. The object of so much shock, sadness, and confusion in her life sitting on her own kitchen counter. Grace thumbed through a few cards. Yes, they were all there—the recipes that had taken on personalities of their own in her mind through the years.

A small envelope was tucked inside, on top of the yellowed cards with their frayed edges. She recognized Lorraine's handwriting: *Grace*. Inside were two pieces of paper. One was Grace's birth certificate—obviously Lorraine had removed it from the safety deposit box. The other was a note:

> Secrets are not good things. Even if held with the best
> intentions. This recipe box has given up its secrets.
> The secrets are yours now. Will these recipes someday
> be Emma's? That is up to you. Finding yourself is like
> the best recipes. The ingredients are there, but what you
> do with them is up to you. You still have time to refine
> the recipe. Your mother, who loves you.

Grace had never had a letter from her mother before. Beyond scribbled notes left on the counter or the hall table, Lorraine was not a writer, but the words in the note were honest and heartfelt.

Leeza's death had reminded everyone how short and fragile life was. After all these years, Lorraine had sent her the recipe box, and she'd pulled Grace's birth certificate out of the safety deposit box. These two things had done so much to shape both their lives, and now, here they were. Grace understood that this was a passing of the baton, of sorts. And it wasn't just her mother sending her a message, it was the universe itself, it seemed.

As she held the recipe box, Grace realized it no longer held her hostage. She would not stuff it into the back of a closet, burn it, or send it back. She would not hide her birth certificate any longer. All the things the box contained were simply ingredients. It was up to Grace to decide how much or how little of them she'd use to define who she would become. She would tell Emma what she'd learned.

But where *was* Emma?

"Where's Emma, Halo?"

"You cannot be serious!" the bird said, his black eyes peering out from his cage.

"That was helpful," Grace muttered as she texted Emma. Then she dialed her cell phone number. The toneless no-answer ring. Then Grace noticed a yellow Post-it stuck to the side of Halo's cage.

Suki
End of Summer Blow-Out

Oh no. Suki was the older surfer kid who had been driving the car and broken his collarbone in the Malibu accident, with marijuana in the car. Suki was trouble. There was an address on Fifth Street, and Grace checked the map online: Skid Row, in downtown LA. *Skid Row!* Where the LA homeless congregated! Suki! The prospects were absolutely terrifying. Grace sent a text to Emma: *I am coming. Stay where you are.*

Amazingly, Emma answered. *I am with Suki. Fifth and Main.* Who knew, Grace thought, what she would find there.

Arriving at Fifth Street in the Central City East area of downtown LA an hour later, Grace was confused. There was no place to park; in fact, she couldn't even get close to Fifth and Main. It was as if a riot were going on. Wasn't this supposed to be Skid Row? The area was known to be a homeless community enclave, where people with transient addresses lived in state-provided housing in cheap hotels, but what she saw after she finally found a parking garage was a street full of tents and stands and colorful tables and booths, a party full of hope. Huge bunches of multicolored balloons festooned an area several blocks long, and music and the smell of grilled food permeated the air. Laughing kids with painted faces and dripping snow cones skipped along, beaming, among play areas. Signs proclaimed: END OF SUMMER BLOCK PARTY! WELCOME!

Grace was wandering through the crowd—probably, she thought, with a dazed look on her face—when she was pushed aside by a trampling mob of shrieking young girls. Edging her way down the street, she saw Jaxon Kerrig, the teenage heartthrob from *The Lost Ones,* flipping burgers in a blue apron, a backward baseball cap covering his trademark curls, surrounded by squealing fans. Standing next to him, in an identical blue apron, under a big, floppy red hat with the brim turned up and caught in a vintage pin, was Emma, handing out juice boxes.

"Emma, what's going on? How did you get here?" Grace asked as Emma thrust a juice box at her.

"Oops, sorry, Mom. We're very busy."

"Who is 'we'? And why are you here?"

Emma dropped her eyes. "Mom. I just wanted to help. It's the end-of-summer block party for the homeless kids who are going back to school. We served over six hundred sandwiches, can you believe it?" Her face glowed. "The kids all get free backpacks full of school supplies."

"Hey, Grace!" yelled Jaxon, with a wave. "We have an opening at the mustard station!"

"So—this is a fund-raiser?" she asked Emma.

"Yeah. They do it every year. The LA Mission sponsors it. They used to have a soup kitchen. Now there's this cool party." She pointed to her apron, which had the Mission's logo on it. "Suki's D.J.-ing pro bono, so he brought me along."

"Suki?"

"He's a D.J. now. We had a big orientation here yesterday. I know I should have told you I was volunteering, but you've been so busy, and I thought you were working late anyhow. And . . ." She beamed, as excited as any of the fans, "Jaxon's here! A lot of stars volunteer today. Check it out. So many people are into this! I'll send you the Twitter feed. Did you know, Mom, that almost seventy-four thousand people are homeless in LA? We have to help!"

It was hard to criticize Emma for trying to do good, but there were still boundaries to be set. "Well, this is great, but don't go off without telling me where, OK? We agreed."

"Sorry."

"Em, toss a juice box!" yelled somebody, and Emma was back to work.

It was like the Cupcake Brigade at the Book Nook, Grace thought, only on a major scale. New London had been a training ground for Emma, small opportunities to learn things that she would then take and make her own. Before, she'd had to express herself in crazy hairstyles, clothes, and piercings, as if her ideas and ambitions were trapped inside her and unable to get out beyond her appearance. Grace realized now that Emma deserved—needed—a larger stage. She'd thought that by being strict and keeping her precious daughter close she was protecting her. But she now could see that she'd been stifling her. Emma was just entering the critical high school years, and she would need her mother's guidance, but she was also ready to take those heady first steps to independence in her own way. Grace stood aside, marveling at her daughter's ease. This was a girl who could handle whatever life threw at her, including a confession from her mother. Grace resolved that it was finally time to tell Emma the truth. Tomorrow.

Grace decided to start the day by showing Emma the recipe box. They would make one of the recipes together. Later that night, she sorted through the cards, looking for something familiar yet Swedish. Swedish pancakes sounded perfect. Opening the cabinets, she saw a box of granola. There was a quart of milk in the refrigerator. She set the recipe box back in its wrappings and grabbed her purse for a quick grocery run before Emma got up. She wanted everything to be perfect.

"We're having breakfast at home? Swedish pancakes?" Emma said suspiciously. "We never make breakfast at home."

"Well, today is kind of special. Your grandmother sent us

SWEDISH PANCAKES WITH LINGONBERRY JAM

Makes about 20 pancakes

FOR THE JAM:

4 cups fresh or frozen
  lingonberries

½ cup water

1 cup sugar

FOR THE PANCAKES:

2 cups all-purpose flour

3 tablespoons vanilla sugar

2 teaspoons baking powder

Pinch salt

3 cups milk

2 large eggs

2 tablespoons butter, plus
  more for cooking

Powdered sugar, for serving

MAKE THE JAM: Bring the lingonberries and water to a boil and cook for 6 to 8 minutes. Skim off any scum that rises to the top. Stir in the sugar, bring to a boil, and cook for another 5 minutes, skimming off any scum. Pour into sterilized jars and process.

MAKE THE PANCAKES: Sift together the flour, sugar, baking power, and salt. Add the milk and eggs and stir until combined, working out any lumps. Melt 2 tablespoons butter over medium low heat in a 10-inch non-stick skillet and stir it into the batter. Pour ¼ cup batter into the pan, tilting the pan to get a nice even coating on the bottom. When the pancake looks dry on top and is lightly browned on the bottom, about 1 minute, flip it and cook for another 30 seconds or so. Stack the pancakes and keep them warm.

To serve, spread some lingonberry jam onto a pancake and roll it up like a cigar. Sprinkle with powdered sugar.

NOTE:

• Use any prepared jam or preserves that you like.

• If you cannot find lingonberries, substitute cranberries and increase the sugar by ½ cup.

• No vanilla sugar? Use plain sugar and add a teaspoon of vanilla.

her recipe box. I thought we'd try a recipe. I ran out before you got up and got some lingonberry jam. That's the key to it."

"What's a lingonberry?"

"It's a fruit that grows in the forest, in Sweden. You've probably had lingonberry jam at your grandmother's house. We always had it when I was growing up; like other kids had grape jam, we had lingonberry. Your grandmother always used to say lingonberry jam is like Swedish summer in a jar. The Swedes love their lingonberries. It's not so sweet, sort of like cranberry sauce. Now, get the milk out of the refrigerator, please."

On her way, Emma let Halo out of the cage, and he hopped onto her arm. "I remember this box thing from Grandma L.'s kitchen. It's kind of old."

"Not kind of, it *is* old. Grandma L. used to make these pancakes for us on Sunday mornings. Look at the card." She pointed out the pale blue, faded handwriting. "That's your great-grandmother's writing. Didn't she have beautiful handwriting? In the days before the computer, it used to be kind of an art. It's her recipe originally. From Sweden. Pick out some other cards and put them on the counter."

Emma laid out the cards as Halo watched with interest. Grace pointed to each successive card. "Your grandmother, your great-grandmother, your aunt, and me. I'm chocolate cake."

"Oh, yeah," said Emma. "The blue ribbon."

"Someday maybe you'll have your recipes in here, too. That's the idea of it. That's why Grandma L. sent it to me. Not so much for me—for you." And Grace knew this was true. She herself had almost broken the chain, and before it was too late, she had wanted Emma to reforge it.

"I don't know how to cook," Emma said.

"You will," Grace said. "These recipes will help you. "

Emma picked up the Swedish Pancakes card. "My great-grandma actually wrote this? This is her writing?"

Grace nodded and picked up another card. This one was written entirely in Swedish. "You know, when I was your age, I used to imagine what these women were like, the ones who wrote these recipes. I used to think they were so far away and different, off in Sweden wearing different clothes, cooking foods with names and flavors I didn't understand, living in different times."

Emma nodded as she thumbed through the cards. "I know what you mean. What is some of this stuff, anyhow? Look at this—pickled—what? Who eats this stuff?"

Grace smiled. "*We* ate it. Your grandmother, grandfather, and me. Grandma L. would make recipes from these cards on holidays, because they would remind her of Sweden when she was growing up, and we'd try them." She pulled out a card.

"*Risgrynsgröt*. Do you know what that is? A rice pudding. The best rice pudding ever. We'd always have it Christmas Eve. The big surprise was there was an almond hidden in it. The person who got the almond in their portion would have good luck." Grace was surprised by the strong wave of nostalgia that engulfed her, taking her right back to her childhood. It was a good feeling; she realized that, once, she'd been very happy.

"Rice pudding on Christmas Eve—huh!" Emma had been used to Brian's family's Italian extravaganzas, which were heavy on fish—and always elicited a *"Yuk!"* from Emma.

"Don't knock it till you try it. Which, this Christmas Eve, you will. Now, you measure the flour."

Together, they made the pancake batter. "You know what I found out from this recipe box?"

"There's a reason for McDonald's?"

"No!"

"I am beggin' you!" Squawked Halo.

"Don't be a diva," Grace instructed the bird. "Now watch this, Emma. Before you put any batter onto the pan, test a drop of water to see if it's hot enough." She threw a spritz of water onto the hot surface and it skittered and sizzled. "See? We're ready. We want to keep the batter thin so we'll have thin pancakes. Tip the pan and then tilt and roll it after you pour the batter in. You try it. We'll use two pans." It felt good to be cooking with her daughter. For a moment, she regretted all those years lost to pizza deliveries and carryout. Well, they would make up for lost time.

Emma squinted her eyes and furrowed her brow in the way she'd always done since she was a little girl, when she was concentrating.

"Here's what I learned—those women who wrote out these recipes were actually not so very different from us. The recipes tell us a little bit about them—how they lived, and even the fact that they took the time to write them out. But the rest is inside us. Inside you."

"Why don't we ever go to Sweden? We could visit Grandma L.'s family. I never even met them."

This was her opening to talk to Emma. Grace took a deep breath. She'd start with the story of her own father. Then segue to Brian and Von. Emma would see that they both had this ambiguity in common. Hopefully, in spite of the shock—or maybe because of it—they would forge a stronger bond. And they could then move on together, hand in hand. Grace realized this was perhaps a bit overly simplistic, but she still hoped with all her heart that things would happen that way. She took a deep breath: "Well, actually there's a reason."

And after her daughter had finished her great-grandmother's recipe for Swedish pancakes with lingonberry jam and pronounced them "awesome," Grace told Emma what she'd found in the recipe box all those years ago.

"I don't get it, Mom." Emma's first reaction was puzzlement. "So your uncle is your father?"

Grace unfolded the birth certificate. "Yes, that's what it says here. That's the paper I found in the recipe box when I was about your age, and that's why I was so upset with my mom, your grandmother, for all these years. I didn't know how to think about what I'd found out, and I didn't know how to ask my mother, so I let it define who I was. It took me a long time to learn that this one thing didn't make me who I was any more than one ingredient can make a whole cake. It was entirely up to me to decide how much or little these things meant in my life." Grace tried to say this as calmly as possible. Certainly she didn't want to burst into tears and upset Emma any more than necessary. "I understand this is probably a big shock to you. I know it was to me when I first found out."

Emma picked up the plates and started cleaning up as though she had this kind of conversation every day of her life. She turned on the water and started rinsing.

"So what do you think, Em? Do you want to talk about it?" Maybe she should have done this in a therapy session, had a professional present.

"I think it's crazy. But stuff happens." She loaded a plate into the dishwasher.

That was it? *Stuff happens?* Grace had thought she'd be stunned. What on earth was Emma going to say about Von—if he were to be her father? Would she shrug her shoulders and say, *"Gee, Mom—stuff happens"*?

"Any other thoughts, Em?"

"Well, it wasn't a sperm donor. And you can't fake your mother. So we know who everybody is, right?"

"Yes, that we do."

"Uncle Carl is dead, right?"

"Yes. Both he and my—dad—died young. You know, my dad will always be my dad."

"And I know my dad. So we already know everybody we need to know."

Well, Emma—maybe not quite. Grace opened her mouth to say something about Von, but the first confession had gone so well she lost confidence, not wanting to screw anything up now. "One step at a time," Grace thought, so instead she swallowed hard, and found herself saying, "Yes, Emma. It's true. Your family is who you create it to be."

At least the secret of the recipe box was now in the open. Grace had imagined something horrendous for all these years, like a nightmare that assumed epic proportions, a dark monster that crawled out from inside the closet and enveloped the room while you were asleep. And then you woke up, and, in the daylight, it was not the monster you imagined at all. Lorraine, she realized, had been right. She had never given Emma—or herself—enough credit. The women in this family were strong. They had resilience. Their heritage was, as Emma said, *crazy*. Everything was not a straight line that meshed perfectly. There were dotted lines, zigzags, broken lines. But maybe they were stronger for it. DNA was as much about love as it was about science. Maybe more. Science did not wake up in the night and hold you when you cried. Science did not cheer when you were onstage or hold the Kleenex box when you had a cold. Science never looked at you proudly when you got good grades. Science never got angry with you for doing something you shouldn't. Science had limits that love would never know. This was the real secret of the recipe box, Grace realized. And Emma—wiser in many ways than her mother—had instinctively had this knowledge all along.

Grace looked outside. The world had tilted, but outside was just the same. It was going to be a sparkling LA day. On the agenda today was braving the mob at Kmart to get school supplies. Maybe they'd try to fit in a bike ride on the beach. She stroked Emma's hair, something she used to do when Emma was a baby. Teenagers rarely stood for this kind of thing, she knew. They were experts at squirming away from affection. But her baby girl was still in there. Which was a good thing, she thought. Not that she didn't want Emma to grow up, but Ken was gone, Leeza was gone, Brian was gone, and she'd pushed Mike away. Aside from Emma, Grace was otherwise more alone than she'd ever been in her life. But did it matter? Work and Emma were enough. For now, they had to be.

It would be good to get to Kmart ahead of the crowd. "Let's go, Em. Remember, last year they ran out of your favorite notebooks." Halo was duly returned to his cage nearby, flipping a somersault as he entered, and Grace and Emma girded themselves for the ritual that every student and parent faces each August.

Grace was searching her purse for her car keys when suddenly a Dalmatian pup scooted down the driveway and leaped up on Emma, its tail wagging, almost knocking her down. Following the dog was Mike, carrying a huge bouquet of white daisies, grinning a bit sheepishly. "Hey," he called out. "Spotty and I were on the Homes of the Stars tour, and we got lost." He handed Grace the daisies and enveloped her in a bear hug, almost crushing the flowers. "I just had to see you and Emma," he said, holding her close. "This distance thing is not working for Spotty and me. And speaking by Skype—I guess I'm old-fashioned. I prefer the real thing. Like right now."

"I missed you, too," Grace said, leaning into him as Spotty ran in ecstatic circles around Emma. She hadn't realized how much, but now that Mike was here, she felt a wave of happiness sweep through her. No, the distance thing was definitely not working.

Emma lifted an eyebrow. "Mom, we can go school shopping later. I think Spotty could use a walk."

Grace escorted Mike into the house and onto the back patio.

"Wow," he said, admiring the canal behind the house. "Water everywhere. I guess that's why they call it Venice."

"In the old days," Grace said, "they had real gondolas. Now it's mostly rowboats and canoes." She put the daisies in water, brought out a pitcher of iced tea, and they settled at the table under the patio umbrella.

"This is pretty sweet," said Mike, surveying the canal. He sighed. "You know, I came here to ask you to come home to New London. But now that I'm here, I see why you like it."

"LA is a great place," Grace admitted. "It has everything." Except . . ." She paused.

"Except?" Mike leaned in and covered her hand with his.

"Except I miss you. But you don't know everything about me."

"What is there to know?"

Grace hesitated. Well, if Mike was going to bolt, she might as well know right now. "My father wasn't really my father. And Brian might not have been Emma's father. I just don't know." She leveled her gaze at Mike, holding her breath.

He shook his head. "That's it?"

Grace dropped her eyes and nodded.

Mike got up, walked around the table, and leaned over, holding her. "Grace, what does any of that have to do with us? I love you and Emma. I respect Brian—does Emma know? Does he?"

"No," Grace whispered.

"Well, I'm here to support you, Grace, whatever you decide. I'm a pretty basic person. For me, it's simple. If you love someone, you love them. That's all that matters." He leaned over and kissed her softly. "Spotty and I would like to invite you and Emma to come home with us. If we leave by the end of the week, we'll get back in time for Emma to register for the school year."

Grace looked at Mike, his tanned face, his sincere eyes, the little cleft in his chin.

And the question now was, how could she *not* leave? This had to be a decision, not a vacation, but the fact was, aside from a job she could do from anywhere now, thanks to the computer program, there wasn't really anything in LA for them. Grace had to admit that, in more ways than one, she'd left her heart in New London, and Emma would be happiest when they put down roots somewhere with a mother she could count on, a mother who was present. Grace would move to the ends of the earth for that, she decided.

————

Together, Grace and Emma were going home. They would finally make a real home. And this time, when Grace returned to New London, things felt so very different. She did not race to the airport alone, and she did not take a suitcase. She, Emma, and Halo took a road trip back with Mike and Spotty, bringing only the things they'd need for the five days in the car and packing everything else into a U-Haul. Grace decided to sublease the Venice apartment to Roberto, who bought most of the furniture with the bonus he received from Ken for stepping into Grace's job. It felt good to be starting clean. The furniture had served its purpose, transition pieces that carried the psychic weight of the divorce from Brian. Now there was a fresh new beginning. She and Emma would stay with Lorraine until she could afford a place of their own. It was funny how things worked out, Grace thought. Last spring, she couldn't have imagined moving back home with her mother. Now she was looking forward to it. Of course, she wasn't deluding herself into thinking this was a fairy tale; there was still a lot to be worked out.

Emma was happy to be closer to her Chicago friends, whom she could visit on weekends, and to Brian. Halo's blog could be done from anywhere, and she was chronicling his cross-country trip, posting pictures of Halo at every landmark along the way under the heading "Halo, the Cross-Country Cockatoo." A newspaper in St. Louis had even e-mailed and asked for an e-interview with Halo. Everyone had seen him on TV. And Artie had to have him written out of the storyline of *The Lost Ones*. Emma was excited to unveil her new look to her New London friends and, most of all, to help with the Book Nook. Getting the shop up and running again in time for the 3F Fall Festival was going to be the first priority. For the first time in a long time, Grace realized, in their lives, as on the open road ahead, both she and Emma had much to look forward to.

chapter 14

"Well, time to roll up the proverbial sleeves," Ken said as Grace and Emma stood, shell-shocked, in front of the Book Nook—or what was left of it. Emma had wanted to drive directly there when they had pulled into New London. The charred wreck of the Book Nook was the sorriest sight that Grace had ever seen. The pictures had not captured the real damage. "Oh, Mom," Emma had said when she saw it, her voice shaking. Mike had tried to prepare them, but the reality was even worse than they could have imagined. Tim had to move out of his apartment above the shop, so he and Ken had gotten a place together in town. There was no telling when the building would be cleared for safe occupancy. "If it weren't for Mike, Tim might have even died of smoke inhalation," said Ken. "Mike is a hero."

"It's just my job," Mike said quietly. "I wish I could have done more. But these old wooden buildings were built before modern code. They're charming, but they're tinderboxes."

"Well," said Tim, taking a deep breath. "There is some good news today. The insurance adjuster called about an hour ago. They are going to pay for the rebuild. We are totally covered for the structure. The decorating part, no, but we can figure that out."

"Yes!" cheered Ken. "We *will* rebuild. Better than ever!"

Grace wasn't sure how this would happen, but she cheered, along with Ken. It was amazing how, in spite of the disaster of the fire, Ken looked happier than she had ever seen him. The tightness that always surrounded him in LA seemed to have unwound, and he and Tim were working together on something important to them both. It wasn't on national television or involving movie stars; it was something small and personal, and that made it even more precious. Not just to Ken, but to all of them.

As they stood in front of the burned, boarded-up porch, a woman with a toddler and a golden retriever came up to Tim. "I hope it won't be too long before you're up and running," she said, touching his arm anxiously. She gestured to her group of young moms across the street in the park. "We all miss this place—and you." She turned to Emma. "And you, young lady! My Max misses your stories, and your beautiful bird, don't you Max? Let us know if we can help."

"People," announced Ken in his best Artie imitation, "there's a hole in the sky in New London, Wisconsin, and we're gonna fix it!"

The first thing that Grace unpacked when they unloaded the U-Haul at her mother's house, while Mike and some of his buddies from the firehouse were carrying in boxes, suitcases, and armfuls of clothes on hangers, was the recipe box. She'd wrapped it back up in the bubble packing that Lorraine had shipped it in and put it in a canvas bag on the floor of the backseat, under Halo's cage. After all, it was a well-traveled member of the family, having crossed the Atlantic Ocean and now half the USA twice.

Unpacking had to happen in a hurry because there was no time to waste. The Book Nook had to reopen for the 3F. It was funny, Grace thought, how so many things in her life had revolved around fall in New London. It would always remind her of Leeza; it was their special time together. That's why she knew things would be all right. Leeza was surely watching over them, if fall was involved.

Squeezing into the house was going to be tight. There were only two bedrooms; Grace figured she would sleep on the pullout in the tiny den while Emma moved back into the red and black "girl-cave," as Grace thought of it.

"I still feel bad about leaving you so suddenly," Ken said. They were looking for knives to slice open the taped-up boxes. "I should never have left you in the lurch like that, but I knew you could do it."

"Now I do, too. You actually did me a huge favor."

"Well in that case, I have another favor for you." He smiled, took her hand, and led her up the stairs, past the two bedrooms on the second floor, to the attic. Grace could hardly believe what she saw at the top of the stairs. The old, dusty attic had been transformed into a room that looked like a marshmallow floating on a white cloud.

"We had a little junk sale," Ken explained. "Lorraine and I cleaned out about twenty years of crapola." The room had been painted shiny white top to bottom—walls, exposed beams, floors. A queen-sized bed with a fluffy white duvet sat in the middle, with white gauze draped from the ceiling beams. White gauze looped across the ceiling and fluttered at the single window, which showed only the blue sky. The only furniture was her old dresser, now painted glossy white with new crystal pulls, and a huge mirror in a white-painted frame. A large white overhead fan spun lazily, rippling the fabric.

Grace gasped. "This is so—lovely. I can't believe you did this. Oh my God, Ken. How did you do this? How did you know we were even coming back?"

Ken shrugged. "All part of the game plan. I admit I had a secret weapon. It's amazing what a fire brigade with a few cans of paint and a spray painter can do. Even Claire kicked in."

"*Claire?*"

"Yes, wonders will never cease. And speaking of makeovers—how about my goddaughter? I take all the credit. The show choir is doing *Les Mis* this fall. I see Cosette in her future." He cocked his head and looked sideways at Grace with that wry smile she knew so well. "I had confidence you'd come back. A Musketeer never leaves another Musketeer for very long. It's a rule."

Footsteps sounded on the steps, and Lorraine emerged from the attic stairwell with a bouquet of daisies in a Mason jar. Smiling, she placed it on top of the dresser. "Welcome home, Gracie."

Grace had always loved daisies. There was a sturdy, undaunted happiness to them. Once, when she was ten, she'd gotten in trouble for picking all the daisies out of Lorraine's garden. So this was, she knew, a special gesture. So many people cared. There was white, there was sky, and there were daisies. *Such gifts*. She didn't fight it when she felt tears wet her cheeks.

———

"Battle stations, everyone," commanded Ken as Tim, Grace, and Mike gathered around a pizza. Tim and Ken were living in an industrial loft that had been a storage facility over a garage. But it had thirteen-foot ceilings and exposed brick walls, and Ken had shipped up his furniture from Malibu. Ken propped up his iPad and displayed a mood board on Pinterest, showing a collection of pictures fashioned like a digital scrapbook.

The plan was simple—keep the atmosphere clean, organic, and modern, with fun, unexpected touches. Add a Wi-Fi hot spot and oversized communal tables made from reclaimed barnwood planks nailed together and protected by specially ordered glass tops. Reclaimed barn wood would also be used to create a mantel for an oversized wood-burning fireplace. "This should be a refuge," Ken said. "There's enough craziness and noise out there in the world."

"This is going to be our new look," he announced. "Natural meets modern. With a touch of opulence, like this crystal chandelier. And reclaimed wood for the walls. That beautiful old wood—it just warms everything up. Then cross that with something modern. But all neutrals. I'm seeing browns, and a white the hue of clotted cream. And candles—scented cylinder candles, and silver serving pieces. Simple. Real. Like a new age barn. We'll rename it the Book Nook Barn."

"But first we have to tear the damaged walls down," Mike said, frowning. He clearly wasn't thinking clotted cream. "And put the new walls up. And the electrical. I can do it, but the timing is beyond tight if you want to make the 3F."

"Well the mayor can speed-push the approvals through. Snoopy will make sure of that. So we're fine, as long as the physical footprint doesn't change. Here's the timetable." He clicked to another page.

Ken's timetable was impossible, even Grace knew that. She could create a work plan, but she didn't see how they could finish the job. Maybe Artie could meet a schedule like this, but in New London there just weren't those kinds of resources, and she told Ken that.

"True," he acknowledged. "What would the Three Musketeers do?" he asked rhetorically.

"Get reinforcements?"

"*Of course*! Call for reinforcements! Bring in Roberto and the A Team! *The Lost Ones* has a two-week hiatus from production following Labor Day. New London, you are about to go Hollywood."

Every night, Grace went home to "The Cloud," as she called her attic bedroom. It wasn't air-conditioned, the summer's heat rose to the top of the house, and the bathroom was downstairs, but she could hear the end-of-season crickets in a chorus outside through the open window, and the ceiling fan stirred the air. Collapsed on top of the fluffy duvet in a white T-shirt, she slept better than she had in years.

The first day of high school was a rite of passage, Grace thought. Somehow, she was more nervous than Emma.

"It's no big deal, Mom," Emma said impatiently. "Everybody's already hooked up on Facebook, so we all know one another already. And I have my friends from the reading group and the Book Nook. Von says . . ."

"*Von?*"

"We're on Twitter." She gave Grace a look. "Since you shut me out of the Skype account."

"You were not supposed to communicate with him. I don't understand, Emma."

"You just said I couldn't Skype. I didn't."

How stupid of her to think she could pull the plug with Emma simply by changing the Skype password. Today's kids were global operators with limitless ways to communicate. Text, Twitter, e-mail, Facebook, cell phone, Skype . . . When Grace was in high school the phone rang constantly, endlessly irritating her parents, but it was just one phone. Now, the same phone was silent, eclipsed by technology. The house was often eerily quiet, even if three people were actually talking to six others. Who knew who was talking to whom? Revolutions could be—and probably had been—planned soundlessly. There was no point, Grace knew, in trying to unplug Emma. Reactivating anything was just a SIM card away. Grace had heard from other moms that there were kids who carried a deck of SIM cards, changing them like outfits to camouflage who they were talking to and what they were doing online. She didn't want to have a relationship like that with Emma. The bigger issue, the eternal elephant in the room, was Grace's secret and Von Vasser. Grace needed to figure out what she wanted.

Emma's new confidence helped her ease into the school activities in New London. With encouragement from Grace and Ken, she decided to go out for show choir. Going back to the high school with Emma brought it all back, especially the tryouts, which were scheduled before the start of the school year. The building itself was different—in the late nineties, the town had built a new high school, and the wobbly risers she and Von had stood on in the gym had been replaced by an impressive new auditorium with theater-style seating, a catwalk, a full lighting and sound booth, and even a greenroom—it was practically professional level! The talent roster was surreal, Grace thought, as she observed a senior rehearsal. Many of these kids were state-ranked singers, and a few had reached the nationals. Since it was competitive, nobody could ever just coast. As a freshman, Emma was going to be watching the older girls, earning her place, learning how to fit in, making her own mark. She didn't yet have a friend like Leeza, but the girls from the reading group had taken her under their wing.

Emma had gone through at least six ideas for her outfit for the first day of school and had settled on a short denim skirt she'd made herself from an old pair of jeans, a man's dress shirt with the cuffs rolled, one of her belted skirts, and flat booties without socks. She debated on a floppy hat with a big pin on the brim, and decided against it. School started before Labor Day these days, something Grace would never understand, but they were somehow going to be ready.

The thermometer hit a record high, and sweat soaked through the back of Grace's sleeveless shirt as she made yet another water run. Grace could never remember an August in Wisconsin that was this hot and humid. She parked in front of the Book Nook and dragged the Styrofoam cooler, heavy with water bottles and ice, onto the front porch. Then she pulled out as many of the sweating, cold plastic bottles as she could carry and carried them inside to pass out to the team. Ken had set up fans, but all they seemed to do was swirl sawdust around the room. Still, nobody was complaining. The scene reminded her of an old-fashioned barn-raising, with groups of people pulling up wall framings, nailing railings, sawing, and sanding. The burned-out areas had been demolished and carted off in Dumpsters, and the remaining space looked raw and new inside the Victorian shell, which would stay. Ken, wearing a yellow hard hat, was immersed in blueprints, while Tim was glued to his BlackBerry, firing off e-mails. Mike had set up a pair of sawhorses and a table on the porch, where he was using a jigsaw to cut angles from lengths of barn wood for the molding. As Grace returned for more water bottles, he looked up from under his goggles. "You know, you're very distracting. I could have cut my arm off."

"Don't shoot the water girl." She tossed Mike a bottle of water. "How's it coming?"

He wiped his forehead with his shirt and gestured to the group inside. "Thanks to those Hollywood guys, we're going to beat our timetable. I mean, you've got some real master carpenters in there. It's borderline intimidating."

"Who do you think builds all those sitcom sets?" Grace said with mock indignation. "These are the guys who can turn day into night, inside into outside, summer into winter—they have the magic."

"Do you think they could muster up a short freeze?"

"I'll put in the request. Do you think we can be ready?"

"The crew's leaving the second Sunday following Labor Day to go back to the show. Everything will be framed in by then, including Tim's apartment upstairs. Electrical, and the sound and security systems are going in this weekend. After that, we close up the walls, and it's just the icing on the cake—and that's your department. Snoopy said he'd rush the Certificate of Occupancy."

Tim leaned out of an open window frame. "Grace, we're counting on you. Fire up that Cupcake Brigade!"

"Right!" Grace snapped her fingers enthusiastically, but she wondered how she was going to do it. Emma was in school, and she herself had work to do online for the production company to keep some money coming in. But Tim's can-do attitude was infectious. No matter how great the obstacle, he'd bounced back with something better and stronger. Grace couldn't imagine how she'd have reacted if her business and her home had almost burned to the ground. When she'd asked him about his apartment above the Book Nook, Tim had brushed off the question, although she knew from Ken that almost everything he owned had smoke or water damage. Instead, he'd focused on rebuilding "for my kids and my moms."

"They're at loose ends. They have no place to meet, greet, and read," Tim had said sadly. "What's going to happen to reading and the exchange of knowledge, news, and ideas in this town? They need their Book Nook." He looked genuinely alarmed. "It's their sanctuary! An island of civility in a world of reality shows and disposable content! Dickens. Faulkner. Dostoyevsky. Maya Angelou. J. K. Rowling. We can't just lose them to—blogging!"

"That's my Tim," Ken said fondly. "I've never met anyone like him. He's out to save the world, one paragraph at a time." For once, Ken was not being sarcastic.

The heat was getting really oppressive, Grace thought as she sat fanning herself on the front porch, trying to figure out a way to bring attention to the bake sale. Fall was always one of the busiest times of the year. The migration of the wild birds was a big deal—and not just the snowbirds on their way to Florida and Arizona. New London was flooded with tourists, and everyone was selling something. The new and improved Book Nook Barn needed to get noticed.

Suddenly there was a loud honk from a car. A red Mercedes convertible had pulled up and parked behind Mike's van. Claire, wearing huge, dark sunglasses and a tennis outfit, was behind the wheel. Sara was in a car seat in back. A huge diamond glinted on Claire's left hand as she waved at Grace.

How did she manage to play tennis with that skating rink on her finger? Maybe her strategy was to blind her opponents. "Hi,

Claire. Sara! Hi, sweetie!" Grace waved at the little girl, who waved back. "Welcome to the construction zone. Be careful with that white skirt."

"Oh, I'm not going in. Sara can't go into a construction zone; it's unsafe. We're on our way back from nursery school. Is Tim on-site? I've got some exciting news. Tell him and Ken to meet me across the street, in the park. You too, Gracie! And Mike, you too!" Her ponytail swung as she lifted Sara out of her car seat.

"What could be so important?" Grace asked Ken as they all dutifully trooped across the street.

Holding Sara's hand, Claire led the group to the center of the small park. "All right," announced Claire, smoothing her short skirt. "Looking directly across the park is the Book Nook. Over on our left is the playground, with the slides and swings. Wouldn't it be wonderful to have a real focal point for our park? Something that will help the Book Nook, too?"

"Put us down for that," Ken said.

"Well—David and the City Council approved it today. We are going to build a town gazebo right in this very spot where we're standing. People will be able to sit in the shade of our beautiful new gazebo and read, or talk, and there can be concerts there, too. Plus, it will look beautiful looking across from the Book Nook."

"Amazing! How is it being funded?" Ken asked.

"That's the best part. It's being generously donated by Von Vasser. In honor of his cousin Leeza. We'll have a plaque and a naming ceremony—Leeza's Gazebo. A permanent reminder of our wonderful Leeza, who loved gardens. Fifty years from now, people will come and sit in the gazebo and enjoy the park and think of Leeza. Isn't that thrilling? Von has promised to come over from Zurich for the opening ceremonies. This will make all the news."

Grace froze. She hoped Mike didn't notice. A gazebo in Leeza's honor sounded wonderful, of course, but it meant Von would be back in town, and she'd finally have to deal with her past once and for all.

"I've already started working on the plans," Claire enthused. "Of course, we'll coordinate the landscaping with the terrace plantings of the Book Nook, so we'll have a synergistic effect. The idea will be to have a tree-lighting and a naming ceremony at Christmas. We'll have an evergreen and icicles theme, with thousands of lights and a candle-lighting in the park. I'll frame the porch and doorway of the Book Nook with the same treatment, and we'll tie it all together."

"We're renaming it—the Book Nook Barn," Ken said. "Let's just hope we open the doors for the 3F. Grace is just planning an opening day bake sale. Then we can work together on the gazebo."

"Well, I have even more *wonderful* news!" Claire clasped her hands in front of herself like a little girl at show-and-tell, beaming. "To kick things off, we'll have a raffle at the dedication event, and Von has also generously offered to donate the prize! The winner will be invited to be Von's guest on a cruise on his boat—have you seen the pictures? It's beyond fabulous! I will insist on chaperoning! It's so wonderful that even though he's so successful, Von hasn't forgotten his American family—isn't it, Gracie?"

Grace nodded imperceptibly. It wasn't easy keeping her expression unreadable as Claire raved on happily about Leeza's Gazebo, but she tried. "Yes. Wonderful." But Grace felt conflicted. As much as she loved Leeza and as much she'd like it to be wonderful, having Von suddenly involved in a project right across the street was not so simple for her.

chapter 15

What was it about Labor Day in Wisconsin that caused the weather to turn overnight? Grace wondered. One day you went to sleep sweating, and a week later there was a slight snap in the air and a dry rustle of birch leaves. Pulling on her jeans to drive Emma to her first day of school, Grace could feel it in the air when she looked out her bedroom window. But who was that outside the house, in biker leathers and helmet, on a motorcycle? It looked like Mike's motorcycle, but he would not be going to the first day of school in a biker outfit. "Emma?" She called down the stairs. "Who's outside?" Grace buttoned her blouse as she came down the stairs. Lorraine emerged from the master bedroom, pulling a robe around her.

The bathroom door burst open and Emma came out, hair flat-ironed and fully dressed, except for her boots. Luckily, it had cooled off enough for her carefully prepared outfit. "I don't know, Mom. None of the kids I know rides a motorcycle."

"I don't like strangers sitting in front of my property," Lorraine said, frowning. She had her cell phone in her hand and was ready to summon the police.

"Maybe he's got a delivery," Grace said. "He looks like a

delivery man, or a messenger." She walked to the front door and cracked it open. "Hey! Can I help you?" she yelled. The motorcycle guy swung a leg over the seat and started toward the door. Halfway up the walk, he pulled off his helmet and shook out his hair.

"Jaxon?" Emma peered out from the doorway, incredulous.

"Oh!" gasped Grace. It was Jaxon Kerrig, the star of *The Lost Ones*. The kid who made the heart of every girl under the age of eighteen melt like sugar in a cotton candy machine was striding up their front walk. "Mom," she said to Lorraine, "this kid is the star of the vampire show Ken and I worked on."

Lorraine pulled her robe tighter and squinted toward the walkway. "What's he doing here?"

"I may be wrong—maybe he got lost on his way to the Hollywood Freeway—but I think he's come to take Emma to her first day of high school."

Jaxon gave a salute in Emma's direction. "Hey, Em! Hi, Grace. When does school start? We don't want to be late. I have absolutely no idea where I'm going, Emma—you'll have to navigate."

"Jaxon! This is so cool!" Elated, Emma ran out barefoot to give him a hug.

Lorraine had made cinnamon buns the night before for the food pantry, and coffee was already on, so they sat around and had breakfast together.

"I had a network visit in Chicago," Jaxon said, biting into a cinnamon bun. "Wow. This is so good, you should bottle it. I went to Northwestern for a year before I got cast on *The Lost Ones*, and when it's over, I'm going back. They've got a great theater department, Emma. A little plug there. Anyhow, it was just a quick flight up here, and I'd promised Emma. My parents always taught me, never break a promise."

"You have good parents," said Lorraine as she refilled his cup.

"Yeah, we're from Omaha." He looked around the kitchen. "This reminds me of our kitchen. This, and being here with your family. Emma, you're lucky—it's so much better than Hollywood. Forget the red carpet. This is what everybody wants. This is the bomb." Jaxon carried his plate to the sink, rinsed it, and placed it carefully in the dishwasher.

Now I see why he's a star, thought Grace. *This is no vampire, Jaxon's a well brought-up kid who can talk to anybody and has values. Kudos to his parents in Omaha.* Grace knew what it took.

"Ken copped the motorcycle for me. If it's OK with you, we're working this into a segment they're doing on me for *Hollywood Close-Up*. That's who got the plane." He spotted a crumb of cinnamon bun on the counter and popped it into his mouth. "Ouch, stop me now. If I gain any weight, they'll fire me. It's in my contract—vampires don't get fat."

Emma let Halo out of his cage and told Jaxon about the blog. She took a picture of Halo on Jaxon's shoulder to post. "How did the End of Summer thing wind up?" Emma asked.

"Record year." Jaxon took a last gulp of coffee. "It was great that you came and brought that amazing D.J. I've told a lot of my friends about Suki; they should get some gigs. But listen, the producers told me they're getting e-mails and fan mail for Halo. We're going to have to get you guys back for a guest shot."

"Cool! What do you say, Halo?"

"*God bless America!*"

"He's very patriotic," Emma quipped, as if she bantered with TV stars every day.

Emma grabbed her backpack, and they were off. As she watched the motorcycle roar off with Emma holding on to Jaxon, Grace felt like she was looking into the future, a time when things would be different, and young men would pick Emma up for real dates, and she felt a twinge because she was not taking her little girl herself to the first day of high school. But she had to get real: If it was Mom versus TV star, she wasn't going to get the votes.

When her cell phone rang as she was checking her e-mail for messages from LA a few minutes later, Grace knew it would be Mike, reporting in from the school. "So that was your motorcycle?"

"Guilty as charged. Ken was the mastermind. He didn't want to disappoint Emma, and neither did Jaxon. At the last minute, it worked out with his schedule, so he came. I was sworn to secrecy, in case it didn't work out. Wait a minute, I see them now. Oh, it's not just them!" He started laughing. "You should see this."

"What's so funny? Tell me!"

"There's a local TV van with a video crew trailing them. OK, three guys are jumping out with equipment."

"That must be the *Close-Up* crew."

"Whatever, the word is out, a crowd of kids is gathering. Emma's taking her helmet off . . . and now Jaxon's walking her through the crowd, right up to the school door. Well, there's an entrance you don't see every day at New London High!" He paused. "Wow! He just gave her a kiss on the cheek, and the photographers are going wild. Emma kept her cool, though. That girl is something. She just went inside, but he's signing some autographs. He seems like a good kid to do all this. Oh-oh, a girl just pulled up her T-shirt and asked him to autograph her stomach. I'd better get over there."

"OK, Ken's on the other line."

"Grace, I'm across the street from the high school watching this, our girl is a star."

"I can't believe you arranged all this, Ken. It's just over the top!"

"I've never broken a promise to my goddaughter, and I'm not about to start now."

"Honesty is in the air."

"Somebody has to set an example! Besides, it's good business. Roberto's buddy produces *Close-Up*. He arranged the whole video thing, and they got the plane. The pitch was: showing the human side of the vampire kid. It's genius, don't you think? I hope you didn't mind the surprise. We weren't sure until the last minute if it would all come down, but I don't want Lorraine to die of shock."

"She didn't even have a clue who Jaxon was, but he loved her cinnamon buns, so she was delighted. Thank you."

"Gotta hop, the windows have arrived. You better get over here, it's a madhouse."

After Lorraine headed out for the church office, Grace was left alone in the house. It was funny how everything looked different now. How the same kitchen that had been so depressing now looked warm and welcoming. How the ratty, dusty attic was now a soft, enveloping space. How her old room was now Emma's lair. Only her mother never changed, Grace thought. Lorraine was always a constant, no matter what storms swirled around her. Grace had once seen that as unfeeling and unresponsive, but now she realized that her mother had always been her rock. In staying the same, she had allowed her daughter and granddaughter to evolve. Lorraine's little nest of a household, tucked under the wing of the solidly Midwestern New London, may not have been LA or Chicago, but it was what it was—always true to itself. And that solidity is what had saved them.

That night, as the three Holm-D'Angelo women sat down to dinner, there was so much to talk about. Jaxon had blown away everybody at school, but there were a few kids who were posting tweets that the whole thing with the *Close-Up* crew was too Hollywood. Emma was too excited to care. The much-anticipated show choir list had been posted, and Emma was on it. Rehearsals began immediately, and there was scheduling and transportation to plan. Grace made a list of parents she could call for carpooling. Lorraine was the new hero of her bridge club, who were big fans of Carrie Flannery and *The Lost Ones*. Who knew? Ken and Tim were hosting a wrap party later for the crew, before they flew back to LA, and Grace and Mike were going to stop by.

In honor of the day, which was the start of so many things, and because there was so much going on and almost no time to cook, Lorraine had made a dish that took almost no time. Grace remembered it from growing up, because it also cost almost no money, and funds had always been tight.

"Actually, this recipe is a Swedish-Wisconsin hybrid," Lorraine explained to Emma as she demonstrated so that next time, Emma could make it herself. "I adapted this recipe from something my mother made. It uses sausage, so we can just use almost any Wisconsin sausage, or even brats. And the other ingredients—tomatoes and chives are in our garden this time of year, and we always have eggs, so there you go. Thirty minutes and three key ingredients, and you're done. Toss a little salad, and it's a nice dinner. Emma, grab some fresh tomatoes and chives from the garden out back, would you?"

The casserole was a hit, although Emma skipped most of the meat and seemed compelled to ask if brats were officially a food group in Wisconsin, to which the answer from both Grace and Lorraine, in chorus, was, "Yes."

Even Halo chimed in: *"OMG!"*

———

The wrap party for the LA crew was bittersweet. Grace was glad that Mike was there, holding one hand, as Emma held the other, because more than once she thought she might start crying. She was thrilled for Tim and Ken, who were like proud parents showing off their new baby, but she also knew that the completion of the new Book Nook Barn meant saying goodbye to her colleagues from LA. They would be leaving in the morning to return to their lives and their jobs. As she walked through the group, stopping to hug Roberto, kiss Tim, and

KORVLADA

Serves 4 to 6

1½ pounds bratwurst sausage

1 tablespoon soft butter

8 Roma tomatoes, peeled, seeded and coarsely chopped

8 large eggs

1 cup heavy cream

Salt and pepper

3 tablespoons chopped chives

1 cup shredded provolone cheese

Preheat the oven to 350°F. Butter a 2-quart baking dish.

Remove sausage meat from casings and brown it in a skillet. Drain the fat and put the cooked sausage into the bottom of the prepared baking dish. Sprinkle the tomatoes evenly over the top of the sausage meat. Whisk the eggs with the cream, salt, pepper, and 2 tablespoons of chives. Pour over the tomatoes and top with cheese. Bake for 35 to 40 minutes or until set in the middle. Let rest for 10 minutes and sprinkle with remaining chives before serving.

NOTE:

- Almost any sausage will do.

- Use finely chopped scallions if you don't have chives, or use another herb, such as basil, sage, or parsley.

- If your tomatoes aren't ripe, use green tomatoes—just chop them into smaller pieces.

- Any cheese will do: Use Muenster or mozzarella in place of the mild provolone, or try a sharp cheddar.

pose for pictures and a video with Claire and David, Grace felt incredibly proud of all they'd accomplished in such a short time. There was still work to be done, but it was mainly the cosmetics. The reclaimed barn wood gave the space unique warmth and a kind of instant history. The wood had gone from giving shelter to framing life. Clusters of people chatted on stools and secondhand chairs. Ken had slipcovered them with burlap and sturdy canvas, and tonight they were covered by sheets and tarps. But dozens of candles flickered, casting dancing shadows on the rough-hewn beams. The books had yet to be arranged in their shelves, but the warmth of the place shone through. "You did it," Grace whispered to Ken.

"No, *we* did it," he said, pouring Mike a glass of white wine. "You know, the fire was a blessing in disguise. It allowed us to create something for ourselves."

Ken and Tim would start remodeling the apartment upstairs next, but they planned to take their time with that. The important thing was that the Book Nook Barn was ready to open for business. Tim clinked on a glass to make a toast. "I'd like to thank everyone here who was so helpful to the rebirth of this store," he said. He listed each and every person by name, ending with Ken. "And finally, to my partner in this shop, and in life— Ken. We all know that Ken is a magician, and he has brought magic not only to this town, but to my life. Ken, you are a very special person."

It was clear from the look on Ken's face, Grace thought, that he would not have been so proud if he had received an Academy

Award. Ken had, at last, found his place in life. How fortunate he was, Grace thought, remembering the young, uncertain boy from all those years ago. How far he's come, turning rejection into triumph, really owning his choices and his life.

Later that night, after all the lights were out and her daughter and mother were asleep, Grace lay upstairs in the Cloud and thought about the past weeks and the weeks ahead. School had begun, and she had to get back to her online work. It was so easy to get lost in a to-do list or use it as an excuse. Grace was facing a week with a hundred things to do, but she really had only one important thing on her to-do list, the same thing that Leeza had reminded her of in her last and final note.

Emma. She meant to be home when Emma got home from school. To never miss a show choir performance. To attend every PTA meeting. To have dinner with her daughter as often as possible. She would do all the things she'd meant to do in LA, but hadn't. It was important to Emma. But it was, perhaps, Grace thought, even more important to herself.

––––––––––––

"What are you doing, Mom? Are you going to cook something for tonight?"

Grace was sitting at the kitchen table with the recipe box in front of her. It was Sunday morning and the house was quiet, anticipating the day. Lorraine had already left for the food pantry to get a jump on the week, and the house smelled of her cinnamon buns. "Sit with me, Em," she said. She opened the box and started taking out the cards, spreading them across the tabletop.

Emma slid out a chair and sat across from her. Halo was tucked into the hood of her sweatshirt, like a feathered papoose, sartorially surveying the scene.

Emma eyed her warily. Grace could tell Emma was worried about what her mother might say next.

"Emma, you know what I told you about Uncle Carl. And we've talked about that. What I didn't tell you about is you."

"Me?" Emma's eyes opened wide. *What more was there to know?*

There was nothing to do but come right out with it. "When I was in high school, I dated your dad for years."

"I know."

"But there was a time senior year when things weren't going so well, and we broke up."

"OK . . ."

"It wasn't for long, but I started going out with Von Vasser."

That got her attention. "You! Went! Out! With! Von?"

"Yes, I did. He was Leeza's cousin, and he was a very exciting guy. Very exotic for New London, a person from another world. He still is."

"Wow. You and Von." She laughed. "You might have ended up on the deck of a yacht, Mom."

"It's possible. But it wasn't that simple, because, you see, I got pregnant with you. I'd much rather have you than a yacht."

For a split second, Emma sat stone still, and Grace could see her mind trying to take this in. Then she just blurted it out. "Is

Von my father? Dad's not my father? Are you saying that no-body is anybody's father around here?" Emma looked like she was going to burst into tears. "Is anything real?"

"You're real, and I'm real, and your dad, Brian, is real. To tell you the God's truth, Emma, I don't know for sure who your biological father is—Brian or Von. There was never a scientific test."

Emma leaned over intently. "I know how to get one online. I've seen them advertised on the Web, Mom. We have to know. What if Von is my father? Oh my God, oh my God!"

"You are the only person I have told about this, except for Aunt Leeza. Even Grandmother L. doesn't know. This is a se-cret that's just for us."

"But don't we need to know, Mom? Don't I need to know? Look how you felt, what you told me. And what about Dad?"

"We can have you tested. It's your right to know, just like it was mine. And your dad's right to know as well."

This was a lot for Emma to handle, Grace thought. But there was, she knew from her own experience, no right time. The dif-ference was, Uncle Carl had been an ocean away and she had never even known him. He had died without knowing his daughter or, as far as she knew to this day, caring to know her. Emma not only knew Von, she was communicating with him. They had a relationship. And Brian, unlike the man who raised Grace, the man she thought of as "Dad," was very much alive. What the two men had in common was they were both fathers who had loved their daughters. Would the fact that Emma might not be Brian's biological daughter change that? Would the risk of the loss of that love be worth the trade-off of knowing the truth?

Grace moved around the table to sit next to her daughter. "So you see, Em, I've been very disturbed by Von's e-mails to you. And you see why we can't go on his boat."

Emma looked confused, and her huge eyes suddenly welled with tears. "But you said he doesn't know."

"I think he has suspicions."

Emma was holding a handful of recipe cards and fingering them. "Were you in love with Von, Mom?" she asked, her head down.

Had I ever really been in love with Von Vasser? "No, it wasn't love. I see that now. I was in love with a fantasy. Brian was reality. In the end, reality is a better choice, even if it doesn't always have a fairy-tale ending."

"Did you have to get married?"

"Actually, no. We chose to. We would have gotten married regardless. Because yes, we were in love. And your dad loves you, Emma, just as mine loved me. We choose our families, in the end. Ken is our family, Leeza was our family, just as much as Grandma L. Or my father. Or yours."

Emma sat bolt upright. "I don't want to know!" She announced firmly. "It doesn't matter to me. Dad is my dad; that's all I care about. And Von is—Von. He's a cool guy, but he'll never be my 'Dad.' " She made quote marks in the air with her sparkly blue-polished nails. "No matter what that test says, I don't care." She wiped fiercely at her eyes with a napkin.

chapter 16

"Our sign has arrived!" Ken proclaimed as he tore the protective wrapping paper off a large, rectangular shape. A dust mask was hanging around his neck and a bandanna was tied around his forehead. "It's twice the size of the old one. You can clearly see it from the park: THE BOOK NOOK BARN."

A special fixture took pride of place in the corner—Halo's permanent perch. A set of small chairs was stacked nearby, as this was to become the center of the children's reading area.

"Check it out!" Tim said to Grace, pointing out the latest find—a bluestone countertop for the communal Wi-Fi table. "Ken scored this from a defunct gardening shop in Appleton."

"We're like a woman in her underwear, getting ready for a ball—halfway dressed and waiting for her stylists to make her beautiful!" Ken proclaimed.

Grace had to laugh. "Not everybody has a stylist, Ken."

"Well, this girl does," he said, slapping a wall. "And here I am! This place will be a sanctuary, like a spa for the mind, for all ages. Simple, modern, and rustic all at the same time." He gestured dramatically to a large heap in the center of the

room, covered by a tarp. "And now for the pièce de résistance."
He pulled back the tarp, revealing a large crystal chandelier
draped over a chair, its crystals dripping and puddling onto
the floor.

Grace shook her head. "Barn wood and a crystal chandelier.
You've outdone yourself. But this must have cost a fortune."

"It cost nothing. Jonathan donated it. Leeza had it in a crate in
their garage. It was her mother's, from Europe, and she had nowhere to hang it. It's on loan until Sara might want it someday.
If she happens to marry a prince and move into a castle. Mike
rewired it. He's coming by later to hang it and put up the sign."

"I think it looks like something from Miss Havisham's
wedding banquet," said Tim, referring to the jilted spinster
in Dickens' *Great Expectations* who left her opulent wedding
banquet intact to gather cobwebs for decades when the groom
failed to show up.

"Perfect!" Ken agreed. "We'll name her Miss Havisham!"

The space was truly going to be stunning. Grace had worried
about Ken leaving Hollywood and all its glamour to go back to
New London, but it was obvious she could back-burner those
concerns. Ken was in his element. Instead of being cannon
fodder for a crazy director, under the gun for ratings, he was
in charge of his own domain here, and working with people he
loved. He was free to create his own world, with nobody to
judge him. In a way, Grace realized, it was what Ken had been
always looking for.

"Grace, step into my office." Tim had set up what he called
his "office," a laptop on a folding card table, over in a back cor-

ner. Grace picked her way around tarps, equipment, and paint cans. "I was just working on inventory. The books will be loaded in last. But I thought we should go over your ideas for the bake sale."

"Emma and her friends are going to pass out baked goods on trays in front of the high school the day before the opening," Grace said excitedly. "And Halo will send out e-mails to all the kids. Emma will set up a reading corner for a sneak peek of her new Halo e-book—and Halo will do a beak signing, or should I say piercing?"

"Dostoyevsky and Faulkner are rolling over in their graves."

"I'm going to feature recipes from our family recipe box and attach a tag with the name of each recipe author to each baked good," Grace continued. It felt good to get excited over plans for the opening. "I thought we could put the goodies under glass domes on old cake stands of different heights all the way down the bluestone counter."

"Love it!" called out Ken.

There was still so much to do. Squinting at the plans, Grace realized they'd forgotten about where people would hang coats in winter. She'd need to source some old barn hooks. What else was missing? Grace was so engrossed in the plans, bent over the table, scribbling notes, that she didn't notice until she saw the red laces in the Converse sneakers standing next to her that Brian had walked in.

She looked up with a start. "Brian!" Reflexively, she smoothed her hair. Not that she cared how she looked. "What are you doing here? Is Emma OK?"

What was that look on his face? She'd known Brian for twenty years, and she'd never seen that particular look. She threw a glance at Ken, who shrugged.

"Are you going over to see Emma? She's at show choir practice."

"Actually, I came to see you. Can you take a break?"

Grace glanced at Ken, who was pretending to be busy but lifted an eyebrow. Ken always had great intuition when something was up.

"I guess so. Is it important? I mean, you didn't call . . ."

"It's important. I thought we'd go for a walk."

When they were kids, "going for a walk" had always been how they'd talked things out, finding a place where the adults couldn't overhear their conversations, or see them making out. "Going for a walk" with Brian, who lived inside his head, avoided all outdoor activities, and loved to quote his alignment with Woody Allen as "Nature and I are two," was code for alone time. In this case, "going for a walk" entailed driving a few miles to the nature center that bordered the river just outside of town, a place Grace loved and didn't often have time to visit. Lovely as it was, the nature center was not high on Brian's favorites list. His comment: "There's a reason they call that place Mosquito Hill." Which, to Grace, was ridiculous. There was a Butterfly House that was magical, and beautiful trails and flower beds. On a less hectic day, Grace might have really enjoyed a leisurely stroll. But today she felt every minute tick by. *Why couldn't Brian have called?* Oh, well. That was Brian—and just another example of their different points of view. Still—he did have a funny look on his face. Nervous, almost.

Brian headed straight for the Butterfly House. Lush plantings lined the path, and multicolored butterflies flitted through the air under the glass dome. It was like being inside a butterfly snow globe, Grace thought. Brian took her hand and she was fifteen years old again. "So—what's the deal? You hate this place, remember?"

Brian laughed. "You're right, it has the two dreaded F's—flora and fauna. I always feel like the butterflies can read my mind and they're on the attack." He swatted the air. "Butterflies should go back where they belong—onto screen savers."

They were laughing together now. "Good thing Emma can't see this," Grace thought. "She'd be putting us back together again." Emma always retained that micro-shred of hope.

"We do know each other like nobody else, Grace."

"The good, the bad, and the ugly."

"When we were growing up, I couldn't imagine being with anyone but you."

"I guess it seemed preordained."

"I always think about how much we meant to each other, you know? And don't you—just a little? Even after all we've been through?" He was holding her hand.

Grace dropped her head. She was having trouble meeting his eyes. "Sometimes," she found herself whispering. And it was true. How do you ever forget the feelings you had for your first love? Since the visit to Chicago, Grace had to admit her feelings toward Brian were poking through the armor she'd put up after the divorce; they were like fresh green shoots through the spring thaw after a long, icy winter. She had left in such a fury, literally slamming the door on her feelings, that she had not really given them a chance to sort themselves out. And now, there was Mike. But on the Scales of Relationships, as the Unbiased Panel of Judges would call it, it was hard to balance a decades-long relationship with a co-parent with one that was brand-new.

"Grace, I think it's amazing what you've done with your life, and Emma's," Brian said, still holding her hand. "She's becoming such an incredible girl, and I give all the credit to you for this amazing turnaround."

"She did it herself," Grace corrected.

"I know what I see. And I see a girl who's secure and confident because her mother is. You were always the most wonderful person; you were the only person who didn't realize it." He dodged a butterfly. "But I always knew. I was such a fool, and you were absolutely right to leave me. But we all deserve another chance, an act two."

Oooh, here it comes, Grace thought, stopping as if someone had pulled a plug and cut all power to her body. Two thoughts remained: 1) *He wants to get back together!* And 2) *Now would be the time to tell him about Emma!*

"That's why I want you to be the very first person to know— I'm getting married."

For a minute, it did not compute. *Getting married?*

Then, the hammer: "I can't wait for you to meet her."

Oh my God, he's marrying someone else!!

Brian seemed oblivious to Grace's shock as he strolled along, leading her by the hand. "Heather is a great girl. She's smart and young. She's twenty-five and has so much energy. She is so amazing. Our meeting was kind of a whirlwind thing—it's interesting how we met—so I haven't been able to introduce her. But Emma's going to love her."

Later, all Grace could remember was Brian's litany of *Heather said*s.

Heather said she couldn't wait to meet Emma—and Grace.

Heather said she would be so happy if Emma could live with them.

Heather said they were going to get married right away.

Heather said Emma would be maid of honor and they'd start shopping for a "fierce" bridesmaid dress right away.

Heather said she would never intrude on your role as Emma's mother.

Heather said she was going to quit work.

Heather said she was pregnant.

Grace found all this impossible to process. The brain must shut down when there was too much information, she thought. Brian pulled out his phone and showed her the screen shot: Heather and her Maltese, Feather. Heather and Feather. The dog was wearing a pink sweater with Chanel double-*C* logos on it.

All Grace knew now was that she had to get out of there and away from Brian. If there were something she could have thrown at him, she would have. But how do you throw a butterfly? Anyhow, it was better not to react. *Don't show him a shred of emotion! He doesn't deserve it! Heather and Feather could have him.* "Well. Congratulations to you and—Heather. I'm sure Emma will be thrilled to be a maid of honor. And a big sister."

What did she expect? Grace asked herself. In a way, Brian had done her a big favor. It was time for both of them to move on.

chapter 17

"The wedding's in a month?" Lorraine was incredulous. "How long has he known her?"

"Long enough to be decorating a nursery," Grace said. She hoped she didn't sound bitter, because she really wasn't. Brian had a right to live his life, to date. What had she been thinking, to imagine he'd be sitting there, indefinitely waiting for her to throw him a bone? She'd clearly been living in a fantasy world. They would always be united by Emma; that would never change. That would have to be enough, for both of them.

Grace and Lorraine were exhausted. Every bowl, spoon, pan, sheet, measuring cup, and mixer had been mustered into service and sat in dripping, batter-spattered heaps on the counters and in the sink. Grace had dried batter in her hair and on her forehead; Lorraine had frosting smeared across her chest— and there hadn't even been a food fight. The kitchen felt like an inferno. Still, there was no way they'd have a large enough baked goods inventory for the opening. The 3F always brought throngs of people into the town, so the volume they needed was huge. The baked treats were a great supercharger for Book

Nook sales, and cookies and cupcakes could be handed out at the festival as bait to get people to divert off Water Street and over to the shop. But at this rate, Grace knew, they'd run out by noon. Now that school had started and there were after-class activities, several of the helpers had bailed, and there were no reinforcements in sight. Grace had to admit that this first 3F since Leeza's passing was hitting her harder than she imagined, and so she seemed a little slower than usual. On top of everything else, Emma was adjusting to the idea of a new stepmother and, understandably, her focus was splintered.

Learning that her father was remarrying was one thing, but the fact that she would soon have a baby brother or sister was quite another.

"Halo doesn't want to be with some dog that gets carried around in a *purse*," Emma had said scornfully. "And who knows what might happen—that stupid dog might attack him! I can never take Halo there. So I can't go."

Grace had tried to talk sensibly to Emma, in spite of her own feelings. "You have to give Dad and Heather a chance, Emma. There are so many blended families these days. And you'll be a big sister."

Emma had rolled her eyes, but when Brian had sent her a plane ticket to Chicago last weekend, Grace had felt obligated to let her go, which meant she wasn't able to help out with the Cupcake Brigade.

Brian had gone all-out, with a trip to the Lincoln Park Zoo, dinner at a glamorous Italian restaurant overlooking Lake

Michigan, and Sunday brunch with Grandma M. Emma recounted the story of how Dad had met Heather at the Chicago Historical Society, where she worked in public relations; he'd been brought in to design a new interactive program for tourists. Heather had taken Emma and her Chicago girlfriends for mani-pedis on Oak Street and shopping in Old Town, and showed her the historic town house in the Old Town Triangle where they'd be moving as soon as they rented the loft. Emma was going to have a room there, she was assured. They were planning to be married at the Saddle & Cycle Club, an exclusive enclave near the city.

Grace couldn't imagine how Brian could afford all this. And he had always disdained clubs. Then it occurred to her. Of course! Heather had money. Brian wasn't materialistic, but this was a definite lifestyle upgrade. It was amazing how women seemed to always put their hearts and souls into turning their men around, only to break up and have the next woman reap the benefits. Not that Grace was bitter, but she did feel a twinge.

"What kind are these?" Emma asked about the cupcakes that were cooling in their pans. Halo bobbed on top of her head, surveying his culinary opportunities.

"Almond and cardamom," said Lorraine. "We adapted a traditional Swedish recipe from the recipe box. I think it came from my father's side of the family. I remember it growing up."

Emma grabbed a cupcake and christened them "Nut Case Cupcakes, in honor of all the nuts in this family."

NUT CASE CUPCAKES

Makes 20 cupcakes

FOR THE CAKE:

½ cup butter

2 cups light brown sugar

3 eggs

1 teaspoon vanilla

2 cups cake flour

1 teaspoon baking soda

1 teaspoon ground cardamom

1 teaspoon ground cinnamon

¼ teaspoon salt

1 cup sour cream

½ cup finely chopped almonds

FOR THE FROSTING:

3 sticks butter, softened

1½ cups dark brown sugar

½ cup powdered sugar

4 ounces cream cheese, softened

½ teaspoon vanilla

FOR THE CANDIED ALMONDS:

½ cup water

1 cup sugar

½ teaspoon ground cardamom

2 cups slivered almonds

Preheat oven to 350°F. Line cupcake pans with 20 paper liners.

MAKE THE CUPCAKES: Cream butter and sugar. Add the eggs one at a time, then the vanilla. Whisk together the flour, baking soda, cardamom, cinnamon, and salt. Mix into the butter mixture alternating with the sour cream. Fold in nuts. Fill the liners ¾ full with batter. Bake for 20 to 25 minutes, rotating the pans halfway through baking time. A toothpick inserted in the center of a cupcake should come out clean. Let cool.

MAKE THE ALMONDS: Bring the water, sugar, and cardamom to a boil. Add the almonds and stir to coat. Keep cooking until the liquid has reduced and is syrupy. Pour onto a buttered piece of aluminum foil. Spread out with a spatula and let cool. Chop or break apart when ready to use.

"I have an idea," Emma volunteered. "These are great, but look at all this. Why don't we buy cupcakes from the supermarket? We'll just take them out of the package and—"

"Emma!" barked Grace and Lorraine in unison.

Grace had to admit that she'd really promised something she couldn't deliver. The cupcakes on top of the work at the store and her online business, plus Emma's starting school, and now this wedding circus were more than she could handle. And Emma was right. It was crazy to be baking all this from scratch. A commercial bakery would probably buy frosting by the vat or go General Mills for a commercial-grade bulk cake mix to use anyway.

"Hel-*loo*!" It was Claire, knocking at the screen door. "Gracie, Lorraine!"

"What's she doing here?" Grace thought, opening the door a crack. Behind Claire she could see a group of young girls in green uniforms.

"Oh good, you're here. Girls, stay right where you are, please." Claire acted like the crack was a wide-open door and somehow ended up inside the kitchen. "Hi, Lorraine, hi, Emma! Oh, my goodness! You are busy. Well, I won't keep you. But I have a little business proposition."

"Um—are we in business?" Grace asked.

"We can be. You have to make a lot of cupcakes. I have a lot of Girl Scouts. So I was thinking, we all want the Book Nook Barn to be a big success when it reopens. And the cupcake sale worked so well before. But with the Fall Family Fest and all, you'll need many more cupcakes. And you could do me a huge favor, Grace. My Junior Girl Scouts need to earn their baking badge. And my friend Sheila, in Appleton, has a similar problem with her troop. So I was thinking, if you'd let us, we'll have the girls bake cupcakes for the sale. I'll supervise this group, and Sheila will be in charge of hers, and we'll be delivering about—let's see, if each girl bakes two dozen, and there are about twenty girls in each troop, we'll be bringing you about eighty dozen."

"That's fantastic, Claire! I am so excited! I can give the girls a basic recipe, and they can decorate the frosting with M&M's. We'll pay for the ingredients. Are you sure they'll earn their badges?"

"Absolutely. Jennifer has been begging to work on her baking badge. The girls watch those cupcake shows on TV and they want to do it, too. So—is it a deal?" She thrust out her hand.

Grace took it. "Deal."

"You know, we're all really glad you and Emma are back," Claire said. "I know I can't replace Leeza, and it must be hard just now since this was the time you always came back to see her, but maybe we can have lunch when things lighten up."

"Sure. That would be nice." Claire had saved her, that was for sure. Of all people—Claire? *Would wonders never cease?*

———

"I now christen thee—the Book Nook Barn!" With the flick of a switch, Tim illuminated Miss Havisham, who sprang to life, sparkling and fiery, as she hung above the oversized bluestone table. For a minute nobody spoke, it was that gorgeous. As everyone was still looking up, there was the sound of a champagne cork popping.

"To the Book Nook Barn!" Mike announced. "The phoenix that rose from the ashes. Literally!"

The glass cake stands stood at attention like soldiers at the ready, awaiting their cupcakes.

The Kids' Corner was a mound of fluffy pillows surrounding a group of weathered milking stools that at one point had served the needs of actual cows but were perfectly sized for the littlest readers. The Wi-Fi was up and running.

"We're ready for the festival," Ken proclaimed. "We did it!" He raised a glass of wine, then hit the remote, and Michael Jackson burst from the sound system. With a flourish, Ken grabbed Tim and started to dance, pulling a fierce Moonwalk.

The playlist shifted to Adele, and Mike grabbed Grace and spun her across the floor, twirling her until she was dizzy and they'd spun out the door and onto the porch. It was amazing,

Grace thought, to actually know someone who could do so much with his hands. Mike was the polar opposite of Brian, who lived in his head, and, needless to say, of Von, who lived only for business deals. Mike radiated an air of self-assurance. The minute you encountered Mike, you knew that he could fend for himself—that he was the kind of guy who could survive in the wild, who'd be able to chop down trees with a penknife, build a shelter and make a fire with a bunch of driftwood, and locate water and edible berries. The kind of guy who could— and did—save lives, not just his own. Ken called him a "throwback," and he was. A throwback to simpler times when everybody knew where they stood.

Dancing with Mike, holding his muscular fireman's shoulders, feeling his cheek rough upon hers with the twinkly chandelier overhead and the moon rising over the park outside, Grace felt a glow, and she was pretty certain it wasn't just the champagne. Mike dipped her dramatically, his hand firmly pressed to the small of her back. Yes, he was a man who literally had her back.

They reluctantly closed up shop. Tomorrow, the festivities started at 5:00, with a classic-car parade down Water Street, but the real action started much earlier when crowds of families arrived for an explosion in the town on Saturday—games, clowns, crafts, a climbing wall, a petting zoo, a band, and kids' sports. Mike would be working with the fire department, and the fire trucks would be on display. There was always plenty of food. It was going to be crazy, and the park was sure to be packed.

The Book Nook Barn would be open bright and early and ready for business.

Grace knew she had to get up to start the cupcake engine at the crack of dawn, but that didn't matter now. She was wrapped in Mike's arms, dancing a slow dance without music. Tonight, she wasn't a mom or a friend or a daughter, or an ex-wife. Tonight, she was a lover.

It was dawn, and the sky was just starting to streak with bits of light as Grace tiptoed into the house with her shoes in her hands. Her room being at the top of two flights of stairs meant negotiating the planks in the floor that were known to be creaky, and trying not to bang into any walls or make noises that would cause curious ears to tune in. She felt like she was sixteen again, sneaking home after a night out. This was one of the downsides of single motherhood—sometimes it felt like your child had more privileges than you. As she slid past Emma's closed door. Grace wondered if she'd really gone so far after all. She'd have to reassess her finances and see if she could afford a place for herself and Emma. Still, that wouldn't give her any real privacy, either. Grace sighed as she collapsed onto her bed. The price of motherhood, as any mother knew, was privacy, and this mother had just walked the walk—of shame. Not unlike when she was a teenager, sneaking in after a make-out session. Except she wasn't ashamed. Not at all. Grace was a grown woman.

After an hour of fitful sleep and a splash of cold water on her face, Grace was back in the kitchen. Yes, Grace thought, it was hard knowing this would be her first 3F without Leeza, but she had to laugh: If Leeza could only see her now, baking up a storm. She'd have loved it. Running water for the coffee, she noticed a message on the table. It must have been there the night before, she thought. It was from Jonathan. He had something for her, and could she stop by later. "How strange," Grace thought.

———

Being at Leeza's house without her still felt odd, and if everything hadn't happened as it had, Grace would simply be here visiting her friends as she did every year. The home radiated Leeza's taste, her touch. It was comforting to feel she was still very much a presence. Grace sat with Jonathan in the kitchen as he poured Cheerios for Sara.

"Sara's a bit young for nursery school," said Jonathan as he lowered Sara into her high chair. "But I'm looking at a pre-preschool for her. I thought it was better than Sara being alone while I was at work."

Hearing this broke Grace's heart. Leeza had been so proud to be a stay-at-home mom and had prioritized being there for Sara. *Life was so unfair sometimes.*

Jonathan handed Grace a package marked "3F." She ripped open the envelope. Inside was a thin plastic case with a disc inside. The handwritten label read "Grace"—in Leeza's handwriting. Grabbing the envelope, Snoopy pointed to his PC, which was set up in a corner of the kitchen.

"You can play it here, if you want," he said. "Or take it home."

Grace couldn't wait. She pulled out the DVD, slid in the disc, and pushed "Play." And there was Leeza on the screen, in her early spring garden, thin and frail, but smiling at her. She had obviously set up the camera on a stand or a pile of books and recorded herself. Grace could see Leeza leaning in and reaching forward to make adjustments before she settled back in her chair.

"Hi, Gracie."

Sara's head snapped up. "Mommy!" she cried, stretching out her arms.

Grace clicked off the DVD. "I don't want to upset her," she mouthed silently to Snoopy.

"You can play it in the den, if you want," he said. "I don't think Sara understands what's happened." His face was so sad.

"I don't think any of us do," Grace said. She ejected the DVD and carried it into the den.

Just seeing Leeza in front of her and hearing her say her name made Grace want to cry. She clicked "Play," and the video began again.

"I wish you could have stayed, but I also am glad you left, you know?" Leeza said. "You need to get back to Emma. And I have a job to do here. I know we talked about a lot of things, but I kept thinking about how we always get together for 3F, and I have to be really honest and say, while I hope I'll be there, maybe I won't be.

"Well, if you're playing this video, that means I'm not around, but don't think I'm not thinking about you. You're probably sad, and I get that; I'm sad, too. But here's the thing. I'm counting on you to move on. You're going to have to live life for both of us now. So do me a favor, and don't waste a minute of it." Leeza smiled. "I know you, Grace, you've always been looking for something else, and I know you think Von may be Emma's father. But Grace, Von figured out the timing of Emma's birth years ago. He knew there was a chance Emma could be his, but he didn't come back even then. Sure, there was the business, but he could have at least called or written to you. You were right about that part all those years ago. He's my cousin and I love him, but he was a coward then, and he's still the same old Von, hiding from life behind his work. I asked him to come while you were here so you could see for yourself how he hasn't changed. I wanted you to stop wondering if a life with him could have worked out, so you could finally move on. It doesn't matter who Emma's biological father is, Grace. Brian loves her dearly, and she has the most amazing mother in the world. It's time for you to be happy, Grace. To have someone in your life you love and desire. Someone who can be a real partner. It's not Brian or Von, Grace, but I know he's out there for you. I'm just sorry I won't get to meet him."

Leeza laughed. "God sure has some surprises in store for us. If he weren't God, I'd be very upset with him for my cancer. Who does he think he is? Well, G., I wish I was there with you to talk this through over our coffee mugs, like we always did with everything, but I've gotta go now. Sara's waking up, and every minute is precious. The point of this long and rambling video is, time is short. Sometimes, shorter than we think. Don't let things drift. Trust yourself, you can do it. You are stronger than you know. Bye, Gracie. What a wonderful friend you are, and I love you." She blew a kiss, and the video ended, frozen on that image.

With tears streaming down her face, Grace could hear Snoopy running water and bustling about in the next room, getting Sara ready for pre-preschool. The sound of life.

chapter 18

I t was amazing, Grace thought, how your whole life could shift on its axis and you just walked on through it, like trying to make it home in the winter when the snow was deep and each step was a struggle, but you did it. The mad rush of the Book Nook Barn reopening and the cupcake sale took up every available inch of Grace's brain and counter space, and that was all she was able to think about until the last customer left on Saturday night.

"How many cupcakes did we go through?" Tim asked as he studied the books.

"One hundred and thirty dozen," said Grace in disbelief as she lounged on the pillows in the Kids' Corner, where a few hours before Emma had given a reading of *Hello, Halo!* featuring a guest appearance by the main character himself. The word got out that Halo the evil bird from *The Lost Ones* was at the Book Nook Barn, and it seemed like every animal-loving kid and every *Lost Ones* fan had packed their way into the shop, hanging out on the front porch, or waited outside on the sidewalk to take the place of the next person who left. Grace's feet throbbed and her shoulders were sore from lifting heavy trays and carrying boxes of books. Every cupcake had been devoured. She must have cleaned up and thrown out a million wrappers. "Thank God for Claire . . ."

"Claire really came through with the troops," said Ken.

"I feel terrible that we pulled pranks on her in high school."

"Why? She was probably not even aware of it. She was ten times more popular than any of us. We were like gnats to her." Ken wiped down his precious bluestone countertop. "Well, mission accomplished, team. We certainly drew traffic. And the lifestyle editor from the *Chicago Tribune*, the food editor from the *Green Bay Journal*, and a reporter from the *Appleton Tribune* all showed up. The *Tribune* wants to send up a photographer and do a feature on our style. And here's the icing on the cake, so to speak—they all want to run that Nut Case cupcake recipe!"

"*Seriously!*" Halo's squawk interrupted the conversation as he bobbed left and right on his perch. The bird always had to have the last word.

Mike surfaced from the basement. "Nobody noticed my new hardwired smoke alarms," he said mournfully. "But," he said, brightening, "the Chief wants to order a sheet cake."

"Did you tell him we don't do sheet cakes?" Grace said, rubbing her aching calf.

"Yeah, and he said you should. There's big business there."

"In sheet cakes?"

"A lot of traditions have died in modern times, but sheet cakes are the one social constant," Ken said. "Birthday? Sheet cake. Promotion? Sheet cake. Anniversary? Sheet cake. Shower? Sheet cake. Holiday? Sheet cake. I've seen them at funerals, graduations, you name it."

Grace laughed. "Well, why don't we just tell them we'll put a bakery in here?"

"Sheet cakes, books—what's the difference?" Ken shrugged. "They're both flat, with writing on them."

Grace felt giddy with exhaustion and from the encouragement Leeza's message had given her.

———

"We did it, Mom! I knew we'd pull it off," Emma said as she shared her scrambled eggs with Halo the next morning at breakfast. Since they'd moved back to Wisconsin, Halo had become a bona fide Midwesterner, preferring mashed potatoes and scrambled eggs to seeds or fruits. "This bird would never have survived in the wild," Grace thought, watching her daughter alternating bites of her own eggs with bits hand-fed to the cockatoo. He would only have made it if they had personal chefs in the rain forest. In addition to scarfing down his own portion, he tried to grab the last bit from Emma's mouth as she pushed him softly away. "We're a great team, Mom. We can do anything. And that's why I want you to come with me to Dad's wedding. I need you there with me." Emma said this last part a bit quietly, but Grace heard it all the same.

Come to the wedding? "What? I don't think I'm invited, Em. I happen to be the ex-wife." Grace would do anything for Emma, but what a nightmare! Emma would be with family she knew and trusted, family that loved her. She could certainly go to the wedding on her own. It would be her first wedding. She was just nervous, was all.

Emma sighed and flounced over to the big ceramic mixing bowl where mail, catalogs, and magazines were dumped. Sorting through, she found a large, square envelope, which she ripped open. "There!" She slapped the invitation on the kitchen table. It was thick and cream-colored, with a deckle edge and a watermark of a floating feather. In honor of guess who, no doubt, Grace thought. "Don't you ever open your mail? Heather said she really hoped you could come. Please, Mom, I want you there."

———

"What!" Ken exploded when she showed him the invitation. "I can't believe Bether invited you to their wedding."

"*Bether?*"

"Brian plus Heather equals Bether. Well, we know this will be an out-of-body experience, but if Emma wants you there, you have to do it."

"I don't know if I can."

Ken looked at her. "Sweetie. You have to go. This isn't about a wedding. This is about closure. Now, let's talk about this cupcake crisis." He pushed up the rolled sleeves of his long-sleeved shirt, part of his new literary look.

"What cupcake crisis? Did somebody get food poisoning?"

"Far from it. We have an absolute tsunami of demand. Everybody keeps coming into the Book Nook Barn demanding cupcakes, and, if not the cupcakes, they want your recipes. You're going to have to get Lloyd's of London to insure that recipe box!" He sighed for dramatic effect. "I tell them, 'Sir, or ma'am,'—as the case may be—'this is a bookstore! Can't you read?' But we have to figure something out to keep all our new customers, so they don't veer off to Dairy Queen and do not pass go. Or call it a day and stick with online. Books and food are like peanut butter and jelly. They just go together."

"Ken, I am barely keeping up with the orders for the production program on our Web site. That's paying the bills right now. The cupcakes are a great promotion, but it's not like we run a café."

"Would a café make us more money, if we had one?" Tim asked from across the room. Unless the discussion was literary, Tim tended to stay on the edge of conversations, then swoop in and make the most insightful comments of all. He was pecking away at his laptop, looking up occasionally over the top of his glasses.

"Cafés have a literary history. Hemingway wrote at a café in Paris, the *Closerie des Lilas*. Which reminds me to order *A Moveable Feast*." He dove back into his laptop to make a note.

"Tim, you are brilliant. We'll do the math. Grace, you'd do the baking. This is potentially genius. A café in the Book Nook Barn!"

Tim raised his hand. "Reality check. We just got through with a HUGE renovation. And we can't just drop a café in from the sky, you know. There'll be code. Health department. We don't have a kitchen, or a dishwasher, or—"

"Details, details. Of course, Tim. All that's true. And thank you for setting the tiller. But, really, we don't need to get the Iron Chef in here. We just need a few cookies and cakes. And tea and coffee. And scones. And muffins. And . . ." Ken stalked around the room, his eyes flickering from one imagined possibility to the next. When Ken was onto an idea, he was like a heat-seeking missile.

"To do the actual baking, we'd need to lease a commercial bakery space," Grace said firmly, remembering the explosion in her mother's kitchen and the Junior Girl Scouts. "And I'd need a helper. There are two teams involved with something like this—selling during the day and baking at night, plus everything in between."

"I wonder if we could put a kitchen in the basement," said Ken.

"That would be expensive," Grace added. "Commercial stoves cost a lot, even used. There's plumbing." That point quieted the room for a minute. "Let's think about it," she said. For once, Grace realized that there was too much going on in her head to make an impetuous decision. There were so many things to consider. Cupcakes were the least of them. Still, the idea was tantalizing. It would give her a real role, working with Ken and Tim. And an additional revenue source. But it meant baking. A *lot* of baking.

Leeza's video had made Grace realize that she'd spent way too much of her life wishing for things to be different: that Brian would be there forever for her; that Leeza would not die; that Von could save her; that her daughter would be a perfect princess; that it was Grace's mother's fault she was so unhappy. None of those things had turned out to be the case, yet she had acted on all of them, making life decisions, as if they were facts cast in concrete. This time, Grace vowed, she would figure out who and what she wanted. Grace looked around at the beautiful space they had all created. The crystals in the chandelier twinkled, like tiny, living stars. The Book Nook had survived trial by fire and emerged transformed into something so much better—the Book Nook Barn. So would they all.

———

What to wear to your ex-husband's wedding is not a question they discuss much on those etiquette advice columns, not even a bridezilla TV show, probably because it's a question most women would not rush to contemplate, and is rarely offered. Grace was different. Having put off choosing an outfit until the last minute, she'd panicked. With the entire contents of her closet spread across her bed, she'd realized she was in trouble. Emma's burnt-burgundy maid of honor dress was hanging on a hook, and she stood with her arms crossed, shaking her head. "Oh, Mom," she said mournfully.

It had, of course, taken Ken to come up with a solution. "As your escort, I feel compelled to intervene. I had a feeling this would happen." With that, he'd produced a beautiful navy blue lace dress that he'd asked Roberto to FedEx from the wardrobe of *The Lost Ones*.

"It was one of the pieces that was wrecked when you spilled the blood. The stain never came out, so Roberto said they were going to pitch it anyway. It was white, but I dyed it in the tub and covered all the stains," he said, tossing it onto the pile on the bed. "I had to dye it twice to get it this dark. Tim will kill me when he sees the tub. Don't thank me, just put it on. It's a wrap dress, so it fits almost anybody. Now about that hair . . ." He'd ripped out a magazine picture of a loosely arranged chignon. "One ponytail, three hairpins, pure gorgeousness!"

And so Grace had ended up walking up the aisle of Brian's wedding, not as the bride, but as the mother of the bridesmaid, wearing, as Ken, noted, something borrowed and something blue. Heather, a petite brunette in an off-the-shoulder white mermaid-style gown and layer-cake veil ("Oscar de la Renta," whispered Ken), was preceded by her sisters and Emma, looking beautiful in her dress, a baby calla lily in her hair. Bringing up the rear, as ring bearer, was Feather, who wore a tiny black bow-tie collar and a satin pillow strapped to his back, causing Ken to dig his elbow into Grace's ribs.

As Grace observed the vows, she felt as if she were watching another person, yet another Brian, certainly not the Brian she had loved and married all those years ago in a courthouse ceremony, her wearing a two-piece maternity dress with an elastic-waist skirt, because he hated formalities. Then, the wedding lunch had been at Dairy Queen. Now, there was a seated dinner in the club's ballroom, with about eighty guests. There were canapés, champagne, a seated, four-course luncheon, and a string quartet.

The worst moment had been the receiving line, when Grace had looked into Brian's eyes. There was no hesitation there: He had chosen his path and was proud of it. Proud of the club, the woman in the Oscar de la Renta dress, the cushion-cut diamond ring he'd put on her finger, proud of himself. He was now Mr. All This. The wedding was clearly a symbol of his success, plowing over all his failures with Grace. And so she'd kissed this stranger who now lived in Brian's body on the cheek and whispered the required "Congratulations." She'd offered a hand to Heather, who congratulated her on Emma, beaming, "I've always wanted a daughter."

"*So grow your own*," Grace wanted to say. Instead, she just nodded and smiled.

"We'll keep in close touch on everything involving Emma," Heather promised. "I know she can't wait to be a big sister!"

Grace murmured pleasantries, and the moment was over. After the bride and groom danced together, and Brian danced with Emma, the toasts began. As soon as she heard glasses clinking, Grace turned to Ken. They nodded to each other and slipped out of the ballroom. Emma would be staying overnight at the loft with Grandma M., who would drive her back to New London the next day. There was nothing to do but leave.

"Well, that was fun, and Bether is official," Ken said as they headed up the long stretch of 94 toward Wisconsin. "But what about your cute fireman, Grace? What's going on with you two? Why didn't you bring him to the wedding of the century?" Ken looked at Grace. He had a point. It was a fair question. Mike and Grace had been spending a lot of time together, and it had been a long time since the not-dating stage. Things were getting serious between them, but Grace still wasn't entirely sure what was in her heart. She'd been hurt by so many men that she wasn't quite comfortable yet with putting everything on the line, even if Mike was different.

"Oh, things are going so well. Why subject him to Bether? Besides, I knew you'd have more fun. Mike doesn't really care for clubs and fancy events."

"Hmmmm. OK, Grace, I'm going to let you slide this time, but you better get your mind straight about what you want. Mike's a nice guy, but even nice guys can't wait around forever, girlfriend."

As they passed the Schaumburg cutoff, Ken announced, "We'll stop at the Brat Stop."

"That sounds great!" Grace agreed. It was a tradition to stop at the Brat Stop—home of the best brats on the planet. Ken always had his with mustard and sauerkraut, and Grace always had hers the exact same way.

Thank goodness, some things never changed. They still thought so much alike. It was not surprising, then, that while they were wiping mustard from their mouths and ordering second brats, Ken and Grace came to the same decision—they had to open the café.

chapter 19

If she were being completely honest with herself, Grace would admit that there were times when she came within an inch of packing up and going back to California. It was emotionally exhausting to be in New London, to deal every day with the ghosts of her past. Everywhere she turned, there were reminders of her father, Brian, Von. But there was also Emma, which more than tipped the balance, and the new future they were creating together. This future, Grace reminded herself, would be Emma's past. She owed it to her daughter to make it a good one. And she thanked God every day for Ken.

The reborn Book Nook Barn had quickly resumed its mantle as the favorite spot for the town's young moms. Halloween had been a hit, with the porch draped in spiderwebs and Ken's scary pumpkins lined up on the steps, candles glowing. Emma had written a special *Halo's Halloween* story and her reading at the Kids' Corner, with Sara on her lap, had strollers stacked out the door.

As the weather got colder and the days grew shorter in November, and the moms in the park and the tourists trickled off, business fell off a bit, but the opening of the café after Thanksgiving and the upcoming holidays promised to bring back the numbers. Claire's Junior Girl Scouts were creating artwork for a special "local gallery" area Tim had designated along one wall. As they hung the framed pictures, Claire turned to Grace. "You know, I don't have much of a gardening business in the winter," she said. "I've been helping out at the law firm, but frankly, that's not very creative. Could you use some extra help with the café? I think I've got the cupcake part down."

Could she! Suddenly Grace had a "staff." After one meeting, Claire had created a detailed project management spreadsheet and a work-flow chart that mapped the trajectory of every cupcake from birth to digestion. Claire turned out to be a great partner, because she was all the things Grace and Ken were not: organized, neat, and detail-oriented. Better still, she'd offered up her own double Viking range as backup until the commercial ovens were installed in the basement of the Book Nook Barn.

Construction had begun on the gazebo, with a dedication date set for the second week of December. The structure itself was simple enough, but the wiring for the sound system and electricity had to be installed before the ground froze. The plan for the build-out of the café was to close down the Book Nook Barn for as short a period as possible before Thanksgiving while the counters were installed upstairs and a commercial refrigerator, stove, and dishwasher that met the code requirements were put in the basement. Mike planned to do most of the work with his off-duty firehouse buddies.

It wasn't easy juggling two jobs, Grace thought, but it would be a while before the café turned a profit, and meanwhile she now had real backup from Claire. Grace was also developing a Web site for the cafe, including recipes. Every evening, Grace and Lorraine sat in front of the recipe box and ran through the recipes, culling and editing to adapt quantities and numbers, and trying to figure out the best rotation. It felt good to be doing this together. Each recipe brought a comment from Lorraine, or a memory, and Grace filed these away in her mind. Someday, she thought, she would tell them to a grandchild. She started writing the stories down, and Emma was scanning them to keep a record. It was ironic, Grace thought, that this recipe box, which had caused her so much pain for so many years, was now the source of so many good things. Inspiration, history, heritage, love—all of those were in the box, not just recipes.

The kitchen table was littered not with cupcake ingredients but with calligraphy pens, markers, little tags, and string, to tie a label around each cupcake. "This is crazy," Grace thought. Searching the Web, she found a resource to make the labels in quantity. A small victory for efficiency. One task down, dozens left to go. She hit "Save" and closed her laptop.

"I am beggin' you!" yelled Halo from his cage.

"Take it easy, Halo." She opened the refrigerator, scooped out some mashed potatoes from a small bowl, heated them, and put them into his cage. "What a drama queen you are, bird!" Grace could not believe how they spoiled this bird. But then, this was not just any bird, but their Halo, the feathered superstar that had his own online fan club. Artie had even offered—actually, pleaded—to fly Emma, Ken, and Halo back so Halo could make a guest appearance. It turned out that Artie had been so enamored of Halo that he'd bought a pet cockatoo for himself and tried it out in a scene. The bird, aptly named Vampira, had clamped down on Artie's ear with a viselike beak, drawing the first real blood that had been seen on the set, and that had been the end of that. "Oh, to have been a fly on the wall for that," Ken had laughed.

As Grace cleaned up the table and organized her materials in a large tackle box—a holdover from Hollywood—she was feeling a bit off because Emma was going to Chicago for the weekend. Brian would be picking her up straight from school. Emma didn't need to take anything but her books, because right after the honeymoon in Bali, Heather had taken Emma shopping at Water Tower Place for a complete "Chicago wardrobe," right down to a new toothbrush, which Emma kept in her room at the town house. That night, the plan was for Mike to take Grace to the bowling alley for pizza and a few games.

Grace heard a car pull up in front of the house. Mike was early. Or maybe she was late; she'd lost track of time. "I hope you don't mind if I take a quick shower and change," Grace called out over her shoulder as she heard the kitchen door open. Be right back. Make yourself at home. Mike would be fine. He was used to letting himself in and making himself at home. She dashed out of the kitchen and up the stairs, pulling off clothes on her way up. She took a fast shower, threw on fresh jeans and a soft V-neck sweater, grabbed a lightweight suede jacket, wrapped a thin plaid pashmina around her neck, and swiped on some lip balm. She shook out her hair and peered into the mirror. Her tan and freckles had faded and there was no sign of the California girl. Yes, it had happened. She was a soccer mom. Oh, well. Mike knew what he was getting. *Ready or not.* Taking the stairs two at a time, she hurried back into the kitchen.

The plan was bowling and pizza, but when she got into the car Grace noticed a fluffy blanket and thermos. "Isn't it a bit dark for a picnic?" she asked.

Mike kept his hands on the wheel, looked at her, smiled, and mysteriously said, "Not tonight."

———

Mike drove them just outside of town and parked the car. Grace was confused; they seemed to be stopped in the middle of nowhere. Mike opened her door and took her hand. He pointed to the night sky. There was a full moon and a million twinkling stars. The sky was beautiful. There was a chill, but not too much. Mike wrapped the blanket around Grace's shoulders and led her toward the trees.

Grace didn't know how Mike had arranged everything, but there in the woods, just at the bank of the Wolf River, was a canoe. He helped Grace in, handed her the thermos, and pushed the boat away from shore. They were away from the lights of town, but the full moon glistened off the water, providing just enough light to navigate. The air was still and, except for the occasional sound of water dripping from the paddle, Mike's strokes were almost silent. After a little while he stopped paddling and let the river move the boat lazily along. He took the thermos from Grace, poured something into a mug, and offered it to her. Grace could smell chocolate and peppermint.

——— —

"*Ummmm*, this is wonderful, Mike." The hot chocolate warmed her from the inside and the peppermint schnapps made her feel a bit giddy. Mike moved with expertise across the boat and held her while they floated downstream, taking turns drinking from the mug, enjoying the peace, the shadows of the trees cast across the river and the moonlight. Leaning against Mike's chest, she could hear his gentle, steady heartbeat. Mike was dependable, but he was a surprising man too. It was the best date Grace had ever been on.

chapter 20

"Fork. Spoon. Knife." Grace felt like a surgeon directing a scrub nurse during an operation, and, indeed, she was conducting a delicate operation on Miss Havisham. She peered up, perched on a ladder underneath the huge, drippy chandelier, calling out directions to Ken, below, for implements to hang among the crystals. As part of the addition of the new café area, he'd come up with the idea of hanging tableware from the chandelier—"uniting the literary with the culinary," as he put it. He'd found some stray pieces of old silver at a flea market and strung them with clear fishing line. Grace's job was to tie them on, one piece at a time.

The countdown to the café opening was on, full tilt. Carefully chosen simple white plates, cups, mugs, and glassware had been set up on the new built-in barn-wood shelves along the wall behind the new counter space. Tall stools had been purchased to pull up for quick bites. The refrigerated case had been installed, the dishwashers were in the remodeled basement, and the inspection was tomorrow. If all went well, the café would open two weeks before Christmas, in time for all the holiday festivities. Ken was racing around town with a punch list, pulling together all the last-minute details, picking up the menus from the printer, and distributing flyers with a free cupcake offer.

The silverware made tinkling noises as it jangled against the crystal. When the last piece was hung, Grace climbed down the ladder, Tim flicked on the lights, and they stepped back to survey their handiwork.

"Miss Havisham has had a facelift," he proclaimed.

"Dickens would be proud of the old girl," Tim agreed. They high-fived. Tim was turning out to be the most stable relationship Ken had ever had, Grace thought. There was never any drama in Tim's life; he'd even taken the fire calmly in stride. "You should have seen him," Mike had reported. "He got onto the ladder like he was walking into his living room." It was a perfect fit for a drama queen.

The Recipe Box Café sign was ready to be hung over the counter inside. The plan was to frame it with tiny white Christmas lights and cutlery to match the chandelier. The name itself had been the result of a family brainstorm at Lorraine's kitchen table. Emma had been flipping through the recipe box, pulling out cards to scan so they could create an online file that could be accessed at any time. "I wonder if Great-Grandma over in Sweden ever imagined that her recipe box would go to America and that her recipes would make it into cyberspace," she said, giggling.

"That would never have occurred to Great-Grandma, I can promise you," said Lorraine. "Even if they had invented computers back then. You should have seen her. I remember her hazily from when she was very old and I was very young. She still wore a long dress. She was not very progressive. I called her 'Tant.'"

"Is there a picture to scan into the file?"

Grace realized she had never actually seen a picture of her grandmother. "I don't think so, honey." It had always seemed that her mother's departure from Sweden had left them with zero family artifacts—no albums, no family pictures, no history—just the recipe box.

"You know what?" said Lorraine. "I do have something." She got up, went to her room, and returned with a necklace. A large silver heart dangled from a thick chain. Grace had seen Lorraine wearing this hundreds of times and never thought about its origin. It was just a piece of jewelry. Lorraine fiddled with the heart and it snapped open. Grace had never realized it opened. It was a locket. Inside was a picture of a stern-faced couple. "Here they are, Great-Grandpa and Tant. These are miniatures. They were popular keepsakes at the time."

Grace took the locket and looked at it before she handed it to Emma. It was a sepia photograph—small, but one thing was clear. Great-Grandpa Carlson had very pale-colored eyes. *Emma's ice-blue eyes?* She slowly handed the locket to Emma. This picture has been here all along, Grace thought. If she'd taken more of an interest in her mother, she might have seen it decades ago.

"They look—fierce!" Emma said. "I won't take the pictures out. I'll scan them in the locket."

"Tant didn't get here, but her recipe box is starting a café," said Grace. "The recipe box café."

"The recipe box café," repeated Emma.

"That's a nice name," said Lorraine.

"The Recipe Box Café," Grace said. "Hmm . . ."

Ken had gone wild when he heard the name. "Of course! These are not ordinary recipes. They're recipes with history! It's a great public relations angle. Put it in the press release!"

So the Recipe Box Café at the Book Nook Barn was born.

———

By Christmas week, it was like the café had always been part of the Book Nook. Business was taking off, even following a two-foot snowstorm, a "Wisconsin Special," as Ken called it, that hit the day they launched the café. The storm had one positive side effect, which was the icing of white that had covered the town and the park, hanging icicles from the bare tree limbs. Intermittent flurries had kept the landscape white. Grace, Claire, Lorraine, and Emma, when she could break away from finals, were in overdrive with preparations for the café. Grace's cards, with a bit of the history of each treat, were a big hit. Her cardamom scones included a note that Scandinavians and northern Europeans consume half the world's supply of cardamom. She got so many requests for the recipe, she posted it on the Web site.

Grace and Claire had designed a cookie tree, which sat on top of its own barn-wood table. About four feet tall, it was hung top to bottom with Leeza's favorite gingerbread cookies cut in the shapes of people, trees, stars, and birds, thickly iced, adorned with pink pearlescent edible beads and dusted with translucent edible glitter flakes. The cookies were hung at different lengths on pink satin ribbons that matched the pink bows garlanding the new gazebo across the street. It was almost too pretty to eat, but the plan was to give the cookies as gifts to the kids who came to Emma's Christmas story circle. She'd written a special Halo story, *Halo's Holidays*.

As if all this weren't enough, Emma's birthday was Christmas Day, and Grace hadn't had time to bake a cake. This happened every year, it seemed, but this year she was more prepared than ever. This year, she was determined to start a new tradition— she'd bake a sheet cake! Emma's sheet cake! Something for all her new friends to share. It was just a matter of when. There was Christmas shopping to finish, gifts to wrap, church, and the food pantry to think about. This afternoon was the gazebo dedication, though, and Grace was determined to blast through her checklist and be front and center when Emma and the show choir performed their holiday medley at the ceremony. She wanted the holiday and Emma's birthday to be special, because Emma would be spending New Year's with Brian and Heather. Brian was going to surprise Emma with the promise of a car when she got her learner's permit, and after that, Grace knew, life would never be the same. Her little girl was growing up.

———

"Grace, there is a very important job for you," Claire called out as she strung the ribbons through cookies and put them on trays. Sara was sitting on Jonathan's lap as he then helped her hang them on the cookie tree to replace the ones that had mysteriously vanished.

"Uh-oh. What did I forget?" She leaned over to kiss the top of Sara's head. "What a good job you're doing, Sara!"

CARDAMOM SCONES

Makes 6 to 8 scones

2½ cups flour

¼ cup sugar

3 teaspoons baking powder

1½ teaspoons ground
cardamom

½ teaspoon salt

1½ sticks cold butter

¾ cup dried currants,
optional

½ cup milk, plus more for
brushing

1 egg, beaten

Preheat the oven to 425°F. Line a baking sheet with parchment paper.
Whisk together flour, sugar, baking powder, cardamom, and salt.
Cut in butter. Stir in currants, if using. Stir in milk and egg until just
combined. Put onto a well-floured board and pat into a 1-inch thick
round. Cut into 6 or 8 wedges with a sharp knife. Put them onto the
prepared baking sheet. Lightly brush on some milk. Bake for 12 to 15
minutes or until lightly browned.

"Your job is to take the afternoon off and get your Christmas
shopping done," said Claire. "I'm taking over."

"What? What about *your* holiday shopping?"

"I did it in July."

Of course she did.

"I have to shop for all the village employee gifts, so I figure I
might as well do everything at once, when the sales are on."

Grace sighed. "You put human women to shame, Claire. But

I could really use the time. Emma wants to have a party for her friends on the twenty-sixth, before she goes to her dad's."

Claire nodded. "I know, so much to think about."

Grace was slipping on her parka when Jonathan looked up and called out to her. "Grace! Before you go . . ." He carefully handed Sara to Claire. "I have one surprise for Emma." He handed Grace an envelope. "Leeza left instructions to give it to Emma for her birthday, from her godmother."

"Oh my God, do you know what it is?"

"It's her high school class ring."

Leeza's class ring. She'd only taken it off when she got her engagement ring. It was like a piece of Leeza. "The timing couldn't be better." Grace hugged Claire, then picked her way through the snow to her car. There was so much to do.

———

Grace headed out, looked at the sky, and crossed her fingers that nothing would interfere with the gazebo dedication at five. The Christmas Eve day sky was overcast, with flurries that threatened something more. She was running across the icy sidewalk on Pearl Street when she slipped and slid sideways into a man in a ski hat and sheepskin coat. Looking up, she saw that it was Von.

"Grace! Be careful!"

"I'm fine, I'm fine." She felt flustered.

"You're always in a rush." He smiled. "You always were, as I recall. Can you take a few minutes for an old friend? We could have a coffee. Or a hot chocolate. I seem to recall chocolate was one of your favorites."

Grace found herself blushing. "I heard you were coming back for the gazebo, at Christmas."

"Well, yes. But I had some banking business in New York, so I just extended my trip a bit."

Von escorted Grace into a small coffee shop and ordered two hot chocolates at the counter. He helped her off with her coat, and they settled in at a table.

Grace stirred her drink as she made small talk for a few minutes, describing the new Book Nook Barn and giving an edited version of Brian's wedding.

"Well, it is the end of an era, I suppose," Von said. "That, and Leeza's passing. The universe has shifted and moved us all on. And where have you moved on to, Grace?"

"Right here, actually. The universe, if you call it that, sent me back from LA to New London. I guess you could say I've gone full circle." A year ago, Grace would have felt pathetic saying that. Now she found herself feeling proud.

"I guess many things did not turn out the way we expected."

"Except you, Von. You're doing what you always expected— running your family's chocolate company. I'm sure your father would be proud."

He smiled slightly and sipped from his cup. "Well, even that may change. You never know."

Grace knew. Von Vasser had that chocolate company hard-wired into his DNA, as had his father before him.

"Grace, one reason I made this trip was because I owe you an apology. A long-overdue apology. I am not proud of the way I acted after we were together that night. It has been all these years, and every year I thought now was the time to say something to you, but the time was never right. And you never said anything, so I thought, well, maybe I shouldn't say anything."

Was he referring to Emma? "Well," she finally said, "we were so young."

"Still, I behaved abominably. I was such a confused young man. I was overwhelmed by my father's illness, taking over the business. I knew Emma could be mine, but I was so afraid of that responsibility on top of the rest, and then you married Brian so I figured I must have been wrong. But I still wondered if it could have been possible."

Grace started to say something, but Von stopped her.

"Please let me finish. I have to say this finally. You see, I didn't think children would be possible for me. As a young boy, I had a life-threatening case of measles. I survived, but the doctors said I was most likely left sterile. My mother was devastated, as you can imagine, but when I was young it didn't much matter to me. Until there was the possibility that our night together had meant I was a father. I was terrified, but I also liked the idea, so I had myself tested. I didn't want to cause a burden to you, Brian, or Emma unless it was possible." Von paused. Grace held her breath waiting for him to continue and then she noticed as a sadness crept over Von's normally stoic face, and she knew what he would say. She knew for sure Emma was Brian's daughter. She took Von's hand. "Oh, Von, I am so sorry. We were so, so young."

Von seemed grateful for Grace's words. "Yes, we were, but still I should not have abandoned you like that. After all this time, will you accept my apology? It is important to me. Leeza's death made me realize, life is so short. Our mistakes should not go without apologies. I wanted so much to make sure you were happy, but there was no chance to make it up to you. At least, not then."

"You don't have to make up anything, Von."

"Well, I did try."

"Thank you for being so supportive of Emma, she—"

"When you were married to Brian, I could never tell you this. But now . . . you see, one of my companies invested in his software business."

"What? Brian never told me."

"He never knew. It was one of my holding companies; he would not have made the connection. I didn't want his business to fail, and I heard from Leeza about his gambling debts. I didn't want that for you and Emma. So we put seed capital in his company. "

"Oh my God!"

Von looked at Grace besecchingly. "Actually, it was one of our better investments. With the technology boom, the company has been quite profitable. We have spun off one of the product lines, and we may sell the company at some point at a tremendous profit."

Now it made sense, Grace thought—Brian's newfound affluence, which she'd attributed to Heather. Brian himself actually was wealthy. Thanks to Von.

"Brian never needs to know."

Grace nodded quietly. "We are secure, Von. With each other. But did you do this because of Emma?"

"No. I did it because of you. I felt I had let you down. That maybe you suddenly married Brian—because of what happened. Because I left."

"That's not why I married Brian, Von. I didn't marry him on the rebound. I loved Brian before I knew you, and I loved him after. Did you really invest in Brian's business just to make your conscience feel better?"

"Not at all. I could see he had a promising business model. It was just bad timing, trying to start a business in a recession. When I heard he was going to declare bankruptcy, we arranged for the investment, but the fact is, he did all the work, he created the products, he made the sales, and he's the reason the company has taken off. I'm just the silent beneficiary of a good investment." Von shrugged. Then he knotted his scarf under his neck. "Well, we'd better be going. I have to practice my speech for the gazebo opening."

"And I have to finish my shopping and make sure Emma meets up with the show choir on time."

"Emma will be singing, then?"

"Yes. You'll hear her. She has a little solo."

"You're very lucky, you know. I'm envious."

Envious? This handsome, wealthy man with yachts, planes, women, and the Mediterranean at his feet? For just a second, they stared at each other. For each of them, the other had been, Grace suddenly realized, the road not taken. Far from forgetting her after their night together, Von had never forgotten. He'd had to contend with his own life management, at first denying—and then wishing for—a daughter like Emma.

"Emma will be happy to see you," she said. "Well, I'd better run. Stop by the new café after the ceremony and warm up. Our hot chocolate is guaranteed much better than this! And Emma will be reading a story to the kids." She paused. "Will you ever tell Brian?" she asked.

"No. There's no need to say anything."

"I won't say anything, either."

But, of course, they weren't really talking about Brian. They exchanged a European-style kiss, on both cheeks, and a chapter was closed.

———

The gazebo dedication was so full of Leeza's presence that Grace almost felt Leeza standing beside her. "She probably is," Grace thought. She had to smile. *Leeza was never one to miss a good party, especially one in her honor.*

". . . And so, Leeza, we who love you, in the town that you love, dedicate this gazebo to you," Von announced. His voice, miked, carried across the crisp, cold air of the park, his breath frosting as he spoke. He stood in front of the gazebo with Jonathan, Sara, Claire, and David. Inside the gazebo, waiting to perform, were members of the show choir, including Emma. Grace stood in the crowd, rubbing her hands in front of her. The night was cold, but hearts were warm. The gazebo looked like a winter wonderland, all flickering candles casting dancing shadows on the snow. "As her family, it is our hope that all in New London will enjoy Leeza's Gazebo." Von ceremonially cut the ribbon across the front archway. Applause burst out, and the choristers burst into song—Leeza's favorite carol, "Joy to the World."

With the notes of the last chord ringing out in the snowy night sky, Grace turned and dashed toward the Book Nook Barn, where the front porch, dressed up in a myriad of tiny white lights, matched the festivity of the gazebo. Right now was the calm before the storm. A soft, yellow glow illuminated the room with a winter warmth. Hot cider and cocoa were at the ready, the cookie tree shimmered, and the new pastry case was sumptuous with cupcakes, scones, cookies, and sugared almonds. Lorraine was behind the counter, holding the fort for early arrivals from the ceremony. The vintage cake stands lined up along the bluestone tabletop were heaped with cupcakes under the opulent guardianship of Miss Havisham. Tim had set out a selection of Christmas books, new sure-to-be-bestsellers, and traditional holiday classics. Tonight, however, was past Halo's bedtime, and Emma never disrupted his routine. One animal would, however, be making a special guest appearance—the new Dalmatian puppy that Tim was giving Ken as a Christmas surprise. At the firehouse, Spotty's mother had had another litter. Grace knew that this was not just any puppy, but a very significant gift—another step in the commitment he was making to Tim and their life together.

Grace was dashing up the porch steps when she saw Mike with something moving under his plaid jacket. A tiny spotted head peered out, yawning. "*Shh*," said Mike. "We're being very quiet so our new owner will be surprised."

Grace cuddled close to the tiny dog. He felt like a squirmy

piece of warm velvet. "Ken is going to go crazy, and something tells me you and Spotty are going to have a houseguest. You know, Ken's giving Tim a surprise trip to LA for New Year's. They're staying in the Malibu house. He's getting ready to rent it to Jaxon, for his parents. So you know what that means— puppy-sitting. But who would mind?"

Mike motioned toward the top of the doorway. "I made an addition." A bunch of mistletoe now hung, tied with a pink bow. He pulled Grace close. "You're standing under it. So now, you owe me kiss. It's tradition." He leaned in, the puppy squirming between them.

Suddenly, Mike sank onto one knee in front of her. In the hand that wasn't holding the puppy he was holding up a pearl ring. "Grace, I thought of so many ways to say this, but it all comes down to: I love you and I love Emma. Will you marry me? When you went back to LA, I was so mad at myself for letting you get away. I thought maybe you didn't realize how I felt about you, so I'm making it crystal clear before any more time passes."

Grace was unsure what she should do next, but saying yes did not immediately come to her lips, and the gazebo crowd would be headed across the park any minute. "Oh, Mike . . ."

Grace felt his eyes caressing her face. He could sense her hesitation and stood up, putting his arms around her. Mike was wonderful, but forever? With a man like Mike, Grace knew their relationship would be over for good if she said no. Could she live without him, his quiet strength?

Mike was leaning so close, his breath soft on her cheek,

whispering in her ear. "I don't have much money, but you'll always know who I am, and I'll always be able to make a life for us. That's why I worked so hard on this place—so you could see what I could do for you, for us. Maybe I couldn't buy the best home on the block, but I could make any house the best home, if it was for you, Grace. For you and Emma. For us."

"Mike," she said, pulling him away from the doorway. "I am so—I don't know what to say. Can I think about it?"

"That's not a no?"

"No." Grace tried imagining being married to Mike. The years would spool out evenly, the line straight and unbroken. Something to count on. But then she realized she would be OK without him, too.

That's when Grace knew for sure.

She wanted to be with Mike, not because she needed a man who could save her. She had already saved herself. But because her life would always be more fun with him in it.

"So is it a non-engagement, then?" Mike asked hopefully.

Grace laughed. "Yes," she said, "yes definitely, it's a non-engagement," and then she kissed him.

––––––

That night, when the last book had been rung up, the cupcake wrappers had been collected, and the last crumb swept up, after Emma had read her story to a crowd of excited kids, after the new puppy had met her proud new dad, after Emma had stopped by another chorister's house for a pizza, Grace found herself back in the kitchen. She and Lorraine were baking Emma's birthday cake together. "Midnight baking. A new tradition," laughed Grace. She was wearing the pearl ring—on her right hand for now.

"It was a wonderful night, Grace. You should be very proud." Lorraine set out the eggs for the cake and handed Grace the recipe box.

"I don't think I need that anymore, Mom. You know, I was thinking of giving it to Emma for her birthday." The recipe box had led to so many things in her life, Grace thought.

"I think she'd really appreciate it. "

As the sheet cake baked and its heavenly fragrance began to fill the room, Lorraine reached into her purse. "And I'm going to give you your Christmas present, early," Lorraine said. She handed Grace a small, wrapped box. Grace opened it to find the locket.

Grace ran her fingers over the heavy silver case. "I know how much this means to you. I'll take good care of it until it's time to pass along to Emma. And here's your gift." She handed Lorraine an envelope. Inside were three tickets to Sweden. "Actually, this is for all of us, next summer. We're going home."

The two of them sat together at the table with the recipe box between them. This was where it had all begun. Where two girls had become young women, a daughter had become a mother, and a mother and daughter had become friends. And they both knew—the tickets were just the icing on the cake, because they were already home.

RECIPE INDEX